"Wright's Wrath has voi‹

importantly a mystery that

until the very end. You wo₁

October K Santerelli

For April

In Memory of David Farland.
I've never met someone so passionate about mentorship and
writing. You are loved and missed.

WIGHT'S WRATH

KEVIN A DAVIS

Inkd
Publishing

CONTENTS

WIGHT'S WRATH

This is the first book in the Khimmer Chronicles series. It centers around Ahnjii and Khimmer, the mind of her adaptive Nightarmor.

Ahnjii is a human dropped into Earth where she is one of the few people who can see the glamor hidden cryptids that live among us. Naively excited in a world new to her, she is soon to find the darker side.

CHAPTER 1

PLAYING with the end of my braid, I blew out a long breath, trying to calm my nerves. I straightened the straps of my bodysuit, then opened the creaking door to William Buford's office.

Human, like myself, he had paler skin, looked older than I'd expected, and wore a loose black suit. Smiling warmly, he rose from behind his desk. An open book rested with a pen left in the spine, perhaps to keep his place. Wavy, short hair hung above his ears. I couldn't tell if he'd forgotten to shave or if he kept his gray speckled fuzz along the chin fashionably trimmed. The room smelled like fried rice from the night before, unless that was his breakfast. My stomach growled.

I stuck out my hand in proper Earth, or at least Tallahassee, tradition. "Ahnjii Fate; I'm here for the interview."

He smiled, pumped my hand, and studied me as he spoke. "William Buford; call me Bill." Letting go of my hand, he pointed to a padded chair and dropped back into his own seat. His nose appeared round and thick. "Ms. Fate, I've been told you have peculiar talents."

Everyone had been clear to keep my abilities secret, but my friend Deanna had set up the job for me and I trusted her opinions when it came to staying out of trouble. I needed a job and did horribly in retail — it got boring real quick. She'd said that she knew a defense attorney who wouldn't want anyone knowing what I could do, if he hired me. My secret would be safe.

"Yes. I can tell when someone's lying," I said. The Aegis monks had called it truthsense, but the name didn't matter.

He pursed his lips and leaned forward, nodding. "You won't be offended if I test that statement, would you?"

"Go for it." I forced my smile down, once I realized I was grinning.

His expression turned bland and nonchalant. "I didn't like Deadpool's humor."

Lie. The thought and feeling were as sure as if I'd lied myself. The wrongness hung in his voice and in the air between us. "That's a lie," I said quickly. Who was Deadpool?

"My daughter likes bunnies."

Truth. "True."

"I didn't have a crush on Melody."

Lie. I detected seven more of his deadpan statements with my truthsense.

His expression grew more serious as we parried back and forth until he finally threw his hands up and laughed. "You're hired. Pay is twenty an hour. Probably eight or ten hours a week, more if I'm in a trial. Otherwise, depositions and jury selection." He paused, touching his lips with a fingertip. "Don't know how you do it."

"Sounds great. Thank you." Deanna had said to ask for fifty dollars an hour, but Bill seemed so excited, I just couldn't.

He stood and reached out to shake my hand again. I had thought handshakes were just for greeting, but I still had a lot to learn.

"I've got a case right now that I need help with. My own client is lying to me. He's admitting to a murder." Bill waved his hand. "I'll set something up and explain it then. For now, get with Doris — you'll be a 1099, independent contractor. She'll get all the paperwork and your contact information."

A 1099? I thought to Khimmer, the mind of my Nightarmor.

Unknown, Mistress.

I kept my smile, nodding, and hoped that Doris was the secretary outside. She'd been nice and might actually explain what 1099 meant.

Doris, an older woman, sat straight-backed at a neat desk with three open portfolios and a monitor. Blonde hair lightened with gray, she looked up over her glasses as her phone buzzed the moment I stepped out of Bill's office. She had an easy smile which broadened as she listened.

I paused awkwardly on the carpet, waiting for her to finish.

She ended with a quick, efficient response. "Yes." Hanging up her phone, she spun her chair toward a filing cabinet. "Congratulations, Ahnjii." Papers rustled. "I just need a little information." Without looking back, a thin finger crooked and coaxed me closer to the desk. "I'll need ID."

I dug into my pocket and pulled out my phone. During what my friend Tyler guessed was my 26th birthday, they'd given me a holder for the cell that had slots for my Florida State ID, an emergency credit card of Deanna's, and folded up cash. "I've moved." Three days ago, and now I had a new job. "I have a different address." I placed the ID with my goofy smiling photo on her desk. Tyler had been there, making me laugh.

"No problem, Dear." Doris closed the folios on her desk and placed out forms. "We'll get to that part, but you should get your ID updated." She carefully studied my clothes, from choker to boots. "Do you have a button-down shirt and slacks or skirt? Proper shoes? For court."

I was wearing a black bodysuit and jean shorts. Nightarmor formed a choker, bangles and bracelets on my arms, a thin unadorned belt, and knee-high boots. Proper shoes? I leaned over to get a view of hers. *Black slippers of leather.* They wouldn't be very good in a fight.

I can form those, Mistress, thought Khimmer. *Would you like me to try now?*

Khimmer had been more intrusive since we'd arrived on Earth. *No,* I thought to them. Everyone had warned me not to change Nightarmor in public. I could get dissected by some government initials.

I nodded to Doris. "Button-down shirt, slacks or skirt, and proper shoes." Tyler and Deanna would have a blast playing dress up. "For court," I confirmed.

"For court."

Fifteen minutes later I stepped out under the brick archways of the massive building that housed Bill's office. The scent of exhaust hung in the air. Strangely, the weather had been cooler for the past few months. Tomorrow would begin the month of February, and Tyler expected it to get warm again. I smiled at the disgruntled man exiting the doors behind me and pulled out my phone to let Tyler know the good news.

"Hey," Tyler answered. Their car started up in the

background. "How'd it go? Never mind, I know you're hired."

I raised up onto my toes. "I am. This'll be way better than the poke place, but no free eats." I hadn't asked, yet I had smelled fried rice. "I don't think."

"I'm parked down the street." Traffic sounded in the background. "I had wanted it to be a surprise. I planned to take you out for lunch to celebrate, but . . ."

"The Pho place?" I rocked from one foot to the next in excitement. Spicy noodles were the best. I grinned and peered into the street, looking for Tyler's beat-up blue car.

"Sorry, love. John never came home last night, and Deanna's freaking out. I can drop you off at your apartment, but I think I should be home to support Deanna."

I felt a little guilty being disappointed about the missed celebration. "I'll go with you to the house. I can walk to my apartment later." If Deanna's boyfriend John hadn't followed his normal schedule, there was a problem. He wasn't the spontaneous type.

CHAPTER 2

TYLER PULLED to a stop in the turn lane in front of me. The SUV behind them blared its horn as I stepped off the curb and jogged around to the passenger door.

Tyler's black, long-sleeved shirt made their light brown skin appear even paler. They wore comfortable baggy pants that ended at their knees. Black hair swung at their neck as they turned from me to the rearview mirror. "Sorry," they said to the driver behind.

I slammed the door, and we pulled into the center lane to cross the intersection. "I think this is going to be a great job." The tree-shaped air freshener swaying from the mirror had a sickly-sweet smell, like old flowers. I grabbed the harness and fastened myself. "I get to use my abilities."

"Be careful about who might notice." Tyler squinted before rummaging in the center console for sunglasses. I kept leaving mine behind, and the sun still surprised me after ten months. It rose overhead every day and got brighter than I could imagine. "What's the job entail?"

I didn't remember the exact words Bill had used, but court seemed a big deal to Doris. "Some stuff, and going to court? I've got to get a button-down shirt and slacks. Khimmer will have to practice making Nightarmor into proper shoes." I glanced over at Tyler's steel-toed boots.

Should I practice, Mistress?

Sure.

Nightarmor's metal sloped into low black slippers, the surface shiny like leather. I lifted my right foot and laid it on my knee to show Tyler. "Proper?" I wiggled my toes, as Khimmer had formed Nightarmor into soft pliable metal that simulated fabric.

Tyler grimaced. "Needs work. I'll show you some examples at the house. Between me and Deanna, we've got plenty." They offered a sly smile. "Did you try that catsuit I showed you?"

"No." I'd meant to, and Khimmer would have been able to form Nightarmor into the one-piece design.

"When do you start working?" Tyler asked.

"I don't know." I'd been so excited, I hadn't asked. "Doris has my phone number." I pulled out the card from my pocket. "Should I call? Ask?"

She said she'd call and schedule, Mistress.

Did she? I didn't have to confirm. Khimmer remembered everything, though they'd been disoriented ever since we'd been stranded on Earth.

Yes.

"She's going to call me and schedule." I tried to sound sure, despite not paying attention.

Tyler's expression had turned tense and worried with tight lips. John being gone overnight bothered them.

"Did John leave a message?" I asked.

"No, which is unlike him. He's considerate with Deanna."

John had been pleased when I'd moved out, or at least

he had never been happy with me living at Tyler and Deanna's family home. He always had something negative to say about Tyler's activities as well. However, he did treat Deanna well.

"What is Deanna doing?"

"Fretting and pacing. We just got back from filing a report at the police station. I texted before I came to check on you."

I put my hand on the rough fabric of my shorts and felt the phone. "Sorry, I didn't check." Earth technology still mystified me. I'd been proud of myself when the phone's map had actually led me to Bill's office.

Tyler chuckled. "I knew you'd call me either way."

We drove past the larger buildings which loomed like gray mountains, as if we passed through canyons. Tallahassee was bigger than any city at home. I'd gotten comfortable with all the basic technology humans used pretty quickly: television, stoves, and cell phones to a certain extent. The people were always in a hurry. Tyler said I should visit New York someday, and be grateful. I'd looked at the photos online.

"What does Deanna think happened to John?"

"Murder and disaster." Tyler's sarcastic tone softened. "She's calling investigators now."

Investigators, Khimmer?

Detectives, like Sherlock Holmes, Mistress.

Sherlock was fun, but I liked his sister more. "That sounds fun, can we help?"

Tyler frowned and shook their head. "I don't think so."

We pulled into Tyler and Deanna's neighborhood where banks and other businesses mixed with a variety of luxurious houses which I'd initially considered mansions, though they didn't have very big estates.

"Will I get to meet these detectives?" I asked.

"Unlikely."

Deanna and Tyler's home was the strangest on the street with tall chimneys, some oddly placed round windows, a pool, a greenhouse, a three-car garage, and a separate building with an indoor basketball court that they used as a skating rink.

Tyler tapped on the steering wheel with one finger in a quick rapid beat. "Last time this happened, I never met them."

"Last time? John's disappeared before?"

Tyler scoffed. "His phone died, and he had to stay on site. Some construction work issue. He's been better about keeping in touch since then, and at least has one of his foremen call if he's outside of signal."

I couldn't consider John a friend, but he had taught me about bars and sports, and Deanna loved him. "I hope it's something simple like that."

We pulled in the drive beside Deanna's huge, black SUV.

Tyler sighed. "Reggae show tomorrow night. I hope this is over by then."

"Dancing?" Next door, hidden behind a fence and brush, children called out as they played.

Tyler smiled, turned off the car, and opened the door. "Of course. It's Reggae."

"My two favorite things."

"Next to skinny dipping, noodles — the list is too long. If all goes well with John, and I'm sure it will, I'll pick you up at 9 p.m."

I grinned at the plan; I liked a lot about Earth. My expression slacked as a guilty chill ran up my neck. I needed to find a way back to Duruce. My duty couldn't be ignored.

When Tyler and Deanna had first brought me to the Ramnath family home, I had asked every day to go back to Slovenia and search for the way to my home.

Tyler had helped pinpoint the location I'd fallen from. Then, I'd gone back to Slovenia for four days with Deanna. She didn't take it very seriously and wouldn't risk Tyler returning to the country. I hadn't found the gate back home. I've been on Earth ten months, most of it spent in the Ramnaths' spare room upstairs, with no way home. Deanna kept promising we'd go back and try again. If I ever did find the gate and get back inside the strange rotunda, then I'd have to figure out which of the six gates would lead home.

"I need to go back to Slovenia and try again."

Tyler frowned, then nodded. "Probably not the best time to bring it up to Deanna. I'm going with you next time. Not that I want to see you go." They darkened and gestured to the house. "Let's see where Sis is at." Tyler led the way inside.

My ears warmed and I laughed in embarrassment. John was missing. Deanna and Tyler didn't need to hear my problems at the moment. I would be helpful, not a distraction. Maybe I'd get to meet these investigators after all.

CHAPTER 3

I'D NEVER MET Tyler's parents, but the Ramnaths were obviously affluent. The two-story house had been stocked with luxurious furniture and lots of electronic televisions. I preferred books. As we walked across tiled floors, I could hear Deanna's irate stomping across the floor above us.

I frowned at Tyler. "Doesn't sound good."

We found Deanna pacing in a sitting room where tan leather couches circled around a large screen. Like me, she had long, black hair, but hers was straight, and Deanna always had on black-rimmed glasses. She tended toward pinks and blues for clothing. Sparkling gems in glittering gold jewelry adorned her ears. Normally cheerful, she had a sharp expression as she talked on the phone. "Isn't this unusual?" she asked someone. I could tell from her tone that she was restraining herself.

She flashed an obligatory smile at us and continued her pacing as she listened.

Two orange tabbies, brothers Jake and Willie, who I couldn't tell apart, watched from the windowsill. I dropped into a soft couch, and one of cats stretched before bouncing over to my lap.

Jake, Mistress.

I scratched Jake's chin as Deanna paced the room listening to someone, peered out a window, and returned.

"I understand, but not a word all day. I usually get a call midday, a text on the busiest day, and now it's the next day and not a word." She stopped, looked at Nightarmor's attempt at shoes, and scowled. "Can you send someone out to the site again?" She came back to stop in front of Tyler. "Thank you. Please call me after they get out there."

Tyler waited as she hung up. "Still no word, I take it."

"I keep telling myself that he's just busy or out of range, but I don't like it. He's gotten better about things like this." Deanna squeezed my Nightarmor shoes. "How can you make such beautiful boots, and such ugly shoes?"

I laughed. *Don't be offended,* I thought to Khimmer.

I'm not, Mistress.

Deanna drew in a deep breath. "I've got Stanton flying over from Valdosta, and this other guy trying to juggle his schedule. The police will do absolutely nothing, but Mother is going to talk to the Commissioner anyway and probably at least get a decent detective assigned."

Red veins clouded the whites of her eyes, and the folds of her eyelids were pink. She'd been crying; that had never happened before. "What can I do?" I gestured to Tyler and myself. "We do?" I didn't drive.

Deanna tried to smile before her lips pressed tight. She swallowed before she spoke. "You're sweet, but these investigators are professionals. I'm sorry. I should have asked. Did you get the job?"

I beamed. "I did."

"Fifty an hour?"

I winced.

"Ahnjii. You've got to move past this people-pleasing. You're overly accommodating." She tsked and shook her head. He eyes drifted away from me before she checked her phone. "When is this man going to email me back? I tripled his rate; surely, he can drop his divorce case or whatever he's working on." She started pacing again. "Tell Bill you need fifty an hour, Ahnjii."

I hadn't needed that much money. Tyler or Deanna always took care of me. I could ask Bill for more later. Jake purred in my lap while I stroked his ears.

Tyler dropped onto the cushion beside me and leaned against my shoulder. "What can I do, Sis?"

"This isn't some internet social justice cause, so I don't imagine anything." Deanna spoke with a sharp tone, then turned away covering her face. "Sorry," she choked. "Sorry."

Tyler jumped up and grabbed her in a hug. "Sis, we'll find him."

I felt awkward. There had to be something I could do to help her. However, it didn't sound like she had anyone I could truthsense. I doubted my training under the Aegis monks would be useful.

I bristled at the thought of John making her feel like this. His typical thoughtless behavior toward others such as Tyler and myself had never mattered, as long as he made Deanna happy. Tyler ignored the slights. I couldn't picture John being in actual trouble; he was as big as Tyler and myself combined and muscled like the construction workers he managed.

"Damn." Deanna pulled back from Tyler. "I need to cancel my appointments at TCC. I'm in no shape to help those kids." She started typing on her phone.

The room faded into silence. Jake purred lightly. I drew my fingertips along his chin in slow repeating scratches.

"Hungry?" asked Tyler.

"Can't think of food right now." Deanna's lips tightened. "What if he broke a leg on site and has been out there all night?"

"Police would have found his truck." Tyler glanced over at me. "I'm making Lo Mein. I'll sauté shrimp for yours. You barely ate last night and didn't eat breakfast. You're going to wear yourself out."

"Stop it. I'm not hungry," Deanna snapped.

Tyler headed for the stairs. "Still going to cook and put a plate in front of you."

I slid Jake onto the couch and jumped to follow. I couldn't resist Tyler's cooking. I loved noodles, and Tyler made them extra spicy for me with crunchy white chestnuts and soft garlic pieces. The delicious aroma itself made the house feel normal for a minute. Even John had said Tyler was an excellent cook.

Deanna did end up picking shrimp out of her dish, partially to keep her cats out of the plate. When Tyler finished eating, Deanna shoved her plate toward her sibling. "I'm going to my room. I appreciate you being here, but there's nothing any of us can do, and I'm getting cranky."

I helped with the dishes but wished I could do more. John needed to get his grumpy butt back to Deanna.

Tyler sighed as we finished. "I'm going to jump online. I've got a three o'clock Discord that I might make, unless Deanna needs me. You can hang out. Pool. Skate. Read."

I shrugged. "I'll go down to Railroad Square and hang. You'll call me if I can help?"

"Of course. I'll drive you."

It was a short walk, but I enjoyed the extra time with

Tyler. We drove through College Town and passed the green sports field to get to my new apartment. The streets were crowded with students and office workers.

"How did the date go the other night?" Tyler waved at the restaurants that bordered the sidewalk under the multi-story student apartments.

I shrugged. "We had sex."

"Ooh, any sparks?" Tyler glanced over, trying to catch my eye.

They didn't understand. "Nope, no spark." In my previous profession, you didn't get emotionally attached to people; it put them in danger. A romantic relationship I couldn't bring myself to risk; sex was about physical release. It had been hard enough to accept friendships since coming to Tallahassee.

Earth was different, I knew, but someday I had to go home and complete my mission. For the moment, I couldn't cross that line between sex and friendship. I'd tried to explain this to Tyler; of all people I wanted them to understand. If I had liked the college boy, whose name I couldn't remember, then there would have been no sex.

We passed the railroad and drove into the student housing that bordered my neighborhood. Tall, blocky buildings rose up neatly, and cars parked in every available spot. Young women and men climbed stairs or walked balconies, though few stopped to congregate. It was crowded and busy, yet somehow isolated. On the other side of the tracks to my left lay a quieter, more comfortable, Railroad Square District where my Fae friend Vivianne and my Nedjir friend Laura worked.

I yelled over the music, "I'm going to go over to Fat Cat Books after you drop me home." I wanted to rinse. Vivianne would be as excited about my new job as she'd been about my new apartment.

Tyler didn't respond. Their dark eyes, augmented with eye liner, focused intently ahead. They often got this way. Tyler tended to get involved in random, what John called radical, causes. If they hadn't, we never would have met in Slovenia. I respected their principles, though I had little to offer because most of their activities seemed to involve the internet in ways I did not understand. At the moment, they probably worried about Deanna and John.

This afternoon I'd have plenty of free time to visit Vivianne and Laura, unless Deanna needed me.

We drove out of the complex of tall, newly built student housing into an older, shorter neighborhood and pulled in front of my gray, stained apartment building of only two stories. Trees shaded most of the property, and cars parked wherever there was space.

I stepped out and leaned back in. "Call me if you find John or have any news."

"I will. Love you."

Ridiculously fake pink birds had been planted in the yard by my neighbor, Mrs. Forster, who peeked out her window on the second floor as I closed the car door. Oak trees circled the property, and the nearby lake left a pungent odor to the air.

I managed to get inside before Mrs. Forster opened her door. She had the end apartment, and I had the one next to her. I would have used the back door to avoid her if I could have gotten it open. Deanna had made John promise to come fix it.

My rooms had no furniture unless you counted the ceiling fan. Deanna approved of the off-white walls and had tried to furnish it, but I'd declined. Laura had said it would be more "me" if I found used furniture. The living room ended in a personal kitchen at the back of the apartment with wood cabinets and gray counters that formed a divider separating the two rooms. The opening to the left led to the bathroom in the back, an empty closet, and my bedroom.

I had let Deanna buy a bed. So far, I had bought a tea pot, a bowl for ramen, and a clear glass pitcher with accompanying cups from the vintage store in Railroad Square. I would need to go shopping for some appropriate work clothes. Before Tyler had picked me up with news about John, I had assumed I'd go to a store with Deanna and Tyler. It would have been selfish to ask considering the circumstances. If I could help find John, I'd do anything.

I stepped into the bathroom and my phone rang. "Hello?"

"Ms. Fate? This is Doris. Mr. Buford asked that you come in now; he has some work for you."

My eyes widened and I stared down at my frayed jean shorts and ugly shoes. I grabbed the end of my braid and flicked the hairs at the bottom. "Court?"

"No." Her tone sounded light, as if she suppressed a laugh. "But can you be here in half an hour?"

Boots, I thought to Khimmer. "I'll be there."

CHAPTER 4

MY FIRST TIME IN A PRISON, I managed to cause my new
boss, Bill, some stress.

The middle-aged guards had found Nightarmor to be
troublesome to their metal detectors. First the gate had
buzzed, then they'd had me remove the boots. Khimmer had
replaced the slippers since I'd never had time to sit with
Tyler and figure out a proper shoe. Their wands beeped
over my belt, which they had me remove as well; the
bangles, bracelets, and choker they let me keep on.

The room stunk of acrid cleaning supplies. The guards
grumbled and argued with Bill, until we were finally
allowed to continue.

As he led me behind an escorting officer, Bill spoke
quietly. "Perhaps a little less jewelry."

Khimmer?

*I can minimize to a mass similar to the choker you now
wear, but it requires an expenditure of energy to maintain it,
Mistress. We can leave a significant portion of material
behind, but I'm loath to take the risk.*

"Less jewelry, proper shoes," I said, braid in hand.

I carried the folder he'd given me on the ride over. It contained the questions he wanted me to verify. I wasn't to speak, just write "T" or "F" for true or false. My writing still had a long way to go, but I could handle two letters.

The guards led us to a room with a metal picnic table in the middle. Bill had said we were to meet his client, a construction worker named Emery Porter, who might have killed some people.

I started to sit opposite Bill.

He snorted. "We sit on this side."

I slid in next to him, opened the folder, and laid it out in front of me. Bill gave me a knowing look and slid the folder so that it tilted from the table to my lap. He didn't want his client to know that I was verifying his statements. In interrogation, the monks had always found it more useful if the person knew they couldn't lie.

We sat in silence until the door opened and a guard led a shackled man in brightly colored garb into the room. A deadpan expression on his face that did not fit his cheery clothing, the prisoner otherwise reminded me of John with a toned, stocky build. The man had brown hair and brown eyes. Beyond the dull gaze, I could see something almost fanatic in his quick inspection of us and the room. He wanted to be free.

As Bill cleared his throat and began to speak, Emery Porter focused his eyes on my boss's face. The prisoner's expression didn't change, but emotions appeared to flicker in those deep brown eyes; first a dullness, then a rage or hate, and finally a sharp intellect that the rest of the expression didn't carry.

Bill walked through some rather boring details that I didn't understand. I'd thought we were here to interrogate.

Waiting for my part to start, I tapped on my bracelets and studied Emery Porter.

"Mr. Porter. This is my associate Ahnjii Fate. I'm going to confirm questions we already have gone through. I need them for my briefs," Bill said.

Lie. I glanced over. Tyler had said to expect lawyers to lie a lot.

"You were alone, except for the victims?"

Emery had a deep, throaty voice. "Yes."

Lie. I marked a small "F" next to the question.

"You killed William Green?"

"Yes."

Lie. Why would someone claim to kill someone they hadn't?

"You killed Theresa Green?"

"Yes."

Lie. Someone else had killed these people, and Emery covered for them.

"You killed Brian Schwartz?"

"Yes."

Lie. Emery hadn't killed anyone, at least none on Bill's list.

Every question Bill asked, Emery Porter lied about. Only once or twice did my boss check my work, and none of those times did he seem surprised. I had a very strange job.

When we walked outside and back to his car, Bill took the folio. "I knew it. Now I just have to prove it. His family has the money for investigators and wants him released. I can understand their concern; he's been missing for a month, then pops back up, caught at a murder scene. Once I get some leads, I'll need you to attend some interviews. You'll be extremely helpful."

"Interviews?" I asked. Did I have to ask for the job each time? That seemed pointless.

Khimmer?

I believe you just did an interview with the prisoner, Mistress.

Bill tugged at his collar. "Yes. It's when we ask witnesses or associates questions. You'll see. Depositions would be if we believe they have something we want on record."

I nodded, but the experience had left an odd feeling. I longed to find out why Emery had lied, whom he protected. I hoped I'd learn the details, but the hint of purpose left me wanting more. It would have to wait until Bill needed me again.

I'd left my phone in Bill's car, but resisted calling Tyler to relate my new experience. I checked my messages in case someone had found John. Deanna crying had disturbed me, but I couldn't do anything.

As he slid behind the wheel, Bill motioned toward my arms. "Less jewelry," he said once more.

My ears warmed and I nodded emphatically. Khimmer could reduce Nightarmor. "Got it."

"Office, or you want me to drop you off at your apartment?" Bill asked.

I could go back to hang with Tyler and Deanna, probably eat dinner, but I felt in the way. They needed to find John, not keep me entertained.

"Railroad Square?" I asked.

CHAPTER 5

THE NEXT DAY, they still hadn't found John. I visited with Tyler for a bit before returning to Railroad Square. Deanna had ranted on her phone from her room. I hadn't stayed long.

Sitting in Fat Cat Books, I lifted the cuddling gray tabby off my lap and deposited him on the chair between myself and my blonde-haired Fae friend, Vivianne. The cat squirmed to return until I stood.

"I'm going to get some Boba tea, then head home to eat," I said.

Vivianne had light olive skin, a tiny nose, and two tall Fae ears that poked through her hair in delicate points. "Glad you like your new place. Get to see you more." The only marring of her features was the slight dimpling on her forehead caused by the sigils engraved in her bone that made humans see her as human without her beautiful ears.

The black beauty that hid atop the bookshelf replied with a long meow before I answered, "I'm closer." I came by every day, or had for the past few, since I'd moved into my apartment.

"You're lonely." Vivianne tilted her head as if sorry for me and blinked her large brown eyes. I found her beautiful in her Fae state, but even people who only saw her glamoured view found her attractive.

"Perhaps." Living alone had proved difficult. There were plenty of people living in the apartment building, but they weren't Tyler.

"You'll get used to it, or find someone to keep you distracted." Vivianne's lips pulled up in a sly grin. She coaxed the gray tabby to climb into her lap. When I didn't respond, she offered a compassionate smile. "Nails. I hope they find your friend."

I flicked the hairs on the end of my braid. "Hate to say it, but John isn't a friend, not like you. I do care how it's tearing up Deanna and Tyler, though." Vivianne knew that part of the reason I'd moved had been John. He'd been clear I should get my own life.

Usually, I would head over to their house in the evening. Tyler had mentioned Reggae, but we hadn't discussed it this morning. "What are you doing tonight?"

Vivianne's smile lifted on one side in a sly grin once more. "Date."

I raised my eyebrows. "Already? You just broke up with . . ." I couldn't remember his name. I checked the back door of the store where another employee worked with the cats before I leaned in conspiratorially. "Fae?"

She huffed and checked the back of the store herself. "Of course he's Fae. Nothing personal, but I've only dated one human. Nails, talk about a complicated relationship."

"I'll drop by tomorrow and see how it went." I winked at her and grinned. "If it doesn't work out — is he cute?"

Vivianne popped her mouth open as she mocked being offended and pointed toward the front door. "Out."

"See you tomorrow." I waved to Vivianne and the kitties as I exited the first door of the bookstore. Railroad Square was quiet with only a couple tourists drifting down the street toward the vintage shop. My stomach growled, and I started for the road that would lead me over to College Town where I could buy Boba tea.

Doris might still call today, since Bill had said there'd be more work. Deanna had walked me through the money I'd need to pay rent and buy groceries. She did want me to renegotiate the pay rate. I'd said I would consider it, but there seemed to be no need; in the same conversation, she'd promised me whatever money I needed to pay bills.

As I crossed over to College Town, the street turned busy with cars and students walking along the sidewalks. As often as I came through for food or on the way to Deanna and Tyler's, you would think I'd know everyone. It was rare that I recognized anyone.

I sipped on a Boba tea while heading back home. Traffic hummed on the streets behind me. Lunch would be ramen after I got home and cooked it. I'd call and check in with Tyler. If I hadn't been worried about John before, I was now.

I took my usual path around Railroad Square toward Famu Way, cutting through the back parking lots. The garbage bins leaked rancid odors that highlighted the city's exhaust fumes. Khimmer had tried slippers again, but the new shoes didn't walk well. I wanted to show them to Vivianne.

Under a pair of shade trees, a woman sat in overgrown grass. She had bright red hair and a thin face; her overly large eyes studied me. I transfixed on the seductive grin that spread across her lips, enough to bring me a few strides closer. My eyes widened when I recognized the Fae ears, elongated, pointed, and nearly buried in the red hair. Dull, coarse hairs curved off the tips of her ears like waves crashing down on her finer, brighter curls.

Vivianne had blonde hair, which I'd wrongly guessed the norm for Fae.

The red hair, along with an inviting smile, sparked an immediate attraction. From what I'd understood from Vivianne, sex between the two species had been common, at least in the past. Lunch might have gotten more interesting.

"A Fae," I said. Not my best opening line.

Her smile vanished, earrings in her tall lobes jostled, and her jaw tightened. "*High* Fae," the woman corrected.

"Ooh. I've heard about you." Vivianne had almost made them out to be a different species. Purer, with less human blood. She wore a low-cut black blouse and a gray-green plaid skirt. The high Fae had a pleasant figure. Her fingers were long, like Vivianne's. Nothing seemed particularly unusual. "You don't look any different."

The woman stiffened, fingers of both hands pointing toward the grass in a rigid display. She frowned. "Seren Province Investigator, Shailagh."

I might have ruined the moment, but the excitement of meeting another of Earth's inhabitants made me smile anyway. I'd tracked down a Fae walking on the road once before, but that hadn't gone very well. Wiping the cold condensation off my hand, I extended it. "Ahnjii."

Shailagh's face softened, and she took my hand. "Pleasure to meet you." With soft warm skin touching, a glimpse of the earlier attraction flashed across her face. Then she settled into a more businesslike tone. "You have a unique gift. I may have some work for you." She wore intricately carved jewelry at her neck and dangling from her ears; as she moved, they reflected light.

I stiffened, then realized how she knew. I'd seen through the Fae's sigil glamor with truthsense, my gift. She'd known ahead of time, and this had been some test, a guise to get me to expose myself. Vivianne had been explicit about keeping my abilities hidden from the high Fae, but Shailagh already knew. I couldn't see Laura or Vivianne telling anyone.

Disappointed at being tricked, I shrugged. "I've got a job." I slurped up a sweet tapioca ball and chewed on it.

"It pays well." She pulled out a small red crystal and displayed it as if I would be impressed.

I wasn't. It likely had some sort of value, like the paper and plastic money that they used in Tallahassee. I tilted my Boba, trying to get some of the last liquid. "I don't need much. I'm good." I probably should follow Vivianne's advice and avoid the high Fae. I could go home and get out of these shoes. I tapped on my cup.

Shailagh's eyebrows furrowed. "It is rare for a high Fae to request the services of a common witch. You do understand that?"

Witch? I'd heard the term before. *I'm no witch. I'm not even from here.*

I would not tell her that, Mistress.

Don't worry. I'm not.

Vivianne had said that the high Fae were able to live centuries. They might know about my world. *She might know about the gates and how to get back.* Khimmer and I had searched for it, with Tyler's help, to no avail.

Be careful, Mistress.

"Actually, I do have a few questions that you might be able to help with. You're really old, right?" I asked.

Shailagh studied me, and not in the flattering way she had at first. Crossing her arms, she spoke. "If you help me find a killer, I will answer one question, but not about the Fae or their activities."

A killer? What did a high Fae investigator do? Did I really care? "One?" What if I asked the wrong question?

Shailagh smiled smugly.

I couldn't pass a chance to find out more about the gates. I had to try. Letting out a breath, I sighed. "Okay, deal. Who got killed?" I fidgeted, needing to get out of these shoes.

"A low Fae." Shailagh didn't lie.

I'm not sure why I was surprised that she'd be helping someone like Vivianne. It made me look at her in a new light. Or at least revise my opinion of the high Fae, which had only come from talks with Vivianne and Laura. I'd have to ask them about that.

I pulled my braid over my shoulder. "When do we start?" I couldn't help with John but didn't want to get too far away if they needed me. I had dancing planned tonight. Maybe Shailagh didn't even plan on doing anything soon. Whenever it was, I should let Doris know when I wasn't available.

"Now," Shailagh said.

I hadn't expected to leave suddenly. It felt wrong to leave while John was still missing. "Argh, I was going to a show tonight. Reggae. Can it wait until tomorrow?"

Her tone carried that arrogance of a boss that expected everything to go their way. "No."

Getting home had been my only priority for months. The urgency had faded with failure, but here lay my opportunity. Wouldn't it be worth anything to find the gates? "Fine." These shoes had to go. I gestured in the general direction of my apartment. "Let me stop by my place. Where are we going?"

"A city called Orlando."

I knew the name. *How far is Orlando, Khimmer?*

I am not connected here, Mistress. However, using what information I have seen, up to ten days of walking.

Vivianne didn't drive; perhaps Shailagh had a car. Tyler would drive us if I asked. "That's a good bit from here. I don't drive," I said.

"We'll use the Lichgate portal."

I frowned. *Translation, Khimmer?*

Lichgate appears to be a proper noun, Mistress. Portal could be a gateway or entrance.

"The what?" I asked Shailagh. Could this be similar to the gate I looked for? I might get more than one answer if I played this right.

Shailagh's eyes widened. "Do you not know of the Lichgate tree?"

A tree or a gate, which was it? "No. How's a tree going to get us to Orlando?"

I waited to truthsense her answer. Our meeting had been no coincidence. Shailagh had been waiting for me. She'd known of my truthsense. I could accept that if she were helping Fae such as my friend. However, trees didn't move and even the oldest stories never told of portals within them.

Shailagh's eyes narrowed. "Your parents never explained portals?"

I winced at the mention of parents. I'd been an orphan all my life, raised by monks, but I had killed my parents days before I'd fallen through the portal and ended up on Earth. My stomach churned at the memories. "No."

As if to center myself, I drew in a breath of Tallahassee air tainted with exhaust. I twitched my head to clear the images of their bodies. Shailagh thought me an Earth witch, knowledgeable of such things as her portals. I couldn't feign comprehension, but I could use the ignorance to get more information. *I need to go home.* My nausea held. "These portals, can they go to other worlds?"

Shailagh took a moment, and I feared I had made her suspicious. "These portals only go to other portals on Earth."

Truth. I would have to see them for myself. "C'mon. I just need a minute at my apartment, then we'll see about all this." I jutted my chin to indicate down the road. I didn't say more; I wasn't willing to stir up more questions about witches or my ignorance. I had a fragile opportunity to learn about portals and possibly the gate that had marooned me here. These shoes were no good for fighting, and I couldn't know what the day promised.

"It goes without saying that I'll expect you to remain confidential about our association, agreement, and activities."

"Of course." This sounded like some rule between high Fae and witches — and I wasn't a witch.

As we started walking, I glanced at Shailagh's feet. Elongated toes stuck out of rope sandals. Tyler had something similar made of hemp. They reminded me of home where shoes were simple.

When we reached my apartment, Shailagh waited outside with Mrs. Forster watching her through the window. Vivianne had said the high Fae avoided most metals, more so than she did.

Kicking off the shoes beside my bed, I had Khimmer

form my Nightarmor into boots more appropriate for travel — or fighting.

I called Tyler. "Any word on John?"

"No. Deanna's holed up in her room, but I can hear her yelling at the investigators or police; I can't tell who."

Guilt surged in my chest. Not only could I not help Deanna, now I was bailing on Tyler. "I've got to cancel tonight, unless I get back into town in time."

"Something fun, I hope?"

"Side job," I answered. I'd heard John use the term and hoped it fit.

"Details?" Tyler asked.

"Later. I'll call when I'm done."

They paused for a moment. "Be careful, Ahnjii."

My pulse quickened at the comment. It didn't slow even as I returned to Shailagh and we began the walk to her tree.

"So, this tree will get us to Orlando?"

Shailagh studied me. "Yes."

"Where else can it take us?" I assumed that she wouldn't tell me an answer to "the" question since I hadn't fulfilled my end of the bargain, whatever that would be.

She shook her head. "That's a strange question. Anywhere in the world where there's another portal."

Trees lined the road, cooling the air and bringing a fresh scent to the breeze. When she turned us off the side of the road, it was into a dirt parking lot with a single car in it and an old couple coming up a path. I smiled and waved as we passed, but the tightness in my chest held.

The sign labeled the area as Lichgate Tree.

I glanced at the woods around us. "Which one?"

Shailagh scoffed and gestured down a trail. "Follow me."

An old oak rose above the smaller trees of the forest. We exited the path onto a large field of grass that spread out from the tree. Ancient limbs leaned on the ground as if the tree were tired and couldn't hold them up. Light green moss grew along the wrinkled bark while pale grayish moss draped from its upper limbs. The woods were alive with birds, and a bee buzzed between us.

I could not see how this could get us to Orlando, but I had never expected one of the six gates I'd found under the waste to deposit me in the Slovenia mountains. I just had to wait and see what she planned.

Shailagh marched up to the massive trunk and whispered, almost cooed, foreign words. At the top of her skirt, she had a thick belt that seemed to bulge in spots. Her fingers stretched toward the ground, as if reaching for it.

A glow lit the roots of the tree. Golden light rose up the trunk, both immersed within the tree and spreading out toward the high Fae.

I stepped back. Nyx's altar held such magic. What gods resided here on Earth? I had believed none. Did Shailagh wield such power? "Is that you doing that?" I asked.

"The tree and I," she said.

My chest tight, I resisted having Nightarmor cover me. My pulse raced. I crossed my arms and studied the bright oval of light. Could I trust her? What powers did she possess? I wanted her answers, but at what risk?

Shailagh stepped halfway into the glow, one side of her body left visible to me. She gestured for me to follow.

I'd gain nothing by abandoning the high Fae. Besides, she searched for someone's murderer. That had been the truth. I had to give her some credit for helping others. I knew I should be focused on John's disappearance and swallowed some guilt rising in my throat for being excited.

I wiped my lips with the back of my hand and nodded for her to continue. I'd have to prepare a question worth all this.

CHAPTER 6

I SQUINTED against the light in reflex, though it didn't hurt. I felt no resistance to my movement, and certainly no tree, but a faint sound like the delightful tinkling of broken glass fell around me. It smelled fresh like standing on a mountain, but warmer.

A full step brought daylight, a blue sky, and a faded wooden fence from someone's back yard. A younger tree than the ancient Lichgate spread branches overhead. Shailagh stood a few paces ahead of me with an unreadable expression.

Unlike the gate I'd come through to Earth, the experience had not been disorienting. Was this Orlando? The air smelled a little more acrid. In a mere second, I'd come an amazing distance equal to ten days of walking.

"Wow." I hopped in place. I wanted to turn around and do it again.

Shailagh smiled at my excitement, so I grinned back and tapped her arm with my fist.

She started at the action, and I realized I'd breached some Earth or Fae tradition. It had been a strange custom for me at first, but common now with me and Tyler. I'd learned it when we went to bars with John.

Shailagh bristled. "Stop that."

I hadn't meant to offend her. Awkwardly, I turned back to the portal where the glow ebbed toward the roots. I looked forward to using the portal again when we returned.

She led us to a squeaking gate at the corner of the house. Who lived here? I'd ask on the way back.

The neighborhood had similar looking houses on quiet streets. Short and dingy, they were unremarkable compared to most of Tallahassee. When cars did come through, they seemed in a hurry as they buzzed past. A cloudy day, the warm air had enough breezes drifting through that I didn't sweat.

"How far?" I asked.

Shailagh answered as though she didn't hold a grudge against my earlier action. "Less than half an hour to the shifting wildlings' territory."

Laura had mentioned wildlings, an Earth species related to her own. "Shifting?" I asked.

"Surely you know of shifters." She'd grown suspicious with my questions about the portal and now studied me, waiting for a response.

I was not the human witch she expected me to be. I'd rarely heard the term except in passing mention from Vivianne or Laura. The topic hadn't seemed important at the time, but evidently human witches knew much of the Fae, Nedjir, and wildlings. Tyler had warned about telling anyone about Duruce, my home world. I had avoided declaring it directly to both Vivianne and Laura; they knew I was human, but not acclimated to the culture of Earth.

Deanna had never really believed it. John had outright

called me delusional. I resisted checking my phone to see if Tyler had left any message about John's disappearance.

Flashing Shailagh a smile, I tried to dismiss my ignorance of wildling shifters. "I've never come in contact with wildlings." I would ask Laura more later, but for now, I needed Shailagh to fill me in.

Her face tightened and she glanced around us. "Just keep quiet and give me an indication if they lie. They socialize in small indistinct packs, so I'll need to find their leader and see if they had any part in the murder."

I tensed at the comment, but could see my benefit to Shailagh. "You believe they are the murderers?" Surely it would be dangerous for Shailagh to enter their territory.

"Unlikely, as it would start a war between them and the high Fae. However, it could be a rebellious action by an independent member of the pack, or a rogue intruding on their domain. This pack controls the wildlings in Orlando." Shailagh's face hardened. "Neither can be left unpunished."

I felt respect for Shailagh and her people. The humans of Tallahassee seemed mired in arguments while the people who hurt others roamed free. Human internet and television told of unending violence that they let proceed unchecked. It rarely affected me directly. Nyx had given me visions of such a war on Duruce, and the memory made me shiver.

Shailagh walked just off the sidewalk where she could, keeping to the grass or dirt. We turned onto a street and a young man watched us from his seat on a doorstep while scrolling through his cell phone. These houses looked in worse condition than the previous; even the concrete crumbled, and holes dotted the asphalt. The air mixed scents of cut grass and plants with the reek of garbage. The cars parked on driveways or lawns had more rust and dents than most I'd ever seen.

Two other men called out from a porch leaning off a house from the other side. I waved.

"Don't start anything in this neighborhood. These are human thugs, not wildlings. There is no pack here and thus no detente in place."

I could see no harm in being polite, but shrugged. "Can't hurt to be friendly."

Still, I noted as the two men rose and watched us pass. Shailagh too, glanced at them, but without fear. In a blouse and skirt, she hardly seemed prepared for violence despite a self-confident demeanor.

The men are following, Mistress.

Three more slid off a porch ahead of us and talked in a small group.

Shailagh leaned down and spoke quietly. "Don't react to these people."

It did appear that they might attempt to intercept us and cause violence. Since I'd arrived, the only need I'd had to defend myself had been at a bar. Simple pressure holds had been sufficient. The men on this street had the flavor of bandits.

I wanted to pat her shoulder reassuringly, but feared eliciting a negative response. Instead, I leaned toward her as she'd done with me. "If they threaten us, I'll protect you." I had considered joining one of the martial art gyms, just for the practice and rush.

Shailagh smiled, and a flicker of our initial attraction showed in her eyes. "Let's aim to get out of here, without any protection."

Perhaps she enjoyed the idea of a fight. It appeared we would have little choice, as the men ahead blocked the path.

The shortest of the three spoke. "What are you fine girls doing in our neighborhood?"

Shailagh didn't respond, but veered us into the street, attempting to avoid them. The men behind closed in quickly with loud footsteps. My heart pounded, and I craved to draw Nightarmor's blade. The men ahead hadn't drawn weapons. For bandits, they didn't appear experienced.

The tallest of the men smiled. They weren't going to let us pass.

I dropped behind Shailagh to take care of the men following. They had no weapons, and I lured the first into attempting a hold. I slammed my heel into his groin and used his arm to toss him to the side. It felt exhilarating to be in combat once again.

The second man leaned in. He stunk of sweat and alcohol. I punched his exposed throat with the fingertips of my stiffened open hand and followed through with a push from my palm to his chest. He dropped to the asphalt, and his skull bounced.

Shailagh had managed to disable one of the men. He lay bleeding from his nose. Evidently, she had skills.

The other two men groped for weapons under their shirts. None of the fallen three would stay there for long. This had to end quickly. If they brought out guns, I'd need all the Nightarmor to protect myself, and I wanted to avoid that.

Sleeve knife.

Yes, Mistress. Out of a bracelet, Nightarmor formed a short blade on the back of my left forearm. I gripped the hilt and brushed past Shailagh.

When the short man drew a small gun from behind his back, I cut a deep slit into his thumb. His weapon clattered to the ground. Two more bandits jogged from the end of the street.

I spun into the other foul-smelling man. Tall, he had a tight black beard on his chin. My left hand snapped up to wind around to the sweaty back of his neck. I slid my knife against his rib for a light cut and the distracting pain it would cause. Holding his neck firmly, I slung his chest down into my knee. I easily gained control of his left wrist before he could recover. When I twisted behind his back, his knees buckled. A flick of my knife sliced open his gun hand, releasing his weapon. I didn't let him fall. I quickly shifted so that my knife pinned the arteries of his neck. "Tell them to go home," I said in his ear.

Dripping blood on the asphalt, he waved off his comrades rising from the ground and the two new men who loped down the street toward us. "Get back," he called out.

Too tall to control with this hold, I dropped the knife from his neck down to his groin from behind. "Let's walk out of here, just the three of us."

I had to enjoy Shailagh's look of admiration. Somehow, her approval meant something to me. My heart raced, but it had felt good to use my skills. Without Queen and country, I couldn't be an assassin, but I could protect myself.

When the two newest arrivals threatened us, I considered cutting my hostage and turning to the newcomers. Instead, Shailagh swung into the man, and they stumbled into the grass, toppling on top of each other.

When we reached the end of the street, I stopped the man and winked at Shailagh. "Should we take the balls as a souvenir?" Blustering, I laughed and pushed him away. He didn't look back as he ran.

Her withering look cooled my excitement. *Take blade.*

Yes, Mistress.

I pressed the knife against the back of my choker, and it melted out of my hand.

Shailagh jumped behind me. "Where did it go?"

I should have been more careful, but energy pounded in my veins. It had been fun. I might be able to use her curiosity. Letting out a long breath, I replied with a light smile. "Hmm. I'll trade you, answer a question now and I'll answer yours."

She shook her head. Her expression ranged from concern to appraising. The latter was more flattering before she turned grim. "Don't pull it on a shifter. Whatever you do, don't kill a shifter. It would start a war."

The skirmish had been invigorating. I'd have to watch myself if things turned ugly with these wildlings. Surely she wouldn't expect me to die just to protect her people from a war. I had my own people. However, I'd be careful.

CHAPTER 7

We walked into a neighborhood with quiet, better main-
tained houses, though still small boxes in comparison to
Deanna and Tyler's house. Few cars littered the lawns, and
I noted three vans parked on the street, but the only traffic I
heard came from the area we'd just left. Clouds had cut off
the sun, but the air felt warm and humid.

Shailagh's expression and stance had stiffened. I swore
she sniffed the air. This street appeared deserted.

Khimmer, is there anybody nearby?

There is a person in front of the van ahead, Mistress.
Their body temperature is elevated.

I could see no one beyond the old, white van with
deeply tinted windows. I turned to mention it to Shailagh,
but hesitated as she seemed stressed enough.

A young woman with bushy brown hair stepped from
the front of the van and stopped on the sidewalk. As nimble
as an Aegis monk, she moved with a grace that put me on
alert. *A wildling.* I'd expected some resemblance to Laura,
but this female looked human. "That's far enough," she
said. "What's your business?"

Shailagh motioned for me to pause. In a calm but authoritative tone, she spoke. "I'm here to parley with Samuel. There has been an incident."

More have arrived, Mistress. To your right.

Someone moved between the houses.

"He's down south — unavailable," the woman replied.

Lie.

"That's a lie," I said a bit too enthusiastically, happy to be of use.

Shailagh never glanced at me; instead, she stiffened, and her fingers pointed toward the grass, like she'd done before. *An odd posture.*

She drew in a long breath and lifted her hands. "I'll agree to any meeting place that Samuel prefers. Just a few questions."

The bushy-haired woman gestured toward the houses where the others hid. A younger man with shoulder length hair ran to her.

I glanced at Shailagh, but the high Fae ignored me. These wildlings hardly seemed threatening, though they likely would make for a good fight; they moved with a fluidity that I admired.

The two of them whispered in each other's ears, then the young man raced down the street and turned sharply to the right. I didn't even hear a dog bark or a car in the silence that followed.

We all stood awkwardly in the humidity. I'd be sweating soon. "So, will we be headed the same way out? I want to check on my new friends." I asked more as a joke to break the boredom, but Shailagh didn't react.

"We'll see," she said.

I tried to stay still, but found my fingers tapping on my armbands. I'd always had a hard time doing nothing. Tyler said I was chatty, but he said the same about Deanna. If I couldn't stay active, like skating or dancing, then talking came naturally. I spent most of my time with Laura and Vivianne because they had jobs that left them available. Tyler had no job, but they had causes, mostly on the internet.

At the moment, Tyler would be home with Deanna worrying about John. Surely they would have let me know if they'd found him. I shifted, suddenly uncomfortable and feeling selfish.

The male wildling raced back and started whispering to the woman. She pulled them aside and sounded angry. Whatever news he'd brought hadn't gone over well. Why had she tried to deceive us about their leader, Samuel? Sometimes people lied about stupid things.

"They don't seem too bad," I said.

Shailagh blinked, glanced at me, then returned her focus on the wildlings. "They're in their human form. Let's hope they stay that way."

Furious, the female wildling marched toward us, offering a slip of paper as if it were vile. "Midnight."

Shailagh took the note. "We'll be there."

I rocked on my heels, then spun as Shailagh started back the direction we'd come. I hadn't expected to spend more than the afternoon on this. I'd actually hoped it would be done soon and I could go dancing. *Not the case.* "What now?" I asked.

"Now we wait until midnight and meet Samuel."

"Where do we wait?"

"At the witch's house where the portal tree is."

I'd never met a witch. "Can I meet her?"

Shailagh studied me. "Yes. You are a surprise, Ahnjii."

"Good or bad?" I asked.

She turned and spoke as if to herself. "Both."

I had insulted her with the arm punch. I'd be careful about that. The past few months I'd learned Earth behaviors from people around me. I spent most of my time at Railroad Square, but also at sports bars with John and Deanna after he was done with work. Organized competitions proved the only use I found for their televisions.

Vivianne, the only Fae I knew, did not act as sensitive as Shailagh. Still, I'd begun liking the no-nonsense high Fae.

We didn't have any trouble in the neighborhood outside of the wildlings' territory. The skirmish had been invigorating, but dangerous. If they'd fired their guns, I would have had to use Nightarmor. The wildlings had proved unfriendly, but hardly a threat.

When we returned to the tree in the tiny back yard, Shailagh leaned against it with a thoughtful expression.

"I've got to pee," I said.

Shailagh gestured toward the house. "She'll let you use her house. It is part of the agreement."

I wasn't sure what agreements high Fae made with people, but I was grateful.

As I walked toward the back door, Shailagh spoke. "Might as well get yourself a chair; it'll be a while until we leave."

A cautious older woman with long graying hair answered, and her eyes furrowed as she glanced from me to Shailagh who waited deeper in the yard. "Welcome. Do you have need?" This was a witch's house, so she was a witch, whatever that entailed.

"Yes, two wooden chairs." I grinned apologetically. "And, do you mind if I use the bathroom?"

Any expression washed from her face as if there could

be no concern, nor pleasantry. Without a word, she stepped back and pointed down a hall.

The house smelled of herbs in a way that reminded me of Duruce. "It smells wonderful in here." I paused close to her, hoping to strike up a conversation. Perhaps I could learn something of witches firsthand.

She bowed slightly and moved to a well-used kitchen, then chairs scraped on the floor.

"I'll help," I said, foregoing the bathroom for a moment.

The old woman didn't resist me, but evaded my grasp as she passed with two wire back chairs. I would have had to yank them from her to help. Her body language told me we would not be having any heartwarming conversation. She headed outside with her face down and Shailagh ignoring her. I headed to use the witch's bathroom.

When I came out, I didn't find the witch, but beside the chairs stood a small tray table with a pitcher of water, glasses, and a paper plate of apples.

Shailagh stood beside the tree. "I'll be back."

I stopped a few paces away. "Where are you going? What am I supposed to do?" Tension rose in my chest. My previous work always required prolonged periods of waiting, but I had expected Shailagh would be here and I'd get to know her better. I let out sigh and dropped into the chair.

She smiled. "Have some apples."

CHAPTER 8

SHAILAGH LEFT me alone for most of the wait in the back-yard of the witch's house. I would have hung with the woman, but she seemed to want nothing to do with us. However, she did bring me two slices of an amazing lemon cake that bordered on more tart than sweet.

I called Tyler after finishing the slice of dessert. "Any word on John?"

"Nothing. He just vanished. I'm thinking of going out to the site myself."

My throat felt thick. I should have stayed with them. "Can it wait until tomorrow? I'll be back then."

"Where are you?"

"Orlando, with a friend." I shouldn't really call Shailagh that, but I hoped. I started to lie and tell Tyler some story about why I was here, but changed my mind. "What is Deanna doing?"

"Crying and yelling." Tyler let out a breath as I heard Deanna calling. "I've got to go. I'll call you if I decide to go searching, in case I disappear."

"Don't!" I yelled, but Tyler had already hung up.

I'd made a mistake coming with Shailagh. If Tyler decided to do something stupid, there was nothing anyone could do to stop it. I should be there. Stomping through grass, I paced. The sun had shifted closer to where I would expect it on Duruce, but that still left a long time before Shailagh and I were supposed to meet Samuel.

I headed for the hose I'd found in the back of the witch's house and washed my face despite the cooling weather. I paced, muttered, and rinsed until the sun dropped to the horizon. Hanging around outside as it disappeared always felt creepy, like some world-ending disaster loomed as the sun dropped over the horizon. I did not know how Earth people lived with that every day. They accepted night as a normal happening, not the cataclysm it felt like to me.

I was in a foul mood when Shailagh returned in the dark. My humor lifted quickly when I found we had to use the portal again. I could listen to that tinkling all day. The smells inside hinted at incense.

We stepped out of a different tree in a similar type of location with a fenced yard, though the brush grew wild and other trees crowded a slightly larger space. Orlando seemed a noisome place, where traffic rumbled loud and constant. Shadows of tall stone buildings rose against the haze of the sky. One had bright lights shining from it.

Streetlights lit the front of the quiet house, and we had to squeeze between a short fence and a camper to get to the sidewalk. The portal's scent of incense disappeared with the thick exhaust. Pollution, Tyler called it.

Shailagh led us through neighborhoods with only two major roads that we had to wait to cross. Her path veered to keep a noticeable distance from the metal poles and cars. What effect did metal have on her?

The large, dark property where she led us stretched

along the opposite side of a residential street. Vines grew over fences and signs, except for the partially open metal gate at the entrance. Quickly the scents of the city disappeared, and I could pick out stagnant water, decay, and fresh growth. The noise from the traffic never died out. Soon our only light came from the city-hazed clouds above.

Some buildings looked ready to fall, metal sheds leaned, and vegetation-filled ponds dotted the sides of walkways, adding to the ever-present odor.

Mistress, those same people are tracking you from behind and to your right.

I glanced, but could see nothing in the shadows. At least in this abandoned complex, if I needed to use Nightarmor, we wouldn't end up on social media like Tyler warned about.

Someone had left ten tiny golf carts under a tin roof. Rot and vines had claimed most. I pointed them out to Shailagh, partly because they were cute, and also because I watched the shadows to my right for movement.

She appeared tense and snapped in a hushed tone. "Stay focused."

As she spoke, a shadow moved from the back of the metal lean-to. A large man with a full beard wove through the rubble like a cat. Samuel, I assumed.

"Shailagh. What business does an Investigator have here?" His voice sounded older than he looked.

Eleven total, Mistress. Forming a circle around us.

Wildlings shuffled in the overgrowth. Did they want to be heard?

Shailagh gestured with her long fingers. "There has been a murder in your territory. A wildling was involved."

Samuel's face rippled. Muscles rose across his cheeks

and nose, pushing the skin in a disturbing way. His tone grew harsh, almost a growl. "Are you accusing us?"

"No. I am investigating, as is my duty. I will ask you directly. Do you think anyone of your people was involved?"

I waited for his response. She had hired me for this one purpose, but if he became violent, I would protect her.

Making fists, he spit out the answer. "No."

Truth. I nodded, realizing I'd been leaning in, both in anticipation and in curiosity as his face appeared on the edge of turning into something else.

Shailagh sighed. "Are there any rogues in the area?" Her tone heavy with regret, I wondered what she feared.

His eyebrows bulged as muscle grew and his jaw seemed to bristle out his beard. "I would not allow that."

Lie. I raised my eyebrows in surprise. "He's lying."

Samuel's jaw pushed out, reminiscent of a muzzle; his eyes widened, even shifting toward the sides to make room for a larger nose. "An empath?" He looked directly at me.

Shailagh laid her hand on my shoulder as she spoke. "Perhaps we should speak in private."

Did that mean I should leave, or his pack?

Samuel's voice sounded off, distorted and thick. "This is pack business."

"Unless a Fae is murdered."

Samuel snarled, spinning away from us. His muscles swelled tight in his shirt. Could wildlings have sex, all bulged out like that?

Shailagh spoke quickly, as if trying to calm him. "I'm sure your pack is searching for the rogue," she said. "I will need to investigate as well. Why work against each other? Give me what information you have, and I will produce the wildling for your execution."

Execution? I'd grown used to Tyler's culture where they used prisons, big ones.

Samuel roared and his shirt split along seams. He had fingers nearly as long as a Fae's, and black nails protruded. His face had elongated into a short muzzle that flattened his nose and turned the nostrils outward. Hair covered all skin. His irises had turned a dull red, a darker version of Laura's bright eyes.

Shailagh stepped away in response.

Full armor.

Yes, Mistress.

I needed to stop this, before any war started. I wouldn't allow him to hurt Shailagh. She'd said not to use my knife or sword. Nightarmor poured over my head and body.

Shailagh swore softly, "Nails."

Spikes. I needed them to know we were not defenseless. Their teeth and claws would be useless against plate armor while the short, thumb-sized spikes would cause minimal damage unless they threw their full weight against one.

Samuel stumbled back, away from me, and fell onto one of the carts. Through Khimmer's vision, I could see the others, hot red two-legged shapes with longer arms than a human.

"No killing," I yelled. "Do you want a war?"

Samuel stood up from where he'd tumbled. No fear showed in his beastly expression, but I'd obviously shocked him. He roared. "Leave."

I could barely understand him, but the others slowed their approach. They had nearly circled us, keeping a wide distance to our backs and sides, drawing closer through the small cars to protect their leader. In Nightarmor they wouldn't be able to harm me, but Shailagh would be vulnerable. I'd be forced to call for blades. I backed closer to her.

His face did not resemble any animal I knew on Earth or Duruce. Still humanoid, he had deep eye sockets and a strong jaw.

"We need to leave." Shailagh spoke with a sharp enough tone that I glanced at her. She leaned far away from me, or my metal armor.

Her eyes had widened and flicked across Nightarmor. *Damn me to Hades.* I'd used Nightarmor despite Tyler's warning. Shailagh and the wildlings all knew. My blood pounded in my ears.

She strode calmly in the direction we'd come. I could see her telltale ears; it seemed Khimmer was immune to the sigils as well. I had to admire her confidence, despite the threat. Shailagh peered at me as we pushed through brush; as her gaze traveled across Nightarmor, her expression was unreadable.

The pack remained as we left, all but one who followed us at a distance. Samuel probably sent someone to make sure we didn't double back. Khimmer's vision made it difficult to navigate in the dark, especially with overgrown brush. I positioned myself between our follower to my left and Shailagh.

Remove armor. Let me know if any others join the one following us. I couldn't undo their knowledge of Nightarmor, but I didn't need to walk out onto the streets in it.

Yes, Mistress.

Nightarmor melted off, and the air felt momentarily cool against my skin. A mosquito buzzed my ear with a shrill whine. The scent of stagnant water hung in the breeze.

Samuel's shifted form would prove a formidable challenge to any unarmed human or Fae. Did they just have two states, human or beast? "So that's what they look like?"

Shailagh's eyes widened as she turned, nearly stumbling. "Where's your armor?"

I shrugged, pleased that I could surprise her despite the mistake. "Don't need it. There were eleven of them, and just one is shadowing us now." I motioned to the left, knowing Khimmer would have alerted me if they'd changed position.

The streetlights flickered through the thin trees ahead, outlining the street beyond the property. Was my part done? I'd already missed dancing and found that I preferred the idea of continuing with Shailagh.

The one following is approaching, Mistress.

I turned to my left, hearing the rustling of someone jogging toward us. "Wait."

A woman in a tight tube top ran up to us. She wore a black braid like mine, but stood half a head taller. Stopping a few steps from us, she addressed Shailagh. "Samuel is weak. He has failed. You will find this rogue, and bring him to me. Clarita." She pulled her cell from a back pocket and scrolled through it. "We found his nest. We tried to track his scent, but he is clever. You Fae have magics that we do not. I will give you the location." She pulled up a map on her phone.

Magics? More than the portal? I grinned at Shailagh. Hoping to help, I pulled out my phone. Did the high Fae have some way to track people with magic? I had a lot of questions for Vivianne when we got back.

Shailagh nodded and I copied the information from the wildling's phone. The wildling offered a sly smile before she ran back into the woods. Clarita planned a coup against Samuel, it appeared.

I'd expected that Shailagh's matter would be resolved soon. The threat of a skirmish had been exhilarating, and I guiltily pushed that feeling aside. Tyler needed me back. I might not be able to find John, but I could be Tyler's friend and support them, as soon as I finished what I'd agreed to do with Shailagh.

I had always prided myself on keeping my commitments with the Queen and the Aegis monks I served with. My last assassination hadn't failed, unless King Dior died by someone else's hand. I would return home for that duty someday.

I followed Shailagh to the street and set the map to give us directions to the rogue wildling. We strode off at a quick, deliberate pace. This sounded more dangerous, arousing my interest. My pulse started to speed up. I couldn't help but smile. "More good times, eh?"

CHAPTER 9

WE DIDN'T HAVE FAR to go, but I did fear that my phone would run out of electricity before we arrived. Earth technology still baffled me. At this time of night, the rare vehicles in this section of Orlando drove quickly and sporadically. We caused a few dogs to challenge, but no thugs hung out on the steps or porches. It was a quiet neighborhood with few working streetlights and bluish television glows leaking from the windows.

The phone's map led us to a broken building with wood panels shoddily nailed over the windows and doors. There had been a fire once, leaving burnt smudges on the stucco above one window. In the back, a loose board offered us entry through a door. Shailagh seemed to cringe when she entered.

The house appeared abandoned. Inside smelled like a cesspit. An insect buzzed in the darkness. I considered calling for Nightarmor just to avoid the smell, but it would only dull the sense. Air still flowed unless Khimmer closed the vents. With the sparse light peeking in above the boards,

I could barely see as it was. "Merciful Rhys, this place stinks."

The smell or perhaps some metal in the house appeared to be affecting Shailagh. She hunched as if avoiding the walls and ceiling. Some of the rooms were dark enough that I could barely make out walls, but she stopped at one.

A shredded mattress filled one corner, and debris littered the floor. From a pouch within her belt, she brought out a thick bone medallion. She separated the disc into two thinner rounds as if opening the cream filled cookies Deanna liked. Each half had been intricately carved with markings similar to the temple writing of Helios.

Shailagh placed one half on the shredded mattress. As she tapped the other beside it, she swayed and sagged. I thought she might fall into the fetid pile.

"You okay?" I asked.

She didn't answer. The bed and floor began to glow in a blue light. Fae magic? In moments, the glimmer clarified into bright blue footprints covering the floor, some decidedly too large for a human. "Are those his tracks? That's awesome."

The effort, or the house, obviously affected Shailagh. Holding one half of the disc, she ignored me, retrieved the other half, and lurched for the exit. The moment she got outside, I could see her straighten and return to her usual self.

Faint blue footprints led in dozens of directions. "How do we know which ones are his?" I asked.

She'd already started following one of the tracks. "They are all his. The brighter trail is the last."

The blue light only displayed close to the disc she pointed at the ground. I hopped along the edge, watching as the rogue wildling's next footsteps appeared. So far, I loved Fae magic. "Where do I get these?" I pointed to her bone discs.

"You don't."

I hadn't really expected she'd give me one, but I faked a pout. Shailagh didn't react, focused on the trail of glowing blue footprints, so I shrugged and trudged along behind her.

We cut through yards and down alleys until we reached a larger road with businesses. The trail led into a gas station where the odor of petroleum and rubber dominated. Shailagh followed prints from puddles of oil to the street. "This is where the wildlings lost the scent."

I couldn't be sure how she knew that. The trail followed one side of the asphalt for a while, and I took on the task of letting her know when a random car approached. Our hunt had stretched past my typical bedtime, and I wished I'd taken the opportunity to nap at the witch's house, a recommendation Shailagh had made.

When the tracks deviated from the road, they led directly to a two-story building, it's side to the street, that stretched back to an empty parking lot. Crickets called, and flying bugs found my ears. The grass grew knee-high near the street. Tiny yellow flowers held their color in the darkness.

Shailagh followed blue tracks to the side and around the back. A window had been smashed open. Litter lined the small gap between a neighbor's wooden fence and the back of the abandoned building. A car passed on the street, moving too quickly to see.

Shailagh studied the metal frame and remnants of glass. "We'll wait out here for it to exit."

I could go in.

Movement inside, Mistress. Danger.

Armor.

As Nightarmor poured over my face, I pushed between the exposed window and Shailagh to protect her. I could see the hot red shape leaping down stairs and bounding toward the opening. "He's coming."

There are more wildlings arriving behind you, Mistress.

I ached to bring out a sword, but I feared that I'd use it instinctively. "We've got other company arriving as well." Perhaps I could have Nightarmor form a dull staff.

The wildling inside leaped from the middle of the room straight out the smashed window. A stray piece of glass shattered at his passing.

I didn't call for a staff; the arriving wildlings could handle him. His weight and momentum slammed me to the ground. Khimmer had buffers in the armor so that my head didn't rap against the helmet, but it hurt.

His strength was easily twice that of mine, and I couldn't pry off his nails when they wrapped around my shoulders. The wildling's teeth ground against my metal gorget, but with no effect.

I could see the shapes of the other wildlings climbing the fence behind us. If I'd been them, I'd have waited at the gas station and tracked us from there. Were they here to attack the rogue? I couldn't risk them hurting Shailagh.

I slammed a vambrace into the rogue. Rocking with the impact, I rolled and threw him off.

Spikes.

Thumb-sized spikes grew off my pauldrons, elbows, and knees at various angles. Armored and sharp, I hoped the beast would be deterred and go after the other wildlings instead of me. His snarl rumbled through the ground as he flipped to his feet and leaped back to me.

Unfortunately, I'd started to rise, lifting my left shoulder. The rogue wildling came down squarely on one of the spikes. *Damn me to Hades.*

The beast howled.

The full weight of the wildling slapped me onto my back. The creature moved with me, its body pierced by Nightarmor. Belatedly it thrashed up. The outpouring of hot glowing blood through Khimmer's vision confirmed that the spike had found the rogue's heart. The rogue wildling flailed in its death throes. The red shape of it dimmed to a fading orange.

Shailagh cursed behind me, "Liam's lips. What have you done?" She had been clear; don't kill a wildling.

The shapes blurred around me, and I shifted again to gain footing, hoping to stand. The arriving wildling who slapped the rogue's body off me seemed angry enough for everyone. The shaggy fur hid any hint of its sex, but I guessed it to be male.

I hadn't meant to kill the rogue, or be the cause of its death. *Fare well into the house of Hades.* I raised an open hand. "My bad. Sorry about that." The spikes had been a bad idea.

Retract spikes.

The wildling ignored my apology and took a few swipes at Nightarmor. They had enough strength to shift me on the grass, but they would never get through the armor. The other long-armed shapes moved around the periphery.

Shailagh stood behind us, fingers splayed toward the ground in that strange way she had. The tree above her looked ominous and threatening. The branches appeared to have sharpened into spears, pointing at me or, more likely, the wildling. Was this more Fae magic?

A hairy leg moved, blocking my view of the high Fae,

and I raised my arms against the flurry of nails. It had become a show of frustration once they realized they couldn't shred through Nightarmor. "Sorry." I wanted to see that tree again. "Sorry."

One of the other wildlings yelled out, "You promised." I recognized Clarita's voice. "Stop!"

Shailagh snapped a reply as harsh as I'd heard from her. "Nails, it was a mistake."

I smiled inside my helmet. She'd defended me.

My attacker backed away. The branches of the tree behind Shailagh relaxed and returned to their gentle sway in the breeze. I sat up to get a better view.

Clarita, nude and in human form, stepped up to inspect the dead wildling rogue. "This could have been avoided."

Clarita was right. I hadn't needed the spikes, but I had thought they would deter the creature. She breathed in deep pulls of air. Six wildlings in beast form paced restlessly around us.

Still, Shailagh did not condemn me. "Perhaps." A non-committal reply that didn't completely exonerate my actions, but close enough.

I liked Shailagh's ability to remain calm under stressful situations, though it did remind me somewhat of the Aegis monks and their training. I didn't want to think of her that way. Slightly bruised from the first rogue's initial pounce, I shifted to my knees.

Clarita hunched toward me and reddened in Khimmer's vision, her voice growing thick. "It's done. But we will report this to your Council, Fae. My pack will demand it."

Her pack. Did that mean Clarita's coup had been successful?

Remove armor.

Yes, Mistress.

Clarita shifted quicker than Samuel had, and hair flowed across her skin like Nightarmor. Thick lips opened for a growl and her nostrils flared. Leading the others, the wildlings leaped for the top of the fence.

Shailagh studied me, watching the armbands that Nightarmor formed. Hopefully she wasn't too upset. "All good, right?" I asked.

Her eyes focused on mine. "There will be — repercussions." I couldn't tell what she meant, but I guessed it had to do with the other Fae. I hadn't wanted to cause her any trouble.

My pulse was slowing with the most immediate danger past. Shailagh's task had taken longer than I'd expected, and I wanted to get back. Tyler hadn't called, so they hadn't gone out on their own looking for John. We could search together. I might not be able to find John, but I could protect Tyler.

For the most part, working with Shailagh had been fun, exhausting, and more than interesting. Hopefully, I'd get a last trip through the Fae portal. I'd done all this in hopes of getting an answer that might get me closer to finding my way home. I'd spent part of the afternoon waiting in the witch's yard coming up with a question that someone with a knowledge of Earth's older secrets might know.

I nodded to the dead rogue. We'd found the killer. "Pay up. What do you know of the portals between planets?"

A long silence hung between us, and I feared she would lie to me or refuse to answer. Finally, Shailagh spoke in an off-hand manner. "There are no portals between Earth and other planets."

My heart sank. Shailagh's words were the truth. At least what she knew of it. There was one, a gate she didn't know about. I'd fallen from Duruce into a place on Earth called

Slovenia, where I met Tyler, Deanna, and John. I needed help in finding it to get back home and had hoped the Fae knew the location. I forced a smile back on my face.

Her demeanor changed and she rubbed my shoulder. "Listen, I'm sorry. I wish I could help. We should leave."

She spoke the truth, and I did have to get back to Tyler. Hopefully she meant another trip through the tree portal. The rogue had turned into a naked, dead human with a hole in his chest.

She rubbed my bare skin with her thumb. "Maybe we could celebrate?"

I grinned. I had been very interested in Shailagh at the beginning, but now I liked her. Once that happened it became difficult — impossible — for me to think of someone sexually. Old habits from a past life. I didn't want to insult her, and she wouldn't understand. "I'd be interested, I mean, you're hot, but I can't, because I've grown to like you." It all came out badly in a big lump. "I don't care what they say about the high Fae being stuck up, we had fun."

She frowned. The breeze brought the metallic scent of death from the rogue wildling. The crickets had gone silent.

My explanation hadn't helped, but I wanted her as a friend. Hopefully I hadn't ruined it.

She sighed, glanced back at the dead wildling, and nodded toward the street. "Let's get you home."

I stepped quickly to follow her, leaving the corpse alone in the back of the abandoned building. First thing when I returned, I would check on Tyler and Deanna; maybe John had come home, and in the excitement they had forgotten to call me. "You're not mad at me? We can be friends?"

Shailagh's expression changed to a near smile, then she frowned in a friendly way. The sigil carved into her forehead left only a hint or two in her smooth skin. "You are very strange, Ahnjii."

I opened my eyes wide and tilted my head. "But in a cute, likable way, right?"

Red hair bobbing, Shailagh laughed. "Yes."

CHAPTER 10

WE EXITED Shailagh's tree portal in Tallahassee with cool air that sent a shiver down my back.

"Will I see you again?" I asked.

The old Lichgate tree stretched around us in the dark with lower limbs resting on the ground. Few stars showed against the glow of the city. My eyes began to adjust to the darkness after the light of the portal. She paused with her side to me as she faced the trunk and took a deep breath.

Shailagh began reforming a gate within the tree. "Unlikely. I do not think my report will go well." The roots of the tree glowed before light climbed up the trunk. "I doubt we will meet again, unless something comes up that needs your unique abilities." The light from the tree brightened; intensely enough that I feared everyone could see it through the woods. She gestured to my shoulder. "Without the spikes, perhaps."

My ears warmed with a blush. "Sorry."

"Lesson learned." Shailagh stepped into the glimmer and disappeared.

Her lesson, or mine? I took a deep breath and exhaled

after the portal faded. The air held the scent of growth and flowers with a hint of exhaust. The trail back to the road proved difficult to find, but soon I walked alone beside the pavement. Litter dotted the grass edge and the tar let out an acrid scent. Frogs and crickets serenaded. No cars traveled from either direction, though I could hear them in the distance. Tallahassee, like Orlando, was never silent, though not as loud.

I pulled out my phone. It hadn't run out of electricity yet. I texted Tyler. "ARE YOU AWAKE?"

"YES. DEANNA'S ASLEEP I THINK."

"CAN I DROP BY?" I was tired, but guilt made me want to stop at their house.

"OF COURSE. I THOUGHT YOU WERE IN ORLANDO?"

"I'M BACK."

Tyler took longer than I expected to respond. "THAT WAS QUICK. WHO DROVE?"

My heart sped and my chest felt tight. I didn't want to keep secrets from Tyler, but Shailagh had asked. Tyler had never mentioned Fae before, wildlings, or any other non-humans on Earth. There were a few stories that I'd read with some creatures, but I assumed them fiction.

Khimmer, how long would it take to drive from Orlando to Tallahassee?

Depending on the vehicle, driver, and road conditions, I would average four hours, Mistress.

It had been longer than that since I talked to Tyler. "A FRIEND. I'M WALKING NOW. I'LL BE THERE IN HALF AN HOUR."

I hated keeping anything from Tyler, but I'd done it for Vivianne and Laura. The more I saw of other people on Earth, the more I understood.

I met Tyler at the pool behind the house to keep from

waking Deanna. "You didn't go looking for John today?" I asked.

Tyler sat at the edge of a poolside divan. "Deanna's investigators didn't want anyone messing up the scene, as she put it."

I let out a breath of relief that Tyler hadn't risked themself. "What can we do?" This visit was nothing more than me easing my guilt for taking off with Shailagh. I was being selfish. "There has to be something."

Tyler stood quickly, skidding their seat on the concrete. "There isn't, and it's driving me crazy. John's been gone too long to be a simple mistake. Three days. I hope he just went to Vegas or something."

Vegas?

Las Vegas, a city in the middle of a desert renowned for gambling and general debauchery, Mistress. Also called Sin City, you may know it from two of the stories we read.

I didn't remember, but it sounded fun. "Why do you think John went there?"

"I don't, Ahnjii." Tyler's tone turned sharp and angry. "I'm afraid something worse has happened, but his parents haven't gotten any ransom demands. The police are taking it seriously, finally, and no one has found his truck. He could be dead for all we know. I don't think he's in effin' Vegas."

I hadn't meant to anger Tyler. My guilt for not being available the day before hung heavy in my chest, however irrelevant. I needed to help. "There's got to be —"

"I'm going upstairs." Tyler's tone eased. "Hang out if you want to, skinny dip, skate, grab something to eat, crash in your old room. Whatever. Just don't wake Deanna if you can help it. I can't keep talking about this. I'm exhausted."

Tyler walked away with a deliberate stride. Beyond the

fences, cars rumbled in the city. The scent of the pool left a slick taste in my mouth. I felt empty. I had nothing to offer Tyler and Deanna after all they'd done for me. Perhaps I was too tired and hungry to think properly. I should get some sleep and talk to Tyler in the morning. As the door to the house clattered shut, I shuffled toward the side gate.

CHAPTER 11

AFTER THREE HOURS OF SLEEP, I woke to my phone
bugling when Tyler called. I needed to change the ringtone,
once I figured out how.

The morning light lit my bedroom through a sheet I'd
tacked over the window. Crust thickened my eyelids with
grit. Nightarmor's bangles, anklets, and bracelets clattered
dully as I sat on the edge of the bed. Cars were rumbling
outside. "Morning, Tyler."

"Sorry about being a jerk. I know how sensitive you are.
I'm driving Deanna to the police station, so I won't be home
for a bit."

"John?" I stood, ready to get dressed.

"No news. They just want to interview us."

I wrinkled the damp towel from last night's quick
shower under bare toes, wanting to help, but it didn't sound
like they needed me. "Want me to come along?"

"No, but thanks. Just didn't want you to plan on coming
over." Tyler's tone remained calm, but lacked their usual
casual demeanor. "They're probably wanting to remove us
as suspects."

My pulse quickened. "How could the police think you did something to John?"

"Common in a disappearance. We know two foremen and a worker saw John that morning at the office before he went to the site. We can prove we were at the house all day except for a trip to Publix, plenty of witnesses for the police timeline."

My shoulders tensed, and my tone sounded harsh when I spoke. "These police are wasting their time." I cared more about Deanna and Tyler than John, which wasn't fair and didn't make me feel like a good person.

"I know. Don't worry. I expected this. Once it's settled, they can continue investigating. I've got to go. I'll call later or if we find out anything. Love you."

After Tyler hung up, I shook off any lingering guilt, relaxed, and headed for the bathroom. I hated that I couldn't do anything to help. Maybe Bill would have some work to keep me occupied. I considered dropping back into bed, then thought about the day before with Shailagh. More than I wanted to admit, I'd enjoyed the skirmishes, except for killing the rogue. She seemed to think that would cause her trouble. I wished that she'd had some answer about my portal home. I wanted to see her again.

I called Vivianne. "What are you doing today?"

I heard a cat howl from the background. "Cleaning litter at the moment. Don't open until later. Want to help?" she asked.

I could hit up the Square Mug. "I'll bring hot tea."

"Me likes."

I smiled and stood. "I've got to get dressed. See you soon."

Ten minutes later, when I opened my front door, I

found Mrs. Forster sweeping dust onto the welcome mat Deanna had bought me.

Dark gray hair cropped short around a pale face, she scowled as I stepped out. "Heading out again?"

"Yes. Tea." I had tried at first to please the woman, but it seemed she liked being miserable.

She propped her broom against the railing and leaned on it. "You were out late. Young people nowadays take too many risks. In your minds, you inflate current and future resources. Pay attention to what you spend, emotionally and physically."

I locked the door, nodding in rhythm to her tirade. She'd burst a vessel if she'd known what I'd been up to. As she paused, I gave her a final nod and trotted down the stairs.

Mrs. Forster continued what Tyler called her armchair psychology. "It's cyclical. Manic thoughts encourage false positivity that yields greater risk taking."

Nightarmor's boots clattered down the steps, helping drown out her words. In the sun, the air felt warm, causing the garbage from the side of the building to taint the breeze. I didn't bother looking up at Mrs. Forster as I turned onto the street, but she'd be watching me.

Deanna enjoyed the Railroad Square Arts District, and it had become a perfect haunt for me when I'd first arrived. There were days and times when well-dressed visitors, such as Deanna, frequented the businesses. I enjoyed the quieter times when I could be the only one sitting at a bench under the pavilion at the Crum Box chatting with Pete the owner or wandering through a gallery without them expecting me to buy. This morning seemed like one of those muted times.

With a couple hot teas in a tray, I bought a croissant and ate it as I walked along the main road that led to the cat rescue and bookstore where Vivianne worked. My phone rang, and I let it go to voicemail. I'd check it when my hands weren't full.

Vivianne wore the blue rubber gloves the bookstore supplied for working with the litter, and I could see how her long Fae fingers stretched them and pulled the tops down to the edge of her palm. She wore a pinkish top that draped off one shoulder.

The room smelled of litter dust with a sharp tinge of cat urine. A gray tabby found my leg and rubbed against Nightarmor's boots.

Pointing to a chair inside the reading room, Vivianne waved the gloves. "Perfect timing. Almost done. You won't have to do a thing."

"Tea, though."

"Yes, tea, thank you."

A lanky, pitch-black beauty of a cat commandeered my lap. Short fine fur covered its muscles, and a quiet purr rumbled along its ribs before Vivianne came out to get her tea. I seriously considered getting one of the rescue kitties for my apartment, but Tyler had suggested I wait and see what my schedule looked like with a new job before I subjected a companion to it.

Vivianne sat down, held her tea without drinking it, and looked at me askance with a light sly smile spreading on her small Fae lips.

"What?" I asked.

"I've got a boyfriend." Her smug look growing on her face, she sipped her tea.

Fifth in four months. "Should I warn him?"

Her eyes rolled up, highlighting long lashes. "I'm not that bad. Just independent. Don't like men controlling me."

"Which is who you pick. You're not just independent, you're fierce about it." I gave her a big grin and teased her.

"Which is great, just they have no warning, and one slight comment and you rip their head off."

Vivianne didn't argue, but sipped her tea while the corners of her mouth formed a pleased smile. She liked it when we focused on her life.

I raised my own cup, enjoying the pungent steam. "And you're competitive. Then, you can flip to stressed in a heartbeat." I smiled over my tea. "But you're the best friend anyone could have. He'll be lucky to be with you. What's his name?"

"Chip." She said the name with a haughty snap, pretending to be insulted by my comments. This was not a new discussion. "You're no one to give relationship advice."

"True, but speaking of, I nearly tossed with a high Fae." I swallowed, suddenly remembering Shailagh's warning; surely Shailagh's prohibition against talking about her didn't include her own kind.

Vivianne spit, hastily brushing off her shirt. "What?"

I knew she'd flip. "Shailagh. Redhead. Are all the high Fae redheads?"

Vivianne sat up, cradling her tea in two hands. "Shailagh? Works for the Council. I've never met her, but everyone knows about her. Don't let her know about your truthsense." She seemed visibly worried.

"She already knew." *And learned even more.* I'd never discussed Khimmer or Nightarmor with Vivianne or Laura. In the first couple months I'd been on Earth, Tyler had built in a healthy concern about exposing Khimmer. I hadn't meant to with Shailagh. "Red hair?" I asked again.

"I never mentioned your ability to anyone. Not even my parents." She shivered. "Nails, be careful. The Council collects more powerful witches. Wouldn't put it past them to use coercion on you."

I shrugged off the concern. Perhaps Shailagh figured out I would be more than a handful for them. Or, she just liked me. "Red hair?" My lanky, black, lap-warmer slid off to climb into an empty chair where he yawned.

Vivianne rolled her eyes. "Yes, some high Fae have red hair, but so do low. I'm serious. You could be at risk."

"Shailagh seemed really nice, in a hard kind of way."

Raising her cup to her lips, she snorted. "Hmmph." Vivianne's first fingers were wrapped around the cup of tea, almost circling it entirely.

During the worst of it, Shailagh's long fingers seemed to be reaching toward the ground. Feeling awkward about rejecting her, I'd never gotten around to asking her about the strange positioning.

"Fae magic. Shailagh used bone discs to track and seemed to make trees move. Is that something Fae can do?" I would have considered those a power from the gods, but that was my world.

Vivianne sipped her tea a bit longer than normal. "Yes. High Fae, especially."

"What can you do? What other kind of magic is there?"

"Me?" She drew in a deep breath and looked at the window. "Plants like me, they grow well around me, and I know what they need, when they need it, if I'm connected to them."

Everything she'd been saying was the truth, but still I felt like she held back. Maybe I asked rude questions. It happened from time to time.

She started to take a sip and stopped. "Wait. Shailagh tracked with sigils and persuaded the trees? Tracked who? What were you doing with her? Had to be something dangerous to call trees."

"I helped her find a rogue wildling, but I think I got her

in trouble when I killed it. I'm not sure why; they were going to execute him anyway."

Vivianne spit tea again, causing the gray tabby walking by to jump with a hiss. "You killed a wildling? Are you mad? Killing even a rogue might cause a nearby clan to retaliate. Where? Here in Tallahassee?"

There were wildlings in Tallahassee? I had learned so much in one day, but I guessed there was a lot I didn't know. "The clan wanted to kill him, but yes, they were pissed I did it instead. No, Orlando. The first leader wanted the rogue dead, but didn't want our help, while the second used us to find it."

"Second leader?"

It did sound like a mess. My phone bugled in my pocket. Perhaps I could find a tinkling tone that reminded me of the portal. "Yeah, I think there was a coup over the whole rogue issue." I dug in my pocket. "Portals in trees, how did I not know this was a thing?" I'd barely scratched the surface of getting to know about the Fae.

Vivianne blinked as I answered my phone.

"Hello?"

Doris sighed. "Did you get my message?"

I pulled the phone back and glared at it. Why hadn't I checked? It could have been Tyler, or about John. "Sorry, not yet. I was carrying tea."

"Okay. Can you make a deposition in forty-five minutes? Make that thirty, now. Here at the office."

I stood with my tea. "Yes. Proper shoes?" I cringed waiting for her answer. Emery Porter intrigued me.

She chuckled. "No. Boots are fine."

CHAPTER 12

I WALKED through College Town toward Bill's office at a brisk pace. Cars sped down nearly empty streets while the students started to drift out of their apartments to the local shops and restaurants. In the short distance from Railroad Square, Tallahassee took on a heavier, exhaust-filled scent.

I straightened the shoulder straps to my bodysuit in the elevator. Doris had me coming to the office, but still I considered my bangles and armbands. I had to buy a shirt and skirt, in case they needed me at court. *Khimmer, can you reduce the jewelry on my arms?*

Yes, Mistress.

Nightarmor poured in a trickle up my arms and joined my choker, though it did not grow in size and weight. The door opened and a young, handsome professional in a well-fitting suit pulled back to let me exit. He focused on his phone. I turned in the hall to watch him enter the elevator.

In the building hung the scent of something fresh-baked mixed with a sweetness which reminded me of food at the Square Mug Cafe. The aroma made me more comfortable.

Doris looked up over her glasses as I opened the office

door. She went back to typing while I approached her desk. "He's in the conference room." Her gaze flicked up to me then she tilted her head to indicate behind me. "Down the hall past the bathroom. Last door."

The large room had a broad window at the end and was bright with the angle of the sun. A long oval table pointed toward the open view, and a brown-haired woman sat to the right while Bill sat opposite to the left.

"Thank you, Ms. Fate," Bill said, motioning to the chair beside him, then to the folder and pen placed in front of it.

The room looked nicer than his office. Glass cased shelving covered the wall behind the woman and fruit bowls decorated the polished wood of the table. It smelled perfumed and musty at the same time.

As before, the folder had a list of typed questions and beside each a "T" and "F" had been printed. Perhaps my handwriting hadn't been good enough before. I'd applied to enough places that I knew to circle the corresponding answer. I smiled, imagining that Doris had printed out the sheet.

"Ms. Olson, I just wanted to make sure of some items and see if we can get closer to finding out how to get Mr. Porter released." Bill blew out a short breath, puffing his cheeks out. His suit looked wrinkled, like he'd worn it all night.

The woman shook her head and managed to speak simultaneously. It was dizzying. "Emery didn't kill them. He would never."

Truth. She believed him to be innocent.

I glanced down at the paper, it wasn't on my list, so I added the two statements.

Bill caught the movement, and continued slowly, as if

giving me time to write. "We all understand that, Ms. Olson. We are all working together here."

He waited a second before I finished writing. "How long have you and Emery Porter been dating?" Bill asked in a conversational tone, like they were talking at one of Deanna's parties.

"Eight months." She smiled, then her face immediately dropped as if saddened.

Truth. I circled the "T" and frowned at the sloppy curves.

"Did you know or ever meet William Green, Theresa Green, or Brian Schwartz?"

"No. I don't think so. Emery didn't introduce everyone."

Truth. Why would he care if she knew the victims? Did Bill wonder if Emery covered for his girlfriend? She would have had to meet them, to kill them.

"Do you know anyone who could have killed William Green, Theresa Green, or Brian Schwartz?"

"No, of course not."

Truth. That would include her boyfriend, or anyone he might be covering for.

"After reporting Emery Porter's disappearance to the police, did you hear from him?"

Her eyes watered and I could feel her sadness. "No. He won't even talk to me now."

Truth.

"I'm sorry to keep dredging through this." Bill partially stood to reach down to a tissue box in the middle of the table. He slid it in front of her. "One last question."

There were no more questions on my sheet. I wiped my lips with the back of my hand and waited, ready to write out his impromptu query.

"Is there anyone that Emery might try to protect? Be

willing to lie for?" Bill flicked across the polished wood with one thumb.

The woman dabbed at her eyes, then nose, wadding the tissue into her fist. "He is very loyal. I suppose, any of his friends, or his brother."

Truth.

I scribbled question and answer on the paper as Bill read a list of names from his file. Evidently, he had a record of all those she might consider friends.

When Ms. Olson had finally left, Bill took the pad. "Good job on jotting this down." He smiled and handed the folio and sheet back to me. "I've met someone with worse writing than my own. Sit with Doris for a minute and let her type these up, while they're fresh in your head."

My cheeks flushed, but he had complimented me too. "Thank you." I gestured toward his file. "I'm guessing we'll be busy with these friends."

His eyes sparkled and he nodded almost imperceptibly. "You'll do well here. Yes, I think we'll be busy once Doris gets them scheduled. "Thank you, Ms. Fate."

Doris smiled genuinely as I opened the door and approached her desk. "How did it go, Dear?"

I grimaced as I handed her the pad. "Sorry about the list of names. They're all yes though."

She laughed, traced fingers across my added scribbles, and placed her hands on the pad. "I printed the list for him. I won't have any trouble with any of this. Sweet of you to be concerned." Her cheeks lifted her glasses when she smiled.

My face warmed. Doris felt like what I always imagined a mother or relative would be like. She was someone who cared and understood. "Good. I'll head out then, if you don't need me to explain anything."

Doris tapped the pad and straightened. "All good. You

take care."

The hall smelled empty and stale, with only a hint of some cleaning supply. I stepped outside into a warmer day and headed for some Boba tea. This part of town had old, tall buildings. The streets and sidewalks were well worn. Trees grew where they were allowed. Some people walked with purpose and speed, while others meandered and even smiled.

Laura would likely be at her studio by now. Sometimes she took longer to show up, but it was worth a visit. She'd told me once that her people, the Nedjir, were related to the wildlings. Having met the wildlings in both human and beast form, I couldn't see how.

The Crum Box had a customer entering the front door, and the air smelled of flowers and not of Pete's cooking yet. The sound of traffic seemed distant in the Railroad Square District, though busy roads surrounded it.

Laura's studio was one in a large metal warehouse left over from a distant time. I stepped through her unlocked door, the bell chimed, and Laura glanced over at me from her perch in front of her easel. She had golden-tan fur, but short and fine like a kitten's, not the shaggy mess that covered a shifted wildling. Her body, from what I'd seen, appeared human in every way under the smock.

The heat hung motionless in the tin warehouse. The painting by the door was a wash of blues and hints of greens with a scene of a deep forest that reminded me of sunward Vale Aganor. As I approached Laura and her easel, the fan beside her wafted the sharp scents of oils and pigments through the air.

I waved my nearly empty cup. "Boy, do I have a story to tell you." After explaining it to Vivianne, I felt I could really highlight the exciting bits.

Placing her paint brush down, she slid off the chair to stand in front of her work. "What have you done now?" Widely placed, round eyes with ruby red irises were midway down her face, leaving a broad forehead distinctively not human. Like the Fae, she supposedly had a sigil carved in the bone of her forehead that made her appear human to humans, but no hint of it showed. Her sphere-shaped head had two softly curved ears closer to a kitten's than a cat's. Her tiny nose and mouth added to the hint of feline. As far as I knew, she didn't shift or change. Humans saw someone very different; I had selfies of us to prove it. My truthsense didn't work against technology like cameras or photographs. How did it feel to go through life pretending to be something else?

"I met a wildling." Figuring I'd work my way up to killing him, I started with the comment to get her attention and then would jump back to the beginning with Shailagh.

Laura's eyes didn't widen — I don't think they could — but dark eyebrows lifted against the short tan fur and long eyelashes pointed up. "What? How? Why?" Her hands waved off the questions and she pointed at the folding chair that she kept for guests. "Tell me everything, from the beginning." She dropped to the paint-speckled concrete floor and the multi-colored smock rose exposing dark blue sweats.

I grinned as I sat, slurped a tapioca ball from my drink, and made her wait. Her ears twitched when she got impatient. Throughout my story, her expression changed, and I knew that she was less entertained and more horrified. I finished in a few minutes, despite my more theatrical attempts, and returned to finishing my drink.

"I hope the wildlings do not take this too personally, though you likely would have known if they envisaged you

harm. They do not spare others from their anger or threats."
She tapped her forefinger and thumb together, as if nervous.
"I might have been the one to divulge your secret. My
apologies that it reached one such as Shailagh. I had not
thought that my family would be in contact with any of the
high Fae. Unless we need a specific sigil, our two species do
not mix. The wildlings are the product of just such
mistakes. Cousins, half Nedjir, half Fae."

Lips left on my straw, I ran through the last comments
in my head. Laura or her family had told Shailagh, or her
people, about my truthsense. I wasn't upset; it had worked
out. "The wildlings are Fae and Nedjir children?"

"The descendants, at this point. Most of us have learned
the danger of such copulation." Her small mouth tightened.
"We tend to keep to our own, unlike the Fae."

Laura stood and took a long blink which I took as
sadness and an apology. She leaned down and hugged me.
"I'm sorry," she said.

I chuckled and hugged her back. "I love you. Nothing to
worry about."

"Still." Laura picked up a long wooden dowel and
poked a small black button installed high on the wall. A
tone rung from a speaker above it. "Dial, Regina," she called
out to a microphone, I imagined.

The speaker rang as if attached to a phone somewhere.
"You don't like electricity. I remember."

Laura tilted her head. "It hurts."

The speaker clicked. "Laura. Is this important? I've got
a problem here." The woman's voice sounded short and
exasperated.

"So do I," Laura said. "I'm with my friend, Ahnjii. The
one I told you about. Did you tell anyone else?"

There was a long pause and the woman's tone apolo-

getic. "Just my husband, but he might have run his mouth."
Regina made a light whistle. "Sorry. What happened?"

"High Fae." Laura managed a self-satisfied frown.

"Oh Tahit. What can I do? Does she — do you need a
place to hide?"

The latter part I assumed she meant for me. I smiled.
The sister seemed nice. "It's alright. I'm friends with her
now."

Laura looked sideways, still speaking loudly for Regina.
"Please ask him to stop talking about this. It's a little late
now, but let's avoid future damage."

With John's disappearance and Tyler's interrogation on
my mind, I hardly considered Regina's slip a problem. I
never would have met Shailagh otherwise. This morning I'd
been a little tired and a hair bruised, but otherwise I
counted this as a win. Bill's case was bringing in some
money, so I didn't have to rely on Tyler and Deanna.
Unable to get a clear direction on getting home was the
worst thing to happen, and that had just been an off chance
anyway. I shrugged at Laura, hoping she'd let it go.

Laura's lips tightened. "And anyone he told. Tahit's
curse. Just track it down and kill the gossip."

"Of course." Again, a light whistle sounded in the background. "This is awkward, but could I ask a favor?"

"What's wrong?" Laura asked.

"I've got a problem. We're trying to purchase some land,
a horse farm, and I think that they, the realtor and the seller,
are lying to me."

Laura's little mouth opened in obvious surprise, then
her long eyelashes blinked quickly. "Seriously? You want to
use my friend's ability after the trouble you caused her?"

I tapped Laura's arm with my fist. She needed to relax.
"Sure. I'd be happy to help."

CHAPTER 13

I HADN'T KNOWN that Laura had a car. An antique, evidently, that had been rewired by a witch in trade for some jewelry. The interior smelled musty, and she warned me that lighting, radio, and just about anything electronic didn't work inside.

Laura's lips tightened when she started the engine, and the light fur on her cheeks bristled.

How sensitive was she to electricity? "How far is it to this property?" I asked.

"Twenty or thirty minutes, mostly northwest on 27." As we drove, she rolled down her window with a crank and I did the same. The wind replaced the car's funky odor with exhaust.

I searched for something to say to break the silence. "You said the wildlings were children of the Fae and Nedjir, but it doesn't seem like you and the Fae get along very well."

Laura's lips pursed, and I wondered if I'd been rude again. She didn't sound annoyed when she spoke. "We've lost much of the history, but we have stories — long poems that don't translate well into English. We got along well enough at one time."

She cleared her throat, changing her tone as if reciting.

"North winds blew cold into Vinka
Brought the Fae, and all they possess
Fae and Nedjir entwined.
The children rise with water's tide
Learn well this warning to never accept, or
Fae and Nedjir mourn."

My brow furrowed. I didn't do poetry well. "So don't jump each other or children become wildlings? When was this?"

Laura leaned her head back. "Guessing by the placement in the Widdakis, eight thousand years ago? Yes, the water's tide is the Great Rise. Your friend, Shailagh, would have better records of all this. The high Fae document everything."

Eight thousand years. They had to know of traveling between my world and Earth, but Shailagh hadn't lied. Maybe I just hadn't asked the right question. I had to come up with better questions, in case she hired me again.

Regina waited for us at the gate, leaning against a fence post. She had a beak and feathers.

"That's your sister?" I asked. I'd expected a similar feline look, like Laura's husband and herself.

Laura nodded. "Oh," she said, pointing to her own petite nose. "Yes, she takes after my grandfather."

I flushed, feeling slightly rude. "I didn't know that Nedjir were different."

Regina approached wearing a gray checkered shirt rolled up at the sleeves, where tiny feathers ruffled. Her eyes were the same as Laura's and her head just as round, but the similarities ended there. The beak appeared hard, though small, and formed the top lip of her mouth, giving it a uniquely oval shape. I could see no ears.

As we stepped out of the car, she spoke. "The realtor's on his way. A couple minutes out, I'd guess." Regina nodded in my direction and gave me a long blink. "Sorry, again." Her bottom beak or lip looked glossy hard, but flexed with her words. "We'll meet him up at the house."

She nodded down a dirt road, lined with a single row of sprawling trees. The air smelled fresh and alive. Plain, green pastures stretched to the sides. A two-story building poked up at the far end. We walked until barns and a more recently built stable appeared.

"You said you made friends — with Inspector Shailagh?" Laura asked.

"She's nice."

Her eyes squinted at the comment. "That is likely the first time I've heard anyone say that."

Truth.

Should I be flattered that I had a good relationship with Shailagh, or suspicious? Tyler said my optimism toward people bordered on naïve. I shrugged. I might never see the high Fae woman again. That would mean my questions would continue to be unanswered, and I might be trapped on Earth, unable to get home, unable to complete my mission to kill the King my Queen had ordered me to, fulfilling the assassination which bordered on personal. Once I killed that man, then I could decide if I would forgive and continue fealty to my queen.

The house had a porch wrapping around the bottom floor and delicate white curtains in the windows. It looked empty but well kept. The barns were all closed and painted a rust red. The dull heavy scent of manure caught the breeze from the stables, though there were no horses visible.

How long would this take? The grumbling in my stomach reminded me we were close to lunchtime.

We stopped in the shade under the last tree of the row. Regina whistled in a long breath. "I don't want him knowing that you are probing his statements. You are sure of your skill? It is like the old truthsense, not just empathy?"

"Truthsense." I confirmed. It was not unknown on my world, but it sounded as if the ability had existed and been lost on Earth.

"We need a signal. Can you shift to one foot if he lies?" Regina asked.

I tapped the back of my calf with the toe of Nightarmor's boot, balancing easily.

She appeared satisfied and turned to watch the drive. "I just don't trust this human."

The realtor drove up in a white SUV and kicked up dust as he stopped. He was a tall man in a dark hat, and he jumped out of the car with too much excitement, a broad smile, and a wave. He shoved his hand out to greet Regina as he approached. The scent from the stables drifted in from a breeze.

"Mrs. Platt, great to hear from you so soon."

"I had a few more questions, if you don't mind."

"Of course, you'll just fall in love with the place more." He pulled up his hat and wiped back thinning, brown hair.

"The price seems too good for a property like this."

"It is. A steal."

Lie.

I lifted my right leg, tucking my toe around the back of my knee.

Regina tilted her head forward with her beak angling down. "All problems have been disclosed?"

"What's to disclose? It's a perfect deal."

Lie.

I left my leg hooked behind my knee.

Regina tilted her head further and her eyes narrowed. Her once pleasant features looked predatory.

The realtor never gave her a chance to ask another question. "This place is going to sell in the next day or two. It won't last on the market."

Lie.

I felt like one of those pink birds that Mrs. Forster had placed out front of the apartment building.

"You'll put a contingency into the contract? Upon full inspection and environmental assessment?"

He dabbed at his forehead with his sleeve. "I doubt the seller will want to wait that long to close, not at this price."

Truth.

Gratefully, I dropped my leg and rocked my knees back and forth to shake out the muscles.

Regina nodded. "Very well. Thank you for your time. We'll pass." She took a step to go around him.

He reached out, as if to stop her. "Wait, you're missing out on the deal of the century."

Lie.

Mid-step, I jumped back on one leg.

She pulled clear of his reach and sighed. "If you'll just disclose the concern, we can consider."

Shifting his hat and wiping sweat, he shrugged and gestured with a dismissive wave. "There might be some environmental issues with the creek and spring, but it's bordered by two other cattle farms, not just yours."

Truth.

"Cattle farm?" Regina asked. "You said it was always a horse farm."

"Yes, horse farm. I misspoke."

Lie.

I lifted my leg again. We needed a better signal.

Regina drew in a deep breath. "Goodbye. We'll pass."

He blustered and begged, but she plodded down the drive toward the cars, and I followed. Assuming she didn't care if he was lying at this point, I didn't hop on one foot behind her.

He passed us in a flurry of dust. We walked in silence, and I could sense Regina and Laura's disappointment.

When we reached the cars, Regina dug into her pants, pulled out a small medallion, and handed it to me. "You've saved us from a loss we might not have recovered from. Payment for services and a token of our apology for not preserving your privacy. My husband is mortified, as am I."

I waved off the offer. Ringed in silver, the black disc had eight decorative points radiating from a stone center; every other ray alternated light and dark blue. It looked like a compass that Tyler had on his dash. "No, I just wanted to help."

Regina stopped, red eyes squinting so her gaze appeared darker. "You must, for my honor." She pushed the medallion into my hand. "It is a compass. Only a human witch, Nedjir, or Fae can tap into the universe enough to make it work. I make no assumptions on your abilities. However, focus your desire into the sapphire in the center, and the glyph will point the direction, if your will and want is strong enough."

I opened my mouth to speak, then looked closer. I could see a small design etched in the center of the sapphire and an arrow point on the edge. My want was surely strong enough. I desired to go home. "Just hold it and think about what I want?" I asked.

"Focus your will into it." Regina gestured toward the compass.

My heart fluttered and I held my breath. *Home. Home. Home.* Tyler and Deanna could get me back on an airplane and back to Slovenia. I could find the gate. I had a plan to test and mark all six portals to find the one leading me back to Duruce. The stone didn't move. *Home.* I shifted and it just remained pointing wherever I aimed it. *Home.* "Home," I said aloud.

My chest drained as if empty. I couldn't look at them. Was I not strong enough?

CHAPTER 14

LAURA and I sat quietly at a table under the pavilion of the Crum Box waiting for Pete to bring out our order. Under the table, I held the compass, feeling the smooth ridges of the inlay with my thumb. Why wouldn't it work for me? It seemed unfair to learn such a gift existed and I couldn't use it.

The scent of cooking wafted from the little building, but my appetite had diminished. The customers at the table behind me were laughing, and it felt like they mocked me. I hated getting in these moods.

"You okay?" Laura asked, for about the tenth time. She did not know of my dilemma, didn't know about home. "Maybe it just needs something you want more."

There wasn't anything I could feel stronger about. I just didn't have enough "will" or whatever power Earth humans, witches, had.

My phone rang, and she visibly leaned away as I pulled it out. Tyler was calling. I stepped off the bench, not to keep the call private, but for Laura's comfort. "Hey." I slid the compass into my pocket, not needing to dwell on my failure.

"Where are you?" Tyler asked. "I'm heading toward your apartment."

"Having lunch with Laura. Crum Box. What's wrong?" Had John been hurt? I hadn't thought about him while I'd been helping Regina.

"Can you come with me and check out John's job sites? The police are getting nowhere. Deanna is — distraught." A horn sounded in the background. "After you eat? I can pick you up there."

Finally, I'd be able to help. "Of course."

"Thanks. See you in a bit."

I hung up as another customer walked into the pavilion. In the warmth of Earth's midday, he wore a dark brown jacket, leather perhaps. On top of his unkempt brown hair sat a straw hat with a purple band. It looked like Tyler's fedora, but without a red feather. The man had been watching me and glanced away while strolling toward a table in the far corner.

I had one leg over the bench when Doris called. Laughing, I shook my head at Laura. "Sorry." Stepping a few feet away I turned toward the sparse trees near the railroad tracks.

"Ms. Fate? Are you available at 4:00?"

The back of my neck prickled. I hadn't expected another interview so quickly, and I finally had a chance to help Tyler. "I, um . . ." It left me little time to help Tyler.

"Ms. Fate? It won't take long. Half an hour at the most."

I rolled my neck. "Okay. Office?" I'd have to change; standing out in the sun had started me sweating.

"Yes, thank you."

I stuffed the phone into my shorts as Pete popped out of his restaurant with plates, smiling in my direction. He worked alone today, but always made the best food around.

My appetite returned as he slid a cup of mac and cheese beside my sandwich. "Need anything else?" he asked.

"Looks perfect." I stabbed cheesy noodles and gave him a quick grin. "Thanks."

By the time I'd finished the hearty sandwich and licked the cheese out of the cup, Tyler pulled up in their car. The meal had stuffed my stomach, and my moodiness had settled. I stunk and needed to change. Laura was just finishing her sliced cucumbers.

I motioned toward Tyler. "I've got to go."

"Good luck," she said.

I'd filled her in on John's disappearance, what little I knew. "Thanks. I'm not sure what help I can be. The police are investigating, and Deanna's hiring a private investigator as well."

"Just being there for people is enough." She stood and wiped her lips.

I wanted to believe in her words, but my mood hung dark like an Earth night. Dust clouded under our feet as we walked. The only other customer, the man in too-warm clothes, never glanced at us. The flowers near the front smelled sickly sweet.

Tyler stood outside as we left the pavilion. They wore dark make up around their eyes. Usually calm, their face looked tight. "Hi, Laura. Sorry to interrupt lunch."

"Perfect timing."

To Tyler, Laura would look like a human woman with light brown skin, wavy, chest-length brown hair, and a broad nose. They'd met a few times when I'd been traipsing around the studios with Tyler.

"I'll see you tomorrow." I flashed a grin at Laura before turning to Tyler. "I'm sorry, but Doris called. I've got a job at 4:00, but that gives us a few hours. Mind if we drop by my apartment so I can change first?" Regret tinged my tone.

Tyler just nodded. They seemed stressed, likely over John or the interrogation. We walked briskly toward their car.

"Are you sure it's okay? I mean about work?" I asked.

"I don't expect to find anything. I just can't sit in the house anymore. Deanna said the investigators she hired have been over everything multiple times. We can't mess anything up."

I'd drive with Tyler out to the site and see what we could find before I headed to Bill's interview. It didn't sound like they expected to find anything, but at least we were doing something.

CHAPTER 15

WITH MY BELLY COMFORTABLY FULL, I climbed into Tyler's passenger seat and tried not to smell myself. The air conditioner kicked on with a low buzz as we started onto Famu Way.

Tyler smirked. "I should have grabbed something to drink for the ride. I'll drop you off to change and pick something up." They reached to turn up their music and paused. "When we're done, can I drop you off directly to your job before four?"

"Works for me."

They pulled to the curb and let me jump out, pulling away as I crossed behind the car.

Mrs. Forster peeked out her window, and I sprinted toward the pink birds and the stairs, hoping to beat her to my door and get inside. Instead, I heard Shailagh's throaty, almost sultry voice. "Ahnjii."

I spun to a stop. Shailagh stood up from the base of the large oak outside my apartment building. Despite her bright red hair, I'd managed to not notice her. She had on a slightly different green skirt. The necklace she wore swirled around the blue-green stone at the center. "What are you doing here?" I asked, then shook my head. "I'm getting ready for work."

She took a step closer. "For William Buford, Esquire?"

A breeze stirred the leaves around us. Someone nearby smoked tobacco. How did she know about my job? My breath shortened and my skin prickled across my neck. Evidently, the high Fae had a good intelligence network, much like the Queen and the Aegis monks had at home. They used spies and informants. One of Shailagh's had talked with Regina's husband, or someone he told. "Yes." I had no reason to deny it.

"Are you working on the Emery Porter case? Have you met him?"

Curiosity gnawed at me. However, I didn't have time for this conversation. Mrs. Forster had left her apartment and swept the second-floor walkway, peering at us over the railing. She'd slow me down. What did Shailagh have to do with Bill's client? I took a step closer. "Why do you ask?" I flushed. Helping the high Fae might get me answers, might get me closer to home than that useless compass. Was that my motive? "Never mind. I have to get changed. I'm helping my friends, then I'm going to work." Grabbing the end of my braid and flicking it, I didn't leave.

"I ask about Emery Porter because the circumstances appear unusual. His behavior, if I understand it correctly, might indicate a situation that could concern the council."

I'd been able to see if Emery were Fae or Nedjir; they had physical differences. "A wildling?"

"No, and the murders didn't seem brutal enough."

"He didn't kill those people."

Shailagh tilted her head. "You truthsensed this? Yet, he admits to committing the crime. Who is he covering for?"

"That's what we're trying to find out." I stiffened. Bill would likely not want me discussing any of this. Besides, how did this involve the high Fae? "How does this effect you?"

"I can't divulge that."

Lie.

I huffed. Was this a negotiation? Deanna explained it as a common practice when she'd lied while buying an antique lamp. "I probably shouldn't be discussing Bill's clients, either." I remembered Regina's actions, and I turned as if to walk away. Truthfully, curiosity had the better of me. If the high Fae had a concern with Emery Porter, I wanted to know.

Shailagh scoffed. "Very well. A deal. You tell me everything about this human and the investigation, and I will honestly impart something which might have bearing on Emery Porter's state, an aspect of the high Fae that the Council would not approve of me disclosing. You will not repeat what I tell you. I will use your information solely in my investigation."

I knew I shouldn't, but the desire weighed too heavily. Besides, it might help me find answers to questions Bill wouldn't know to ask. "Agreed."

She gestured in the air. "There is an ability, restricted by the accord, that allows the Fae to control humans. Your people called it enthralling. Your knowledge of it seems to have been lost in the history of your short lives. No witch has ever mentioned it to me, at least. Among my people, it is illegal to create thralls, but some Fae have, on occasion."

Did Emery protect a Fae? *Is that who murdered those people?* "And, I'd be able to tell if someone in the investigation were Fae, with my truthsense."

"That would be unbelievably lucky for me. However, I

doubt they would allow themselves to come to anyone's attention. There are very few high Fae who live outside our control, that we know of. They do not live amongst humans."

I shifted uncomfortably and glanced up at Mrs. Forster. How did humans on Earth coexist with all these other creatures? We only had humans on Duruce. On Earth, the high Fae seemed more in control than anyone else. "Why do you think Emery Porter is a thrall?"

"The magic leaves a trace inside the thrall's head. A link to their connection. You would not be able to see it. High Fae, or even more powerful low Fae, can see a faint white glow to the eyes." She shrugged. "One of our low Fae works in the prison system and spotted it yesterday. I've been assigned the case." A sly smile crossed her lips. "Then I learned that I knew someone who had a job working with this Emery Porter."

I hadn't seen a glow, but the failing compass proved I had little abilities beyond truthsense. Shailagh hadn't lied. Emery Porter, a thrall, protected someone, likely the Fae who controlled him.

Shailagh studied me as if waiting for a response. Could Shailagh enthrall me? If she could, we likely would have had sex by now. The air seemed to still, as if waiting for me to answer.

Tyler drove toward us down the street. I needed to help find John. "Crap." Thralls would have to wait. I moved toward the street. "Meet me here when the sun disappears; it will be after my next meeting with Bill, and we'll finish this conversation."

Her eyebrows raised and an annoyed expression passed over her features, then her lips fought a smile. She liked me.

CHAPTER 16

I JUMPED into Tyler's car and let out a tight breath. The air conditioner chilled the sweat under my arms and neck.

Tyler frowned. "I don't think you've changed, unless you have another black bodysuit with a fresh cheese drip on the side of your left boob." They started driving before I had my belt on.

Hades, I stunk. "Where?" I scooped off thickened cheese, rolled down the window, and flicked it out. "Sorry if I smell. I got stuck talking with someone."

"The wanna-be psychologist lady?"

"Mrs. Forster? No." I paused. "I'll find out more tonight. Where are we headed?"

"There's a job site southeast that John was supposed to visit the day he disappeared. A parking lot for equipment and supplies. The police and investigators have checked it, but I need to do something to try and help." Tyler's lips tightened. "Deanna is beside herself."

We passed the airport, and Tallahassee seemed to come to an end. There were other roads with only a few farmhouses visible. Bogs dotted the side of the small highway.

After a few minutes, we turned down a dirt path with room for one car. The trees let in plenty of light, but the woods looked like a tangle to walk through.

The construction site had a wire fence built around a trailer, a bulldozer, and some equipment on flatbeds. A large chain locked the gate. Tyler pulled to a stop just halfway out of the road.

"What are we looking for?" I asked.

"Hell if I know." Tyler jumped out and dug into their pocket for keys.

I could see tracks in the dirt. Plenty of footprints crisscrossed the yard. I didn't see anything they were constructing, but a small section of trees and brush had been cleared outside the fence. The scent of swamp and decay mixed with fresh pine and growth.

We had to find something. The number of footprints told me that someone had been over the area many times. Paw prints indicated they'd brought a dog to sniff John out. Tire tracks pulled close to the fence where Tyler had parked.

The gate creaked when we entered. The dirt held so many footprints, even the best tracker would not have made any sense of it. Shailagh's magical discs would work well in this situation. Could I work a deal to get a pair? I drew in a slow breath. I might need a magic that I didn't have, like for the compass.

From the mess and tousled sheets, someone had been sleeping in the trailer, but it smelled musty, like no one used it. The heat had built up inside, making me sweat immediately. I jumped out as soon as I could and headed for the gate to walk outside the fence along the cleared property.

At the corner, a twisted piece of root caught my attention. It almost appeared crafted. Looking at the turns of roots reminded me of the carvings in the bone Shailagh had used, similar to the temple writing of Helios. I picked it up and smelled a metallic taint. The ground had dark stains that could have been from someone bleeding.

Tyler came up behind me. "What did you find?"

I straightened and showed him the odd twisting of roots. "Strange, huh?"

Immediately Tyler's eyes averted. They winced and squinted left toward their car. "What?"

I moved the roots, and again Tyler turned their gaze. "Can you see this?" I asked.

Tyler tried, then stepped back, face down, and turning pale. "I feel sick."

Fae magic, but what kind? I held the roots sideways to them. "Can you see it now?"

Tyler flicked their eyes up and took a deep breath. "Yeah, a root."

I turned it so the design faced them.

As if in pain, Tyler closed their eyes. "Unnh."

I'd need to ask Shailagh, or Vivianne. There was no reason to torture Tyler. I tucked the roots in the back pocket of my shorts. "Over here, is this blood?" I'd likely had more experience than they did, but I also wanted to see their reaction.

They knelt, fingers poised over the largest stain, but not touching. "Maybe, I don't know. But the police were out here."

And likely the police couldn't stand to look at the twined roots any more than Tyler. If this were some sort of sigil, then the Fae were involved. I had a more important question for Shailagh than anything to do with Emery Porter.

Blood didn't bode well. "Maybe the police should check this again. Or Deanna's investigator."

Tyler nodded, staring at the stain the size of a dollar bill. "What was that root?"

I didn't want to explain about the Fae and betray Vivianne's trust. Shailagh's involvement made it more difficult, but if the Fae were part of John's disappearance, then everyone needed to know. I'd find out more and talk with Vivianne before I made that decision.

"I'm not sure. I'm going to ask around."

Tyler didn't pry, but stood slowly, pulling out their phone. "I need to tell Deanna. She's going to freak." They typed with a frown. "I like it better when I'm the one in trouble."

My stomach churned as the phone dialed. Deanna and Tyler had helped me every way they could. They'd nursed me back to health after I'd first arrived on Earth, helped me acclimate to a foreign world, bought false documentation so the authorities wouldn't imprison me, and gave me food and shelter. The clue I wouldn't tell them about was one they possibly couldn't use, but it felt like betrayal just the same.

"D, I found something out here at the Lost Lake site. There's a spot that could be blood. Why don't . . ." Tyler took a deep breath as Deanna's voice rose. Waiting patiently, they continued, "Why don't you get your investigator out here? They can meet us, or I can leave a marker."

Tyler didn't look at me as they listened to Deanna's reply. Embarrassed and awkward, I strode around the car and road, looking for more blood. The woods smelled partly of decay, turned earth, and fresh growth. Other than the two ruts dug into the grass, little proof of civilization existed beyond the construction site. If John had been attacked out here alone, no one would know. I might hold the key to his attacker but couldn't explain how or who.

"Okay, I'll wait." Tyler knelt down. "She's calling the investigator. The police should have found this."

I guessed that Deanna would be yelling at the police soon. Tyler and their sister came from a wealthy family, not nobles, but something similar. She tended to utilize that status when she needed something.

I was across the road looking through brush when Tyler's phone rang.

"Yes, we'll wait. Twenty-five minutes." Tyler glanced at me and nodded when I didn't object. "Yes. We won't leave. Or disturb anything." Deanna talked through each of their answers, so they commented in quick snippets. "Bye. Yes. Call them. They should have found it."

At least they'd be able to see the blood now. I'd done something helpful. If the sigil was what I believed it was, then no one except me could have seen it. Whatever lie it told, I didn't react to it. Tyler needed to know about the Fae, but first, I'd talk to Vivianne. Betraying secrets was not something I could accept. I didn't have to mention her.

When the wiry man with a piercing glare came out to investigate, I stayed away, hoping that Tyler would not mention the strange tangle of roots. The man seemed skeptical but took pictures and a sample.

We left the investigator after a couple minutes and followed the road to its end, dirt parking that looked rarely used. Tyler suggested that hunters used these roads.

I wanted to believe I'd helped, though it was selfish.

When we returned to the city and came in sight of the airport, I checked my phone. There was still enough time to change clothes before my afternoon job.

I had to speak loud over the punk music. "I need to

change." A shower would be better, but I could throw some deodorant on and cover the worst of the smell.

Tyler gave me a thumbs up and smiled. They didn't hold my secrets against me. All during my search for the gate back home, they'd accepted that I wouldn't disclose what I was doing, but recognized its importance to me. In my previous life, I hadn't met many friends like that. Well, *any*.

We pulled up along the road so I could jump out and fly upstairs, change, and make it to Bill's office in time. Tyler would give me a ride.

Shailagh stepped out from behind the tree and I froze. "Are we ready to continue our discussion?" she asked.

Traffic buzzed up and down the street. Voices carried in the wind. The sun hadn't drifted out of sight yet. Had she been waiting there the whole time? The passenger door to Tyler's car was still open, and I closed it quickly. It slammed too loudly. "No time. Got to change and get to work."

She didn't respond; instead, she looked over the car and her expression turned into a coy smile. "Hello. Aren't you lovely?"

Tyler had stepped out to see who had startled me. They grinned at Shailagh's greeting. My stomach hardened. They didn't need to know each other. I couldn't stop it, but I didn't have to introduce them, and I certainly didn't need to stand there and watch them eye each other.

"I've got to change and get to work." Flushed, I headed for the stairs, hoping to make the door before Mrs. Forster came out of her apartment. I was in no mood for her rambling.

CHAPTER 17

I ROCKED ON MY TOES, waiting for the elevator up to Bill's office. One seemed on its way down but stopped at each floor. The other hung on the second floor.

I'd reacted badly with Shailagh and Tyler, though I had no romantic or physical intentions with either of them. They were my friends. Jealousy had never been an issue for me. I had let it get in the way of asking her about the root, not that I'd want to do that in front of Tyler, but it hadn't even crossed my mind.

The walls of the hall were a dull beige, and the tile floor was scuffed and well used. The red numbers above the elevator door stalled at two. I straightened my shoulder straps and glanced up and down the halls to make sure we were alone. *Khimmer, reduce jewelry.*

Yes, Mistress.

Nightarmor poured up to my choker. Khimmer would request to return as quickly as possible since it took energy for Nightarmor to condense this much. I never understood, but I'd grown to expect the bangles and armbands so that when they were gone, I felt naked in some way. The door to the elevator opened and I stepped inside.

When I reached Doris, I pointed down the hall to the conference room. She glanced over her glasses and nodded. "They are waiting," she said.

Bill introduced me to Derek, a large man, both tall and wide. He was a co-worker of Emery Porter. Bill started with the same questions he'd asked the girlfriend, though this list extended back to the day of the disappearance.

"When was the last time you saw Emery Porter?" Bill asked.

"That's the weird bit. It was after he was reported to have disappeared. I saw Emery at a grocery store down in Crawford. Cops didn't believe me."

I marked off the "T" and tapped the pen, already bored.

"When was this?"

"Three weeks ago. He looked like hell. Didn't even respond to me when I called out to him. I was in line, so I didn't go over to where he was. Should have. He just put down his groceries and left the store. I reported it to the police. I think they thought I was mistaken, but it was him. Worked with the man the past eight years. A little hair didn't change him."

I scratched some notes and got the basics.

"Hair?"

Derek gestured around his own face. "Beard and long hair, like he hadn't shaved or nothing."

"You're positive it was him?"

"Yep. He heard me, too. Not that he showed an expression for all I yelled when he started to leave. People thought I was crazy, but he just looked at me dead in the eye. Kinda crazy like inside, but vacant on the outside. Didn't run or nothing, just walked out."

I chilled at the description, and wrote the question as answered true. *Thrall.* Everything Shailagh mentioned came back to haunt me. Could her people really do that to humans? What else?

"Other than the grocery store, when was the last time you saw Emery Porter?"

I had to write this one in, as we'd already used the question previously.

"Before he disappeared. The crew went out for dinner at this BBQ joint. We'd been on site in south Tallahassee. I was headed home. Emery planned another night on site. The crew was local. A few of us left, and Markie hung with Emery 'til they split up. Emery was supposed to go back to the trailer on site, then home the next day."

Bill pulled up his notes. "The site, off LL Wallace Road?"

"That's the one."

That Shailagh's thralls could be real, and Emery Porter one of them, gave me the chills. Earth was a very strange place and a bit more dangerous than I'd first suspected. It might be that John had somehow gotten caught up in all this, no matter how unlikely that seemed.

The notes climbed up the edges of the page when I ran out of room. I'd have to go over all this with Doris. I could barely read my own scratches.

Would Shailagh be waiting for me? How much would I be willing to tell her about Bill's business? The information could be important. If it led me to find John for Tyler and Deanna, then it would be worth the indiscretion, especially if Bill never knew about it.

Doris looked at the paper and her eyebrows shot up. "Where did you learn to write?"

Sitting around the pool with Tyler, but Doris probably

didn't need or want a real answer. English letters were strangely designed with lots of curves. I had a difficult time combining them correctly. "I'm sorry. Horrible, isn't it?"

I leaned my hip on her desk casually, though I itched to speak with Shailagh.

CHAPTER 18

THE HALLWAYS SMELLED like pizza and made my stomach growl. I rode the elevator down alone. Other than Doris and Bill, the building appeared empty.

It had taken longer than I thought to go through the questions with Doris, and I asked if I kept her from leaving on time. She'd laughed at my concern and called me sweet. I had liked the comment, though she didn't know me very well.

I shifted the straps on my bodysuit. *Khimmer, return jewelry.*

Yes, Mistress.

Nightarmor coiled down my arm returning the black, gold, and silver bracelets and armbands. The door opened as they finished, and a security guard glanced as he passed. He had a tight build with a darker complexion than mine. I returned his smile.

I had to get back to Shailagh and hoped she waited at my apartment. If Emery Porter had been enthralled, I wanted to know more about all this. Could she help fix him?

If he didn't kill those people, he didn't deserve to be punished.

I'd bring up the twisted root to her this time.

At the door, I turned back as the guard walked away; uniforms and suits fit better on Earth.

The street stunk of exhaust, but I made my way quickly home. I watched for the high Fae as I approached, and her red hair gave her away as she sat at the base of the tree. It was a wonder Mrs. Forster hadn't called the police. Shailagh leaned up to walk over and meet me near one of the pink birds.

Relieved, I offered her a big grin. "Dinner?" I nodded toward my apartment.

"No. Can we walk?" She'd obviously learned the area as she led us toward the water.

The lightly wooded area smelled like marsh, but vegetation grew on the top of the water like a proper pond. The sun had dropped to the horizon, where I found it most comfortable. I still had not gotten used to it moving, nor being so high overhead midday.

"Did you talk with Emery Porter? Anything that would confirm my suspicion?"

I took a deep breath and explained the relevant portions of Bill's interview. It didn't exactly feel like betrayal, but I'd gotten used to being committed to the Queen and her Aegis monks. I would never have discussed their activities.

We reached the water's edge and Shailagh nodded. "Enthralled."

"Can we fix him?"

She laughed. "No. The only recourse would be to have one of the oldest enthrall him to them, and they would never do such a thing. Whatever high Fae he is enthralled to would have to die to break the bond, and we will not kill them. This human will never be free again." She turned and bowed her head slightly. "I regret that."

I didn't understand completely, but there were similar myths about followers of Helios, fanatics who would blindly die for their devotion, supposedly entranced by the god. I couldn't discuss that with Shailagh, though.

She knelt to pick one of the water flowers. "A dominar, a wight, I fear. I could use your help again, if you are willing to replicate our deal."

"A wight?" I asked.

Shailagh's head twitched, then she stood, holding a pink blossom. "I suppose, if I ask you to help, you should be aware of the danger. As we high Fae age, there are some of us who grow into our magic, leaning toward our nature with physical manifestations. Some embrace this change and exude wood or bone from our bodies, becoming Osiri or Orobru. Once begun, they take on those aspects. The most extreme of these among the ancient high Fae we consider wights, as they develop an ability to cycle their physical form in a perpetual rebirth. They often outlive their natural Osiri or Orobru lives, but become consumed by wood or bone elements. They live with forms both in decay and regrowth. Most can be erratic and dangerous."

I tried to imagine what physical changes she could be describing of her people. How could people grow wood? Bone made more sense.

"You will help me find this wight?" She asked in an assuming tone.

A bird call echoed across the water. Leaves crunched under Nightarmor's heel as I shifted. I wouldn't want more people enthralled, even if I couldn't benefit from an answer. I might need to ask her something concerning John. "Two answers."

She smiled. "Only one."

"Two." I straightened, as if unmovable.

"Do you not know that Fae are empaths, more so than your human witches? Like yourself, but not to your degree of surety. It is clear you care about Emery Porter, and any other human at risk." She nearly laughed through her comments. "One answer."

My cheeks warmed. I guessed that an empath could know what I felt. If it came to choosing, I'd pick a question about John for Deanna's sake. "That's not fair." I tried to make myself angry, but I liked her. "Why do you even need me then?"

"Mine are a vague sense, a hunch if you would, whereas yours are definitive. They would have to be, to see through a sigil." She tilted her head and wore a gentle smile. "We'll start in the morning, if you agree."

I faced the water. "Morning then." My stomach had been reminding me of dinner anyway. I'm glad she didn't plan another all-night excursion. I needed sleep.

She turned toward the road, and I followed. The shadows from the trees shaded the street. The temperature had dropped.

"What do you know of Emery Porter's whereabouts prior to his disappearance?"

I'd just written some of this during the interview. "He was supposed to spend the night in a trailer, somewhere on LL Wallace Road, south Tallahassee."

She stopped. "Correct. I have the location. There is a portal within a thirty-minute walk of there."

I smiled at the idea of using the portal. Hopefully Doris didn't call me in to work. The more I learned about the high Fae, I could see why Vivianne warned me not to get involved. She'd be headed home by now, or I'd ask her about thralls and wights. *And roots.*

I spun toward Shailagh. "I have something to show you, not part of the question I'm asking, but I'm hoping you can help." I couldn't wait until she found the wight for her to answer.

"What is it?" she asked.

I had left it on the kitchen counter when I changed. "Roots."

"What?"

"Come back to the apartment, and I'll show you."

An expression washed over her face too quickly to be sure, but I guessed that she considered a more intimate invitation than I'd been suggesting. I just wanted her friendship.

"In the morning," she said. "Sunrise. I'll be outside."

"Sunrise." She hadn't refused to discuss the roots. If she told me what I needed to know about the roots, then maybe I could sneak in a question about the compass as well.

When I raced up the stairs to my apartment, guilt warmed my face. I was using Shailagh to get the answers I wanted. That felt wrong, if I considered her a friend, but friends shouldn't have to make deals to tell each other what they knew. Keys in hand, I made for the door. I didn't tell Tyler everything I knew. Mrs. Forster rattled the locks on her door. I slipped inside and let out a breath. In the morning, we would search for the wight.

Earth had become complicated.

CHAPTER 19

I woke to my phone's alarm in the dark and slapped the floor searching for it. The temperature had dropped, leaving my room chilly outside of the blanket.

Khimmer, cover.

Yes, Mistress.

Nightarmor flowed into a thin, pliable outfit that covered all but my hands and head. Tyler called it my wet suit, and the pictures they'd showed me compared, except I didn't need a zipper.

I stumbled for the kitchen and turned on the light, my phone still in hand. I usually woke around this time anyway, but it had been a rough couple of days, and sleeping in would have been preferred. The strange, twisted root sat on the counter. What would Shailagh think of it?

Tyler texted as I waited for the tea's water to boil. "CAN'T SLEEP, WANT TO SKATE?"

I did enjoy early morning skate sessions. I'd learned on the wood floor of their basketball court. "CAN'T. WHAT ARE YOU DOING UP?"

"RESEARCH. THERE'S BEEN A RISE IN MISSING

PEOPLE IN THE COUNTY. WHY CAN'T YOU SKATE?
WORK?"

I took a deep breath. Deanna and Tyler had been
dealing with John's disappearance for a few days. It had to
be wearing on them. The teapot whistled, and I poured a
quick cup to start steeping. I couldn't tell Tyler about
Shailagh. "I'M WORKING WITH AN INVESTIGATOR TO SEE
WHERE OUR CLIENT DISAPPEARED."

"WHAT DOES THAT HAVE TO DO WITH HIS
MURDERS?"

"THAT'S WHAT WE WANT TO FIND OUT." A lame
response, but I couldn't tell Tyler what I suspected, not
without betraying Vivianne's secret or her people.

"WHERE'RE YOU GOING?"

"SOMEPLACE OUTSIDE OF TALLAHASSEE." The tea
had a rich aroma, an Asian stock from what I understood.
Deanna had given me a bunch as a housewarming gift. It
was one of the nicer Earth customs I'd experienced.

"OKAY. I'LL CHECK IN LATER." Was Tyler disappointed?

Carefully, I dropped to the kitchen floor and drank my
tea, leaning back against the cabinets. I didn't have much to
do to get ready for Shailagh except dress and eat some corn-
flakes out of the box. Tyler had tried to get me to eat them
with milk, but they tasted worse and got soggy. We had our
philosophical differences when it came to breakfast.

I dressed and walked outside, where the sky had turned
gray before the sun would come up. I enjoyed the colors of
sunrise and sunset, but the midday, night, and twilight gave
me the creeps. The sun shouldn't move like that. I wore
only a bodysuit and shorts, so the morning chill bit when I
stepped out of my apartment. It would warm up later.

Shailagh waited at her tree. The gray sky cast a questionable pallor to her skin. The sun would brighten her hair as it livened the world.

I pulled the roots from my back pocket and held it as I approached. Her eyes focused on it immediately; she did not have the same aversion as Tyler.

"What is that?" she asked.

"Have you ever seen anything like it?" My eyes flicked to the side, and I felt some qualms over using our friendship.

She took it from me. "These are sigils, a complicated set. Normally this would be carved into wood."

"Fae then."

"Or Nedjir, though they can't manipulate roots like we can. They would have preferred carving in stone for their work." She flipped the twisted pancake back and forth. "Beautiful work. Humans can't look at it, right?"

I nodded. Why would the high Fae hide John's disappearance, or had it been coincidental? I had no proof, but worried that John was somehow connected to Emery Porter. I had never realized the Nedjir worked with sigils. In fact, I remembered Laura stating that the sigil carved into her bone had been done by a high Fae, at an expense. The Nedjir had given me the compass though. Hades, I'd left that upstairs by my bed.

"Have you ever heard of a compass that points toward what you want?" I asked, blurting it out before I realized.

"Yes. Nedjir stonework. They tie into the universe's threads with glyphs. They are quite adept at the skills they know, but not very adaptive. Sigils were taught to the high Fae long ago, but we have mastered their use and even overcome photographic and electronic images. The onslaught of human technology over the past century has proved challenging."

I took a short, tense breath. "What does it take to make these compasses work?"

"A connection to the universe." She shrugged. "The heavy lifting is done in the creation, like sigils. Even a human witch can use them, though few Nedjir or high Fae would let them have one. The devices are notoriously unreliable and high Fae consider them a waste of time. Someone such as yourself would have no problem, obviously, but you might end up following a useless loop." Shailagh tapped the roots with a long finger. "Where did you find this?"

I stumbled mentally. Why did the compass not work for me? Shailagh made it sound easy. I had to be using it wrong, or perhaps that's what she meant by unreliable. "A friend is missing. We found it at the construction site he was working at."

Shailagh stiffened. "What? Why didn't you mention this?"

"Mention what?"

"Your friend has gone missing at a construction site where a Fae sigil exists. We are headed out today to a construction site where Emery Porter disappeared, before becoming a thrall which is also connected to a Fae."

Cold washed down my back. I'd considered there might be Fae involved, just not the wight. Deanna would be devastated. "Can a wight use sigils?"

She scoffed. "Of course, they are ancient high Fae."

I'm an idiot. "You think John's a thrall now?"

"It certainly is a coincidence worthy of consideration." Her tone made me feel embarrassed.

I hadn't wanted to face it, but it had been at the back of my mind. The wight had to be located. "Tyler says there's been more missing people lately."

"At construction sites?"

"I never asked."

"Well, don't alarm them, but see if you can get details."

I pulled out my phone and stared at it. How had I ignored this? It made horrible sense. This couldn't happen to Deanna and Tyler. Well . . . and John. There had to be some way to fix this. Kill the wight? I glanced at Shailagh who waited for me to type. Why did they avoid killing people who would do this to others? These were their elders, I could understand that, but wouldn't freeing people matter? Maybe humans didn't. Again, I could see the concerns Vivianne had with high Fae; they seemed self-absorbed.

If I had to choose between Tyler and Deanna or Shailagh; Tyler would win. I didn't have a true friendship with John; however, they cared about him. That was enough.

What was I supposed to have Tyler look up without alarming them? "Details, like where and when?" I asked.

Shailagh stared absently. "Yes. I think I know what might have set a wight into acting like this."

"What?"

"You humans tend to tear up natural forest regularly. Perhaps the wight feels threatened by some construction. They might believe they are protecting themself by attacking construction workers at sites."

People like John, I thought.

CHAPTER 20

As THE SUN ROSE, we walked to the Lichgate portal in chilled, dry air. The temperature hadn't warmed very quickly, and the morning traffic whizzed past throwing dust, leaves, and fumes. The road quieted as we reached the wooded residential section, but we continued in silence.

If John had been enthralled, then his only freedom might be the wight's death. Could I do that? I had sent many to Hades, but all at the call of my queen or in defense of my own life. Shailagh would oppose any attempt, I assumed.

At this time of the morning, no one visited the languishing, ancient tree. John's possible predicament diminished the excitement of going through the portal. Even the tinkling glass couldn't cheer me. We exited in open woods with the sound of a semi rumbling down a nearby road. The ground felt soft under Nightarmor's boots, and the scents of growth and decay hung heavy in the cool air.

"We've got about a half-hour walk to the location, if the maps are right." Shailagh pointed toward the woods where I'd heard the traffic and kept in step with me.

I hadn't known the exact location of the site, but she seemed to have her own sources. "Maps?"

"Archaic, compared to human technology, but sufficient for us." She gestured toward my clothes. "Aren't you cold? Why don't you bring out your . . ." Motioning at her shoulders, she let the description trail off.

"Nightarmor?"

She nodded. "It would seem warmer for a human than what you're wearing. When did you acquire it?"

Khimmer, how old was I?

You were six years old when I chose you, Mistress.

"Six," I said to Shailagh.

Her eyebrows arched in surprise. "That seems young, for such a weapon."

I laughed. The memories were vague, but I'd been sparring with the Aegis monks at that age, since before I could remember. It had only become more intense after Nightarmor could protect me.

"How did you get it?" she asked.

I hesitated and she focused on the tree branches and brush we walked through. I didn't feel comfortable letting her know; only Tyler truly knew everything and believed it.

You should not answer this, Mistress.

Heat flushed up my cheeks. *I know.* Khimmer had been unusual since we'd come to Earth, intruding at unexpected times. That and their difficulty finding locations had me concerned. I relaxed my hands and responded to Shailagh, "I'd rather not talk about it."

Her jaw tightened slightly, but she shrugged. "Understood."

I felt awkward, like I'd snubbed her. "So, where's this map?"

A smile tugged at the edge of her mouth, and she tapped a long finger to her red hair. "In here."

I brushed aside a cobwebbed branch. A silver car sped on the road we made our way toward. I'd be lost already if I relied on memory. "You know where we are going?"

Her smile bloomed. "Perfectly. High Fae remember everything. Our nimbus is larger and denser than any other creature on Earth."

"Nimbus?" We reached the road and stopped.

"I'd rather not talk about it." Shailagh stepped onto the asphalt.

I stumbled as I followed. Surely whatever the nimbus was couldn't compare to exposing my origins. She was being spiteful because I hadn't answered. "Understood," I mumbled.

LL Wallace Road branched off the two-lane highway away from the sunrise. I prodded about the compass again, but Shailagh dismissed my questions, holding onto her resentment over not discussing Nightarmor. With John at risk, I needed to focus on what lay ahead anyway.

At the construction site where Emery Porter had intended to go, vines had grown up the chain link fence, and the gate swung open. Sprayed in dark green paint across the side of a white trailer were the words "No Mud No Lotus." Several piles of concrete block rested near the front in tight cubes, and weeds grew along the edges of everything.

"It appears deserted." Shailagh walked us around the trailer and tested the door, but it was locked. She had a couple inches on me, so she could look directly in one of the windows.

"Anything?" I asked.

"Food wrappers and bottles." She looked back to the

door and stretched both hands toward the ground. Long fingers arched out as if they reached for the soil.

A spiked vine crawled from under the trailer. I stepped back, as it moved more like a snake than a plant. Its light green tip pressed at the edge of the door while the shaft twisted and grew. It grew up the frame until it reached the latch where the end dove between the seals and disappeared inside. Shailagh appeared to stare beyond the door as she worked her Fae magic. She began to grimace as though in pain.

A light click sounded and the door popped open wide, the vine dropping free and recoiled back under the trailer. I shivered slightly. I'd never seen a plant so alive.

Shailagh hesitated, then stepped inside carefully without touching the frame.

I examined the door. Still locked. I pushed at the latch, and it slid easily. *Khimmer, could you do that? Reach inside and push in on this latch?*

Would you like me to try, Mistress?

Not now. Later. Remind me.

Even with the door open, the sun barely lit the interior, and it took me a while before I could see much, but the single room had a stale, sour smell like someone had left food sitting out. The wrappers were mainly chips, and the bottles were from beer.

Shailagh appeared withered. Hunched over, she moved slowly, standing in the middle and glaring from one item to the next.

The bed covers were rumpled to the far side and draping off the edge. I grabbed them and peered underneath, examining for blood. The floor, a dull green-gray carpet, didn't have any dark stains. "Should I be looking for anything specific?"

Her voice was hoarse. "I don't see any signs of a struggle. I don't smell blood, but it reeks, so look anyway." She gestured limply. "Could you check the bathroom?" As I passed, she crept for the door.

"Does the metal bother you?" I asked. Vivianne had an aversion to it, but it hadn't seemed this bad.

"Yes." Her voice rebounded as she cleared the steps. "It is not as bad as a modern vehicle. The construction seems mainly wood and aluminum. The metals that affect me are under the floor."

The bathroom had its own miasma, but there was no blood. When I exited, Shailagh was studying the ground carefully. "Hey, could we use one of those cool glowing things?" I asked.

She shook her head. "First, daylight makes it difficult, but more importantly, I can smell too many humans in here. I don't think they use clean sheets, so the results could be the wrong person. I wouldn't be sure that I had the right trail. Last, it has been weeks, so the energy would have faded to nearly invisible, even in the dark."

We walked together inside the fenced area, then outside where some trees had been cut down and others had been painted with an orange mark. We circled back to the gate.

Shailagh sniffed the air. "After your description of the other site, I had hoped for something. Perhaps it has been too long. I don't smell any blood, but after this much time, the elements could have washed it away."

I swallowed, but my throat remained tight. Was that it? We'd failed? I felt bad for the others, but would I get an answer? John might rely on us finding something here.

"Would the wight have enthralled Emery Porter here? How does the enthralling work?"

"I believe the wight is holed up somewhere and would

have its human thralls procure the man. It would need to be in sight of a human to turn them into a thrall."

We both stared at the trailer. The green spray paint looked similar to the graffiti Tyler liked, except not so artsy.

I looked at the large, painted words, checked that I had a signal, and called Tyler. "What does the term 'No Mud No Lotus' mean?" I asked.

Keys clacked in the background. "There are multiple references: a book by Thich Nhat Hanh, tattoos, and a conservation group in Tallahassee. What's the context?" Tyler asked.

"Spray painted on a construction trailer?"

"Conservation group."

I'd have to find this group.

CHAPTER 21

I STOOD with my phone to my ear and Tyler waiting as I stared at the words. I understood the concept of a conservation group; they wanted to keep nature and avoid buildings, but I didn't understand why they'd advertise on the side of Emery Porter's construction trailer.

Shailagh watched, and I didn't want to seem too stupid, but I had to ask, "Why would they paint their name on a trailer?"

Tyler answered quickly. "A protest, likely. I'm assuming this is a natural piece of land where there isn't much construction?"

"Very natural." Fresh air and woods surrounded us. After we'd passed a neighborhood, I had only seen a cell tower along the walk.

Behind the fence, trees had been cut and others painted with orange stripes. Could the wight be one of the conservationists? I still had a tough time understanding if the particular high Fae who concerned Shailagh would have antlers on its head or trees growing off its back. I couldn't imagine a sigil hiding perpetual decay and rebirth, but I was relatively new on Earth.

I didn't have much to work with, and Shailagh needed something to keep going. "Where would I find these conservationists?"

Tyler's keyboard clattered in the background as they sighed. "Let me see if I can find you anything." The typing seemed nonstop. "Deanna's been crying and screaming on the phone all morning. I'm worried, Ahnjii. I almost hope John just ran off to Vegas."

I couldn't tell them that I was helping, in my own way, without disclosing a worse scenario. I felt badly whenever my focus narrowed to my own selfish wants when I wasn't paying attention. "What did they say about the blood?"

"Running it now at a lab, that's what she's screaming about. I don't know what good it will do if we find it is John's. That root still bothers me. I wish I understood why I couldn't look at the front of it, but could see the side."

My heart sunk. I hated keeping secrets from Tyler; they were the first friend I'd ever had, and the one I didn't want to hide things from, but I did. Silent, I just stood there flicking the end of my braid.

After an awkward wait, Tyler spoke. "Okay. You're in luck. They're doing a table at a flea market today. You want me to pick you up and we'll head over there?"

I slumped. "No, I'm still with the investigator."

"Oh, okay. I'll text you the address for the flea market and their office."

I wanted to comfort Tyler, offer some company, but it would have to wait. The conservationists likely wouldn't have anything to offer. They could have put the spray paint on at any time. Shailagh knew about wights though, and my best chance to find John was to use her knowledge. Guilt flushed my cheeks, yet I didn't want Shailagh to know that I used her as much as she needed me. We had mutual needs, but I couldn't say I didn't want my question answered either. I needed to get back home.

"Thank you. We'll hang out when I'm done, okay?"

"Sure." Tyler would be sitting in the house with a distraught Deanna.

After I hung up, the text came through, and I opened it in the maps. The crowded streets of downtown Tallahassee took up the screen. "Tyler believes the people who spray painted the words on the trailer might be here. We should talk with them. Perhaps they know something."

"Doubtful." Shailagh shrugged. "I don't have any better options." She looked at the screen. "I know the area. It's less than an hour's walk from Lichgate."

I tried to sound cheerful. "Let's do this."

CHAPTER 22

As WE WALKED along the dusty parking lot, I knew I had been to the flea market before with Deanna and Tyler. The white, barn-like building already had a noisy crowd with one especially loud, unhappy child in a stroller. The sun and long hike had warmed me to a more comfortable mood, though I prayed that somehow, we'd learn something useful.

A musty odor clung just under the entrance and grew as we moved into the shade. Shailagh appeared immediately uncomfortable in the crowd. The stalls reminded me of the market beside Rhys' temple, except there were mainly clothes instead of farmer's produce.

"Do you want me to find them, then come get you?"

She shook her head, but a grimace held tight around her lips. "I'll be okay."

The din around us grew as we worked through the crowd. My stomach tensed, not from the throng, but the dread that our investigation would lead us nowhere. What would I do then? Give up and hang out with Tyler, knowing all the while that John might never be found? I couldn't do that; it would haunt Deanna and Tyler forever. I would find John for them.

I spotted the top of a large green flag in the back with stenciled lettering. From what I could make out, it might have been the same phrase as what was spray-painted on the trailer. "Over there." I gestured in the direction for Shailagh.

Eyebrows tight, she kept blinking and glaring at whomever came close to her. I grabbed her hand and pulled her behind me as I made a path through bodies.

I recognized the hat first, the straw fedora with a purple band. Tousled light-brown hair and now appropriate warm jacket confirmed that it was the same man who had come to the Crum Box when I'd been having lunch with Laura. His eyes flitted away as he turned toward a booth with tie-dyed dresses. Was he following me? Shailagh bumped into me as I stopped.

"What?" She pulled away from me, from Nightarmor, but kept my hand.

I had a choice. I could drag us after him or continue to the conservationists. With a new knot in my stomach, I pulled us toward the green flag with the identical phrase as the trailer.

A lovely woman with black flowing hair sat at the table, largely ignored by most of the crowd. Brightly colored pamphlets spread in front of her. "Sign the petition for the wetlands. Save our natural wildlife. Keystone species are at risk."

The people seemed to consciously avoid looking in her direction. I could see the phrase "No Mud, No Lotus" printed on flyers as well.

She smiled when I approached, and it deepened when

she saw me pulling Shailagh behind by the hand. "Sign our petition?"

"Actually, I have a question."

Shailagh released my hand and stood at my shoulder.

The black-haired woman nodded. "Happy to give you information. It's an important cause. Please."

I tapped the phrase on the pamphlet. "You spray painted this on a trailer on LL Wallace Road. We are hoping . . ."

Her face tightened and she squinted suspiciously. "Who are you?"

I stammered at the interruption. "I'm Ahnjii Fate, this is Shailagh." My finger still rested on the pamphlet. "We want to know if you saw anything unusual a few weeks back. We're looking into Emery Porter's disappearance."

"No," she lied. Then her eyes widened. "Emery Porter? The man who killed those three people?"

He hadn't, but I didn't think the explanation would help. "He disappeared when he was supposed to go back to that trailer. We just hoped . . ."

"Wait." She waved me off and dug out her phone, speaking to herself as she typed. "That was the name of the owner. I never put it together. Over a month ago."

Shailagh had a stern expression and moved beside me to the table. "Did you see this Emery Porter?"

The woman at the table didn't look up and continued to type. "We had no idea he was a murderer, or rather, would be."

"Do you have any information about his disappearance?" Shailagh's voice had an urgent undertone.

Dropping her phone into her lap, face down, the woman stared at us. "Why should I tell you anything?"

"He's innocent," I said. "Covering for someone." *More believable than the truth.*

"His disappearance might lead us to the true killer," Shailagh added. It didn't come through as a lie.

The woman shook her head. "Who are you?"

Shailagh nodded and retrieved a card from her pocket. "Investigators."

Before the woman could take the card, her phone rang. "Did you have any idea?" she asked the person who called. "No, I didn't put it together either. I've got two investigators here, about his disappearance." She glared at us, then shook her head. "No, not police. They want to know if anything strange happened at the site."

We waited while she nodded, listening to a distinctly male voice. Finally, she studied us again and lowered the phone, cradling it in her palms. "Off the record? No names?"

I shrugged and Shailagh said, "Of course."

"We may have noticed this Emery Porter marking trees in the morning. They were going to cut down nearly an acre. Then, he just dropped his spray can and walked into the woods. He never showed back up, but in the morning his truck was gone. After that, the site was empty."

What kind of clue was this? "Did you see anyone else there?"

She picked up the phone. "Anyone else out there, that day or after?"

A shy young man stepped up beside me, picking up flyers, and glanced at me with a timid smile. The woman behind the table readied the clipboard with one hand.

"Just the crew the week before," she said hastily to us, putting down the phone. The smile was for the young man. "Sign the petition?" she asked him.

Shailagh tugged at my elbow. "We need to go back."

I agreed. "Thank you."

The woman didn't look at me.

We moved back to the center, where the crowd wasn't as tight, but I was searching for the man with the straw hat. I didn't find him with the dresses. I spun in a slow circle. He'd moved around to our other side. He studied pottery three booths down from the conservationists.

Shailagh called out as I worked through the people. "Where are you going?"

She would follow, and I didn't want to lose him. With my ability, it always seemed best to face things head on. He started to move off, and I double-stepped to stand in front of him.

"Are you following me?" I asked.

He shrugged and gestured to both sides as if surprised. "No."

Lie.

"Why are you following me?"

He continued to lie. "I'm not."

"You are. Who are you?"

Digging into an inside pocket of his leather jacket, he pulled out a card and a fake smile. "Darren McGyver, Novelist. Urban Fantasy." The card had a sea creature with odd tentacles and his name. "Perhaps you've seen my books."

His smile faded as Shailagh joined me, and his shuffled back step indicated reservation if not fear. Did he know her? She leaned forward and sniffed.

"Witch," she said under her breath.

I blinked, looking between the two. "What do you want?" I asked him.

He didn't answer and just shook his head. What would

a witch want with me? How did Shailagh know he was a witch? His expression hardened and he adjusted the straw fedora.

"What do you want?" I repeated.

His jaw set, he just stared at me, refusing to respond.

"We don't have time for this." Shailagh spoke in a sharp growl. "Stop following." She hadn't seen him before, but trusted me. I liked that. She tugged at my elbow, and we moved away. I glanced back. He still watched us, the crowd streaming around him.

CHAPTER 23

WE RETURNED to the site nearly at lunchtime with my stomach growling and my entire body hot from walking. I couldn't get the strange man, Darren, out of my head. Tyler barely responded to texts, but he promised he wasn't mad at me. I considered searching the trailer for snacks, but the sour smell might have killed my appetite. Shailagh headed straight for the moss-draped woods with the orange stripes painted on the trunks.

We found the paint can nearly covered in leaves. Now what? Shailagh seemed better at investigating than I was. I looked into the cool dimness of the woods and considered telling her that I needed her help to find the wight and John. "Do we just start looking in there?"

Shailagh studied the area around. "Pine and oak. We won't find a trail."

I hadn't learned the names of the trees. Deanna knew plants, but we didn't spend much time together in the woods. I knew she had an oak tree in her yard, but these didn't look exactly the same. Moss dangled from the upper branches.

A tangled square hung from one of the tufts of moss. "Is that a sigil?" I asked.

"Hmph." Shailagh smiled. "You're good. That is a combination of sigils, like your roots. These woven branches would entice a human to investigate deeper in the woods, nothing more." Straightening, she stepped in the direction of the sigil and gestured at the trees ahead. "Look for more. This would only work for a few minutes before a human would wander back."

We found another quickly; Shailagh had an innate sense of direction and appeared to draw a line leading us to more. A rank odor rose as the water pooled in some areas. It hadn't rained in a couple of weeks, which seemed unusual for Tallahassee, but in the woods the ground seemed low, moist, and spongy.

My thoughts drifted as she led. Darren McGyver bothered me the most. "Why do you think he was following us? Or me? How did you know he was a witch?"

"Who? Darren?" Shailagh huffed, but answered the question. After leaving the flea market she'd been sharp and unresponsive during most of the walk. "Strong empaths notice each other. It is hardly difficult. I'm surprised you don't." She peered at me. "How could you have this ability, at this strength, and not have interacted with witches?"

I stiffened. I'd brought the discussion of my origins back into focus. "I just didn't. I'm sorry." Hopefully, this wouldn't send her into another round of sulking. I didn't like it when she was mad at me. "What does he want?"

"How would I know?" she snapped, then calmed. "Perhaps he senses your ability and was reaching out, witch to witch."

No, he hadn't approached me. "I saw him the first time

when I was having lunch the other day. He didn't say hello then or at the flea market."

She shrugged, but I sensed that it concerned her as well. Perhaps she just was focused on finding the wight, like I should be.

A stone mound rose ahead that vegetation softened and the trees shaded as they leaned into the empty space. Gray porous rock jutted up higher than my head, and dark crevices likely held animal dens at its base.

"Someone went to a lot of work for Emery Porter," Shailagh said as we passed under another sigil.

I began to wish I'd carried water. More of the odd rock formations poked up in the woods around us, some so small that I tripped when I stepped on stone instead of the soft earth. I should have brought snacks.

"I'm hungry," I said.

Shailagh pulled out a wafer from a pouch at her belt and then paused. "I'm unsure if humans can eat this." She placed the high Fae food on her tongue and dug her finger into a different section of her belt. "Do you like pistachios?"

I'd heard of them. "Probably."

She pulled out a gray, cloth bag and tossed it to me.

I untied the cord and pushed my nose into a savory scent. I pulled out a gray-green nut, squeezing against a rock-hard surface that hardly seemed edible.

Shailagh snorted. "Pry off the shell and eat the nut inside."

Greenish, the little nut inside was amazing, if a bit salty. I barely looked up as we walked, and I left a trail of shells behind.

The last sigil hung over the lip of a formation where a dark crevice below looked large enough to climb into. We continued past, but could find no other markings. Shailagh's step quickened, searching alternate directions.

"It seems the sigils ended," she said.

The trail led to either the stone or the small cave under it. Circling around, I pulled out my phone and turned on the flashlight Tyler had shown me. It had been a few days before I'd gotten a lamp for my new bedroom.

Kneeling into wet mulch, I held my phone out, trying to get a view. I braced on my elbows and crawled in leaves and moss to get a glimpse of the interior. I could fit inside, but I doubted a large man could squeeze in comfortably.

I flinched at a movement, then laid my ear into the leaves to get a better angle. Something shifted inside. It clung to the upper back corner against porous rock. I fumbled at my phone to get a picture.

Climbing inside with it didn't seem prudent, not until I knew what it was. All I could see was dark rock, but there had been some motion. Little light made it through the opening, and I blocked most of it. I listened for breathing or some confirmation that I hadn't imagined it.

My face and hand felt exposed.

Khimmer could see in the darkness.

Leaves crashed behind me. Footsteps raced toward us.

"Ahnjii," Shailagh called out.

I rolled to see outside and dropped my phone. A lanky man with baggy, stained pants and a worn blue t-shirt sprinted toward Shailagh. Full-bearded, his mouth opened wide as if he might bite her. His eyes showed too much white. Leaves flurried in his wake as he leaped.

Heart racing, I scrambled, sliding on wet mulch. Somehow, he'd sneaked up on us without Khimmer or Shailagh noticing. Had he been following while we tracked sigils, or had he been waiting here?

Shailagh had turned toward her attacker and her fingers reached out for her Fae magic. The wild brute landed on her before I sat up.

CHAPTER 24

I JUMPED TO MY FEET, dripping pungent mulch.

Shailagh pushed the man off. She had surprising strength for her frame.

He had barely rolled over before he scrambled at her again.

Khimmer, light armor.

Yes, Mistress.

Nightarmor poured into light, flexible metal that covered all but my head. Was this a thrall? It had to be. *Khimmer, search the area.*

Just small animals, Mistress.

When Shailagh threw the man off again, I leaped in and caught his wrist. Too strong, he swung free of my grip and nearly landed a punch to my temple. I had no intention of using a blade on an unarmed man, if I could help it.

I blocked him and took his right arm in both hands, twisting wrist to elbow in an attempt to force him down. He didn't react to the pain. His shoulder released with a light pop. The best Aegis monks could handle such pain, so I was able to avoid his response.

He spun backward, injuring his arm worse, and aiming at me with his other elbow. I dropped, not the safest move, but necessary with both hands engaged. Leaning into his knees, I buckled him. Moving my grip to his right leg, I leaned my shoulder forward and forced him to fall back. Then I jerked up, flipping him.

I jumped free to find vines racing through the leaves.

Shailagh had recovered and stood with her hands outstretched, calling her Fae magic. The plants veered around me, or at least my Nightarmor boots. In a flash, our attacker lay wriggling but bound on the forest floor.

Mistress, snakes.

The writhing vines had covered the rustling that now clearly sounded. From my left, the sun-dappled leaves fluttered as light gray and darker snakes wove toward us.

"Crap." I'd never liked snakes, at home or on Earth. *Helmet.*

Yes, Mistress.

Khimmer's vision made the situation worse as Nightarmor poured past my eyes. Pale pink lines wove toward us from every direction. It seemed the entire forest had been infested with the reptiles.

"Sorry, Tyler." They had a love for the cold-blooded creatures. *Sword.*

I had protection, Shailagh did not, and I was using her to find this wight. I jumped to her back, but she already had her magic working. Tree branches sharpened and darted down, stabbing pink squirming shapes and yanking them into the air. Limbs moved with an impossible swiftness. The woods seemed to roar with their movement, creaking and rustling from every direction.

Still, some snakes made it through to my feet, and I slashed at their necks, biting into soft earth. I spun at each hack, looking for those that might get too close to Shailagh. It left me dancing at her sides, and I tried not to let Nightarmor get too near her skin. There couldn't possibly have been this many snakes in the immediate area. How did the wight control them? Perhaps we were close to the ancient high Fae and could rescue John. I risked a higher glance to the woods around. Dying snakes hung in the trees.

I lunged as one twisted a step away from Shailagh's feet, tangled in vines. It stilled as I lopped off its head, sending it to Hades and beyond. I had no time to whisper prayers.

It was just a few minutes later, panting and sweating inside Nightarmor, that I slashed the last snake without realizing the attack was over. I paced a circle around Shailagh while my heart pounded.

The trees rustled back into shape. Random leaves dropped with a silent, swaying float to the ground. In a moment, the forest turned silent.

I detect no further threats, Mistress.

Leaning on the sword, I nodded. "Yes, yes, I got that."

"What?" asked Shailagh.

I'd spoken out loud. "It's over."

"It seems so." She gestured toward the thrall.

The body was motionless and the color a dull red.

Khimmer, remove helmet.

I stepped toward the man. His blank eyes stared up at the trees. Sunlight flickered on his face. He'd died during our battle. *Fare well into the house of Hades.* His death lay partially on my hands. No blood or tight vines about the throat, so a snakebite, I assumed. It did not seem the wight had very good control. It had to be close.

I spun toward the crevice. *Helmet.* From this far away and through the rock, even with Khimmer's vision, I couldn't see what hid inside.

"What is it?" asked Shailagh.

I gestured toward the darkness. "Something is in there."
I would have to find out what.

CHAPTER 25

SINCE NOTHING THREATENED us from the crevice, I needed a moment to get my breath.

Remove helmet.

Blood trickled down the side of Shailagh's ankle. "You've been bit."

I'd risked her life. Nearly all snakes on Duruce were deadly, some within seconds. I had no idea about Earth snakes. If she reacted, I had no healing skill or potions. The healers on Earth were abundant and skillful, but very far from us.

She waved off my concern, smiling. "No need to worry. I'll be fine."

"It could be venomous. Toxic." I chilled. I thought I'd caught them all. Instead, I'd put her life in danger to find John, or more accurately, to help Tyler and Deanna.

Her smile just grew. "Our metabolism is different. We have more control of our functions. Humans have a sensitivity to organics which high Fae do not. If you ever see a nail, or any metal, protruding from me, you can pull it out and rescue me."

I stared at her ankle and the drying streak of brownish blood. There was no argument, she surely knew her body better than I did. Still, I had let one of the snakes reach her. Taking a deep breath, I turned back to the rock.

"How could this wight make the snakes attack?"

"A dominar has a higher level of persuasion than other high Fae." She flexed her fingers, as if stiff after the use of her magic. When I didn't respond, she continued, "Most high Fae can persuade humans and animals to act a certain way, as if it were their own idea to a limited degree, for a short period. A dominar has the ability and usually the practice to make the compulsion permanent and directed to obedience, thus thralls. Our dominar would have to be near or in contact to enthrall humans, but within miles to get this many snakes to act." She pointed to the rock. "Whatever creature is hiding in there, it is not a serious threat. I would sense the wight if it were that close."

Was a wight and a dominar the same thing? I hated asking questions and being annoying, but if I wanted to save John, I had to know. Shailagh seemed in a reasonable mood for answering questions. "What's the difference between a wight and dominar?"

"A wight is an advanced stage within the high Fae life cycle. A dominar is a banned vocation, a decision to develop and use abilities we have agreed to put aside."

"So it might not be a wight turning people into thralls."

Shailagh took a deep breath, as if pondering her response. "We know where most of the high Fae are, even the more reclusive. None of them are here. We have lost wights, as they shun us the way we might avoid the low Fae or humans."

We had some cranky old priests in some of the temples who grew too close to their gods. It sounded similar. Rested,

I nodded toward the rock. "Pull me out if something tries to bite off my face?"

She chuckled. "Of course."

Dead snakes littered the ground, some slashed, others that had dropped out of the trees. This hadn't helped us get closer to finding John. We walked to the stone outcrop, and I retrieved my phone. If I wore Nightarmor's helmet, I would be able to go in deeper, but I wouldn't see my phone well, and the image would be distorted. I reached for my braid, but my armor pinned it down my back.

Khimmer, helmet.

Yes, Mistress.

Lying on my back, I pushed my head under by digging my heels in the mulch. Rock scraped on the back of my helmet, but I had plenty of room.

The creature was the size of a large cat and clung nearly upside down. Its back to me, the head was twisted around to watch me. I could make out large eyes and long, rabbit-like ears. It appeared scared, not threatening. I didn't sense any danger. It hadn't moved.

Remove helmet.

Is this wise, Mistress?

My jaw tightened, but I remained calm. *Remove helmet.*

Nightarmor poured down to my neck, and I could see nothing. The space smelled musty with a hint of spice, like cinnamon. Pulling up my cell, I opened the camera; I could barely make out more than the eyes even at an arm's length away. The creature appeared the color of the rock itself. I took a picture, and the flash forced the large round eyes closed. It whistled lightly.

I had never seen such an Earth animal before. It clung as if fearful, and I wanted to help. "It's okay, I won't hurt you." I found the flashlight on my phone and shone it around the small cave.

The creature whistled, blinking when I lit it up. Gray and mottled like the stone, I could barely make out features, but it seemed to be holding on with tiny paws and a long bushy tail.

"Ahnjii?" Shailagh asked. She crouched at my boots.

"I'm okay. It's cute."

She shifted outside. "We should check the area and other construction sites out here."

Large eyes blinked, and the animal whistled. Did it want me to leave? I probably scared it. *Remove armor.*

Mistress?

Khimmer, stop questioning me. Remove armor.

Yes, Mistress.

Liquid Nightarmor poured back into choker, belt, bands, and bangles. The creature whistled three short notes. It had a tiny mouth, smaller than a cat's, that shifted when it made any noise. Vivianne would have loved it. A little pudgy for a cat, but still adorable.

What did it eat? I rolled my head to each side, moving my phone, but I didn't see bones or debris. Wet sand covered the inner portion against the rock. I could feel the damp soaking into the back of my bodysuit.

I dug into my shorts and pulled out the nearly empty bag of pistachios. "These are good." Maybe I could get a better look if it came down to eat.

It whistled in response, but made no move to climb down.

Using teeth and one hand, I pried a shell off a pistachio and then raised the nut up to the animal. Another whistle sounded, curiosity. Two gray whiskers grew from around its mouth, reaching out toward the morsel. They worked like two flexible chopsticks and prodded at the food. Carefully, they pulled it from my fingers and retracted, bringing it directly to the little mouth. With a series of whistles, it rolled the nut against its lips and ate it. The whistles that followed I believed were in approval. Its ears raised, pointing back against the cave wall.

I shook the remaining pistachios in the bag. "Come down. Have some more."

As if it understood me, the little hands and feet slowly worked the plump form down the rock. Neck still turned, it kept its eyes fixed on me. The tail worked the stone, hairs changing color as it moved, and I could hear no nails.

"I won't hurt you." I tilted the phone against my forehead to illuminate the cave while I used both hands to fish out another shell and snap it off the nut. As my little friend dropped to the sand and turned, I offered it the snack.

As it ate and whistled in contentment, the feet and bottom half of its portly belly turned dark tan, blending in with the sand.

Shailagh leaned in closer to me. "Ahnjii, we should go. What are you doing?"

"Feeding your pistachios to this strange Earth creature."

"Great." She sounded annoyed.

"I won't take long. I promise." What was I doing?

While I opened another shell, the creature produced a third noodle-like whisker.

I believe it wants more, Mistress.

Most of my initial understanding of English had come with the aid of Khimmer. They could categorize words and inflections better than me. The long hours talking with Tyler, then Laura and Vivianne, had expanded my vocabulary.

Can you understand it?

The whistles are unique, so I have correlated them against perceived circumstances and reactions. Basic emotions of fear, pleasure, and desire. Some yet unidentified.

I sensed the animal as well, perhaps with the empath abilities that Shailagh suggested I should have.

When I offered up the empty cloth bag, to show it that I had no more, I swore the whistle sounded despondent. It touched the pouch, then my finger. As it reached the knuckle on the top of my hand, its own color turned to match the light brown of my skin. Light fur covered tiny digits without nails. The stronger scent of cinnamon came with proximity.

"Ahnjii?" Shailagh wanted to leave, that was obvious.

"I'm coming. Sorry." I apologized both to Shailagh and my new friend.

Can you find this place again? I thought to Khimmer. They'd been having a hard time with location since we left Duruce.

Yes, Mistress.

"I'll be back," I whispered to the creature.

Liquid eyes blinked and the whistle definitely sounded sad.

CHAPTER 26

RELUCTANTLY, I grabbed my phone and started to wiggle out of the small cave.

My new friend whistled with disturbing sadness. One of its noodle-whiskers reached out after me.

"I've got to go." I felt horrible. When I pulled clear of the crevice, the scent of cinnamon gave way to the foul smell of wet soil and dead snakes.

Shailagh stood at my feet, watching me with a wry smile. "Humans and their attraction to lesser animals." She stopped and widened her eyes, looking back at the crevice.

The animal had followed, more visible in the sunlight even as its short fur turned the color of the mottled leaves it crawled through. I leaned up on my elbows while it studied Shailagh with large eyes and whistled cautiously.

"What is that?" Shailagh asked. Her hands darted to her side.

I gestured for her to stay calm. "It's safe. Some sort of Earth animal." I swallowed. "It lives in the cave."

"I know animals, and this is not from this planet. It is more akin to an Upre symbiont than anything." Her fingers pointed rigid toward the ground. I couldn't let her use Fae magic on my friend.

I shifted closer to the creature, dropping one hand next to it, and holding my other toward Shailagh. "It's still not dangerous." I smiled nervously. "It likes pistachios." *What's an Upre?*

Khimmer, be prepared to protect the animal.

Mistress?

Don't question me. I tried not to let my frustration show, keeping a smile pasted on my face for Shailagh. I needed her, but I wouldn't let her kill a defenseless animal.

My friend decided for us all, as it crawled first into my lap, carefully up my front, then holding onto the straps of my bodysuit to lie on my chest. Large eyes focused on mine, and they gave off a contented whistle. Their furry tail managed to circle my side, just under my breast, locking their pudgy form in place.

"Do you want to come with me?" I asked.

Their whiskers had receded to thick bumps around their lips. Their face and shoulders had turned the color of my skin; farther down they were the black of my bodysuit. Wavering their nostrils, they whistled.

That was a yes, right?

I would concur, Mistress, but this might not be wise.

Shailagh shifted a step back in the leaves. "This is not a good idea. First, we have no idea about this creature. Second, it has tried to camouflage against you, and you look malformed. We can't go in public with you looking like that."

I stood, and my friend whistled in surprise. Iridescent wings the size of my hand fluttered out, then disappeared back into their fur. "Easy, it's okay." I offered Shailagh the phone. "Take a picture. I want to see."

She shied back from the device. Was that from metal? I flipped the phone around, took a selfie, and grimaced. My new friend mimicked my skin and black top perfectly and created the illusion of flesh where there shouldn't be. I wouldn't have much trouble here, in such a rural area, but from the Lichgate to home the traffic got heavy.

"Let's scoot you down a little." Around my stomach would just look like Bill's extra padding.

They whistled low, disappointed, but let me shift them down.

Despite the meaning, I liked the sound. "What do I call you?"

Liquid eyes watched me as they shuffled down to my waist, but still, the same low whistle.

"Woo? Do you like that name?" I took the following whistle to mean agreement as they settled in, turning black like my shirt, and forming a third boob with their head. I didn't care. They were adorable.

"So you're going back to your apartment." Shailagh had relaxed, but had developed a frown. There was no question in her tone, just condemnation.

"I'm sorry. But yes, I've got to get Woo settled in. Then we can . . ." What could we do? The trail had seemed to grow cold with no more sigils. "What is your plan?"

Shailagh took a long breath, shook her head, gestured into the woods, and started walking. I followed. Woo felt warm on my belly.

"The snakes came predominantly from the southwest. Between our contacts we should be able to find any construction sites southwest of here; perhaps the wight has used this stratagem in other locations."

"I can ask Tyler." I checked my phone, though none of the bars were lit up.

As she led the way, I couldn't see her face, but Shailagh seemed annoyed. "Yes. Do that. Then we can get back to the business at hand, after you put away your little pet."

Be careful, Mistress, wildlife can be very unpredictable.

Shut up.

I was delaying finding out what happened with John, but Woo obviously wanted to stay with me. I couldn't leave them under a rock if they'd rather be with me. I disappointed Shailagh, and felt a little guilty, but I wasn't going to abandon Woo.

"Not a pet," I said.

Woo whistled an agreement.

I'd get Woo settled in the apartment, then we could continue the search for John and the wight. Tyler and Deanna deserved my help.

"Call it what you choose." Shailagh's long strides were taking us quickly through the woods.

I didn't even know which way we were going. "Woo. Their name is Woo."

"Stupid name, and a waste of time."

Flushing at the comment, I rested a hand on Woo protectively. It felt like I had a big furry belly. "Maybe we just take a break for today?" I regretted the comment and sharp tone at once. I needed Shailagh to find the wight.

Shailagh didn't speak for a minute, giving me time to squirm. "Perhaps."

CHAPTER 27

SHAILAGH DROPPED me off at Lichgate, where Tallahassee exhaust tainted the air. She left me to walk home alone. I didn't mind, as we seemed to be at odds about how to proceed. At least, I wanted to get Woo settled in before continuing. Where did Shailagh live? It couldn't be a house or farm. Wouldn't there be too much metal? Vivianne had explained that some construction served her kind better than others, and she worked in a building. As a high Fae, Shailagh seemed more sensitive.

The sun had reached its disturbing place directly over-head. Walking with Woo across my belly along the warming streets of Tallahassee, it was hard to miss it.

The traffic, noisy and fuming the roadways, didn't stop and notice our passage, so I assumed Woo's camouflage worked. However, Woo whistled quietly in spurts each time the cars rumbled past. Khimmer and I both interpreted it as stress.

I patted their side. "We'll be home soon."

Shailagh had been surprised by Woo; perhaps the Fae knew nothing of this Earth animal. Knowing Laura's predisposition to electronics, I tried not to call her very often, but the Nedjir might know something about Woo. Other than pistachios, I didn't know what to feed them.

I dialed Laura, and she answered on her speaker. "Everything okay?" She sounded concerned.

"Yeah. Why wouldn't it be?" The topic of thralls and rampant snakes might have to wait.

"Normally you visit on Saturdays, and, well, you're calling me."

"Right. I've got an animal with me that I've never seen before in any book. Shailagh doesn't know what it is either, but she mentioned Upre."

"An Upre symbiont? That could be extremely dangerous. Get rid of it."

I couldn't. I rubbed Woo reassuringly. I crossed through College Town and garnered more looks from students than I had elsewhere. "Would Shailagh know what this Upre symbiont looked like?"

Laura paused before responding. "Yes. What does it look like?"

"Cute. A tubby rabbit with big eyes that can make its fur change color. Long tail. Oh, and wings, but they keep them hidden." I ran a finger down Woo's back, finding the fold where the wings were tucked.

"Can you bring it by? I only know symbionts by description and drawings."

Given the looks from the students sitting outdoors at the table, I didn't think the Railroad Square Art District would be inconspicuous. "Can you close up and come by my apartment?"

Laura had come by the second day I'd moved in, just to see. "Okay," she said. "When?"

"Half an hour?"

"I'll be there. You want tea?"

I was parched and starving. "Dark goddess, yes. And a snack."

"Have you eaten?" A brush tinkled in her jar in the background.

"I found I love pistachios."

"Me too, but I'll bring a sandwich or pastry."

"Love you."

Laura laughed. "Love you too. Be careful."

When I got to my apartment, I had fished out my keys and made it in my door before Mrs. Forster opened hers.

"Home," I whispered. I nudged Woo off my belly and shifted them around so they sat in the crook of my arm and could see the rooms. We walked into the kitchen, and Woo trailed a noodly whisker to touch the counter. "Formica," I announced. Deanna had disapproved, but said it was expected.

I had made the complete circuit of my tiny apartment and stood looking out the back window of the kitchen when Laura knocked. Woo spun and plastered to my chest, wings fluttering a quick iridescent purple and gold in the sunlight. "It's okay. It'll be my friend Laura." I peeled an arm free of the Woo-shaped growth of skin on my chest and opened the door. "Come in."

Mrs. Forster's broom flicked across concrete.

I jumped behind the door. "Quick."

Laura's large red eyes stared at the mass on my chest. "What . . . ?"

I feared she might drop the teas and bag in her hands. "In, in."

She obliged, maintaining the same distance as I closed the door. Even her furry ears seemed to tilt in to study Woo. I turned from side to side, hands in the air.

Woo kept their eyes on me. Large and wet, they didn't blink, and Woo didn't whistle. "It's okay," I said. "This is one of my best friends, Laura." I turned, hoping that Woo could catch a view.

Mistress, you should be careful.

Leave me be, Khimmer.

Laura sidled toward the kitchen. "I'm putting these down. That's not a symbiont, not even close. Those are fleshy and thin and reside in a human's chest, covering the heart. I've never seen anything like it. An octopus can camouflage, but not with fur. Surely the high Fae would know about a creature like this."

I'm not sure why, but I felt proud. "I named them Woo."

Woo made a low plaintive whistle.

Reaching the counter, I could smell the tea and something deliciously mysterious and sugary in the paper bag. "Okay, Woo. Can I put you down?" I didn't get an assenting whistle, but moved over to the window and sink, shifting them around. The tail stubbornly held about my waist. "Let go."

I lifted them up and placed them on the counter. Dropping to all fours, Woo looked like a gray speckled ball as they changed color. The fluffy tail moved off my waist and wrapped around my wrist; despite the illusion of pure fuzz, the inner muscles and bones felt firm and strong.

"See," I said. "Not dangerous."

Laura remained on the other side of the counter that divided the kitchen and living room. She watched with a smile, warming to my new roommate.

"Cute?" I asked.

She nodded her head and reached for one of the teas. "Yes. Can't argue that."

Woo whistled in what seemed agreement and snuffled along the counter, letting go of my wrist.

As we had tea and I ate a sweet, flaky pastry with a hint of fruit, Woo investigated the kitchen. They managed to open one of the empty cabinets and whistled in excitement at the dark recess it offered. They climbed out to continue exploring while Laura and I settled to the floor and watched. Laura's concern with Woo seemed to be receding.

"Where did you find it?" she asked.

I'd become so enamored with Woo, the morning's adventure seemed a distant swirl. I didn't understand much of what Shailagh had told me.

"In a cave." I tapped on my armband, distracted. "What do you know of the older high Fae? Shailagh says they begin to change?" How far into the wight conversation did I want to go with Laura? I hated keeping secrets from friends. Should I hide this?

Laura's rounded furry ears twitched before she turned toward me. "You need to be careful dealing with her. Our people trade with the high Fae for necessary sigil work; they are masters in the art and more necessary now that technology has taken over."

I lowered my tea and started to respond, but she held up a finger to continue. Her small lips pressed tight, highlighting her feline features. Woo sauntered past, finally heading out of the kitchen.

"There is a history between the Nedjir and Fae, going back thousands of years. So far that we don't have all the details. They betrayed our friendship, and our ancestors fought against their tyranny; this they do not deny. They likely have records of the treaties. We are very careful, not knowing the particulars. They have similar accords with your people, though the most learned witches do not seem to know this." She pointed a furry finger until it nearly touched my nose. "You cannot know what those agreements are, nor when you might interfere or nullify some aspect. The result could be a disaster for yourself, or your people."

It sounded ominous, and fit with a comment or two of Shailagh's.

My phone rang, and we started at the obnoxious tone; Woo whistled from the bathroom. Tyler was calling. I hadn't thought about what they'd been going through.

John missing, the wight, Emery Porter, and the dead thrall in the woods came crashing back into my world. I had to face reality again.

"Are you busy?" Tyler asked in a quiet tone. They could drag themself into some dark places sometimes.

I wanted to hang with Woo longer, but Tyler sounded ragged and worn. I felt my chest tighten, anxious at the thought of seeing Deanna and Tyler. I kept a secret from them. *Many, actually.* "You want to come over?" My eyes blinked wide. How would I explain Woo?

"Can you come to the house? I'll pick you up. I don't want to leave Deanna alone for long."

I sighed. "Yes." I offered Laura an apologetic smile for cutting our time short. "Pick me up in about half an hour?"

Woo hung upside down from the door frame to the bathroom and whistled. Their fur had turned a rich pink with undertones of tan, and their fluffy white striped tail curled up to grasp the wood. Dark eyes watched us both. They liked it here. I didn't want to leave, but Tyler needed me.

Laura giggled. "Can I come by in the morning? Visit?" Woo had another admirer. "I'll bring tea."

CHAPTER 28

WE FINISHED OUR TEA, and I walked Laura to the front door. Woo had returned to the kitchen and climbed to settle on the counter, camouflaging with a pale tan and dark pink. The apartment had begun to smell like tea, pastry, and Woo's cinnamon scent. If they weren't camouflaged, would Woo be tan, pink, or a mix?

When I opened the door, the afternoon air had grown humid and funky smelling from the exhaust and nearby pond. Shade covered the ground in front of the building.

Shailagh waited by the tree she'd become too fond of. "Crap." I wanted to change before Tyler picked me up. Luckily, she hadn't completely given up on me.

As I shut the door behind us, Laura followed my gaze and stiffened. Her ears pointed straight up. "Why is she here?" she asked.

I heard the chain sliding on Mrs. Forster's door and raced for stairs. "C'mon."

Shailagh stepped forward, watching us descend. She stopped in front of one of the pink birds. Her red curls rolled in the breeze. Expressionless, I couldn't tell if she was mad at me. The tree beside her appeared sedate and lazy.

"Be careful," Laura whispered as we reached the bottom of the stairs.

Uncharacteristically, Shailagh waved. "Visiting, Laura Nelson?"

Laura stiffened and it seemed the short fur on the back of her neck rose as high as it could. "Yes, Investigator Shailagh."

I hadn't realized they had met before. Laura hadn't mentioned it, so maybe Shailagh just knew about Laura. My Nedjir friend darted for the road, leaving me standing on the other side of the pink bird from Shailagh. Mrs. Forster's broom swished above, likely finding some leaves for my doormat.

"What have you told her?" Her expression unreadable, she glanced toward my apartment, perhaps thinking of Woo or Mrs. Forster. "Can we walk?"

"I don't have time. I've got to change and go out." My earlier snap at her seemed to be forgotten or ignored. I should be out looking for John, and if I hadn't committed to meeting Tyler and Deanna, I would have brought up the option. "Tomorrow morning? We can check out those sites. I'll ask Tyler for help identifying some of them tonight."

"I've got the list. We should go now, while there is some daylight left." She smiled, but it came out stiffly.

"I can't, I promised."

Her expression turning somber, Shailagh nodded her head. "Very well. I will start off on my own this afternoon. Your help today is appreciated, but our deal is that you help me find this wight; we have not done that yet, and if I find them on my own, I do not consider that a fulfillment of our deal."

I swallowed down a protest. She had a valid point. My agreement to Tyler suddenly felt secondary to finding this wight, and I still needed Shailagh's help. I wanted my answer but had been snippy and then made plans with Tyler. "Understood. Morning?" I needed to change clothes. A quick shower might even help. Unsettled, I stood there. "What if you run into more thralls, or snakes?"

Shailagh chuckled. "Worried?"

"Yes. I don't want you to be hurt." Heat flushed up my neck, and I glanced toward Mrs. Forster, broom in hand, watching us from above the second-floor railing.

"So sweet." Shailagh dug inside her belt pouch and pulled out an earring, a silver pin with an engraved sphere and a simple backing. She tapped it against a matching orb in one of her tall lobes. "You don't have to wear it, just hold it against your skin. Neck, ear, forehead."

When I touched the jewelry, a spark snapped between our fingers. I sucked in a short breath. Fae magic was involved, and Laura's caution caught me. "I'm not going to be enthralled, am I?"

Shailagh laughed. "Not by me. However, I had hoped for you to become captivated by my charms."

It seemed she did not harbor any ill will from my earlier outburst. I took the post and placed the ball against my neck.

The thought came through as an emotion. *Here.* I felt a sense of amusement and her physical attraction to me and the sense of presence; where she was.

"You'll be able to focus on me if I send to you, much like the compass you asked about. General emotions will go through it as well. If you were in danger, and used this, then I would know your direction, possibly even sense the location, along with your fear or anger."

The mention of the compass just deepened my blush. "How do I use this, to send you anything?" Any power I had was too weak for the compass.

She frowned. "I can't believe no one found you and trained you. Focus on where you are, then focus on the sigils engraved on the silver; push it."

My face had heated to the tips of my ears. Still, I thought of my apartment, the trees, the pink bird and imagined it going through the jewelry to Shailagh. In that instant, the earring seemed both cold and hot, a noticeable presence at my neck, drawing in.

Shailagh smiled. "Perfect. You should have been trained properly." Her expression darkened. "But I would not trust that Darren McGyver witch."

I pulled the jewelry away from my neck, more amazed with the intricate carving than worried about her warning. I'd made it work. Excited, I had to resist punching her in the arm. The sweeping above had stopped, and I flicked a look up. Mrs. Forster had forsaken her premise and watched us openly. Tyler would be arriving soon. I still hadn't changed and fought the regret of not accompanying Shailagh. "I have to go."

A gray car sped down the road and passed; I stiffened, suddenly not wanting Tyler to come by when Shailagh was here. "Morning?" I asked.

"Unless you get out before nightfall tonight." She tapped her earlobe. "Just let me know."

"Okay." Magic Fae jewelry hidden in my hand, I skipped for the stairs.

Mrs. Forster resumed her sweeping, nearly blocking my path. "If you had a solid job, purpose, then you might not be out all hours relying on risky behavior to give meaning to your life. You're young and have a future to plan for."

I smiled as I reached my door. "I've gotta pee."

"And these strangers outside . . ."

I closed the door behind me and from the bathroom, Woo whistled an admonishment for having been abandoned.

CHAPTER 29

A FEW MINUTES LATER, after Tyler messaged me, I ran down the steps clattering in Nightarmor's boots. Tyler looked ragged, dark-eyed and staring out the front window of their car. They wore a dark, low-cut top that clung tightly to their scrawny figure. The black around their eyes could have been more sleeplessness than make up. Had they even slept?

The car smelled like soured energy drink, and a green can sat in the middle console. I slid into the front seat, then leaned over and gave Tyler a hug. "You okay?"

Tyler shrugged. "I don't know what to do." They hugged me back and we sat there for a minute. "I'm really worried."

Leaning back and putting on my seat belt, I couldn't respond. I wanted to tell Tyler about the wight, and what I was afraid had happened to John. How would saying anything help? I should be out looking, but I'd been selfish about Woo and difficult with Shailagh. If we found John, could I do anything? Would I kill this old high Fae, despite Shailagh's beliefs?

I'd lived a simpler life before. When the Queen told me to kill someone, I did. The rest of the time I trained, read, and ate. I'd had no friends, no companions, and certainly no conflicts, until the end.

We cut through a bustling College Town on the way to Deanna and Tyler's house. Tallahassee had always been a strange city to me. On my world, the cities weren't as tall, except for some rare, ancient palaces that defied architectural abilities. The city I grew up in had a defined city center filled with workshops, storefronts, and temples.

Tallahassee never seemed to end. Just when the businesses appeared to relinquish to residential neighborhoods, with albeit strangely built mansions or clusters of squat homes, a new binge of shops sprang up. To the south, you could pass into farms, but along main roads, the storefronts persevered.

We pulled up to Tyler and Deanna's house, something I would consider a mansion. Around the corner off a side street, Deanna's car sat in their drive. "She's home." I made the comment more to break the silence than alert Tyler to the obvious. They didn't respond.

Their garage stretched along the side closest to the huge barn-like structure that housed the basketball court and its wooden floor where we loved to skate. Maybe we would end up skating.

Inside, the house smelled of cooking spices and incense. We climbed all the way to the second floor only to hear Deanna outside by the pool talking on the phone. Her cats watched her from the window, turning to regard me and Tyler with judgmental stares. They tolerated petting, but made it obvious they preferred Deanna's company. I stroked Jake or Willie and leaned over to see the pool area. Deanna walked a lap around the edge, her cell phone to her ear.

"We could swim." I offered. The situation had become awkward with Tyler silent and moody; besides, I found it difficult to do nothing.

"No, Deanna's upset enough. She doesn't need you skinny dipping in broad daylight." Tyler pet the other tabby.

I saw no reason for clothes if you were going in the water. People on Earth had different ideas. My stomach grumbled, and the tabbies peered at me.

"Hungry?" Tyler asked.

I hadn't had lunch, and the pastry that Laura had brought just stoked my appetite. "Yes. Pho?"

Tyler shook their head, motioning toward the stairs. "I'll make veggie burgers — and see if I can get Deanna to eat as well." Tyler always cooked vegan meals, but neither Deanna nor I minded. She would get seafood when we went out to restaurants or if Tyler offered her a meat option.

From the pool deck, Deanna saw us in the kitchen and stormed in after her call. "I hired an ex-FBI agent. These other two investigators are incompetent." She choked a sob and grabbed me. "Where is he?"

I held her, but stared at the tile floor blankly. Even if I didn't know where John was, I feared I knew what had happened to him. Hiding what I knew tore me up inside. My stomach tightened and churned, turning the savory scent of cooking patties nauseating. I wanted to say something comforting, but it would only be a lie. Shailagh had done the right thing, heading out to search for the wight. I'd selfishly focused on Woo, thinking it wanted to be with me. I'd made a mistake coming here with Tyler when I should have gone out searching.

Tyler flipped burgers, and the pan sizzled. "This new guy, is he local?"

Deanna pulled back sharply. "Atlanta. Booked a flight while we were talking. He'll be here at 8:00 tonight."

"I'll pick him up." Tyler moved to the island counter and sliced an onion.

"Thanks." Deanna grabbed my hand. "You found the only real clue. Can you think of anything we can do? I know I've asked you this before. I'm out of my mind." She did look slightly ragged, without makeup and her straight black hair tied into a frazzled ponytail halfway down her back.

"Where have they looked?" I was curious, but I mainly avoided her question. Chest tight, I tried to smile.

Deanna yanked off her glasses and dug in a drawer for wipes. "Every construction site the company has open and a couple they just finished, the office downtown, his father's condo, and the Pensacola and Jacksonville offices and sites." She tore open a wipe to furiously rub at a smudge I couldn't see. "My friend got the police to search a square mile around the site where you found the blood — dogs and everything."

At least they had checked the woods. If there were sigils there, they might have been led down them, or turned aside. Were dogs affected? "I don't know where else to look." Some place south and west perhaps, where Shailagh searched.

Deanna put on her glasses, grimacing with red eyes, and tossed the wipe and wrapper into the garbage. "I think the police have given up. The detectives take my calls and give me BS about where patrols are searching." She sobbed and hit the counter.

Tyler placed a tomato slice on one of the buns and moved to their sister. Hands on her shoulders, they moved her to a chair and gently sat her at the counter. They kissed her frizzed hair before returning to the stove.

I stood nearly shaking. My duty was to search for the wight, not eat dinner. I needed Shailagh.

Tyler didn't speak as they slid plates toward us; mine had jalapenos dripping out of the bun, which helped ease my queasiness. I'd eat and then leave. Tyler would find it strange, but I couldn't help it. I'd been a fool.

Deanna poked her bun, but didn't eat. Tyler sat beside her and picked up their sandwich, speaking. "Take a bite, Sis. I'll get back on the forums, but I need to know you're eating."

Shoving her hands in her lap, she shook her head, more side-to-side as her shoulders and torso swayed. "I'll puke."

I ate at the edge of the counter, taking a bite, but I found it hard to swallow. Usually, they might rib each other, but in this situation, Tyler showed a different side. Envy stirred inside me. They had family to support them, and I'd killed mine. I flushed, taking another bite to hide the shame. They had taken me in, and even tried to help me return home, though they had no idea what I was looking for. I couldn't begrudge them their relationship. Tyler had said I was family.

I ate while she stared blankly across the room. Finally, I spoke. "I wish I could make this better." I could try. I had to.

"I'm afraid," she said. "John wouldn't just ghost me and his business. The blood you found. Someone had to have hurt him. His father still won't come down. He said there would be a ransom if it were anything other than an unannounced trip. Idiot." Through sobs, Deanna jumped up and headed for the stairs. "I'm going to sleep, or at least lie down." She stopped at the bottom step. "Wake me up in time for you to get to the airport. I'll text you the flight number."

I stood as she disappeared upstairs. Her footsteps trailed

into silence. The light outside still shone on the backyard. Chairs sat empty beside the pool. Wind trailed ripples through the water. The wight had John, I could be sure.

Tyler said, "She hasn't slept, and won't, most likely. I'm worried about her, and John, of course." They smiled with more of a grimace around their eyes. "I tried to get her to use her degree and psychoanalyze herself, but that just pissed her off. I'd hoped you being here would give her someone new to talk to. I guess she's all talked out."

I couldn't help but feel this was my fault. At least, I should be using Shailagh to find the wight. My chest emptied, thinking of John acting like Emery Porter. First, I had to find him, then decide what to do about the connection to the wight.

I wiped my hand on a napkin. "You shouldn't leave her, so I'm going to walk home and see what I can think of."

Tyler shrugged and pushed aside their half-eaten burger. "C'mon, I'll take you home.

CHAPTER 30

WE PULLED up to my apartment with the sun still well above the horizon. Woo would be upset that I'd left them alone, and would again, but I couldn't take them with me.

I grabbed the sour smelling energy drink. "I'll throw this away."

Tyler responded with a slow, dejected nod. "Thanks."

"How long before nightfall, do you think?"

Tyler pulled up their phone, tapped, and scrolled. "Two hours 'til twilight."

The odd gray period before the sun disappeared. "Okay." I had time to contact Shailagh and do something productive.

When I stepped out of Tyler's car, both doors of a parked truck opened, and two thin men climbed out. I froze when I noticed their clothes were muddy and baggy, reminding me of the thrall earlier in the day. Their glares confirmed my concern before they ran toward me. How had the wight found me?

I tossed the energy drink at the closest, a man with gray

streaks in his beard. He held a short knife and swatted at the can, spilling sour contents over his shirt.

Fair game. I dropped to a crouch behind Tyler's car to keep out of sight from the apartments and Mrs. Forster. *Vambrace and blade.*

Yes, Mistress.

Nightarmor formed metal from elbow to wrist on both arms. From the one on my left forearm, a sheathed blade rose from the top.

With the gray bearded man to my right, I rolled to meet him first, drawing the younger man away from Tyler where they sat in their car. Crouching low, I forced him to adjust his planned attack. He stumbled before I kicked a heel into his knee. The impact jarred him, but I slipped sideways to avoid him jumping atop me. Thralls appeared to feel no pain. On elbows and knees, he missed me and skidded on empty ground. The men stunk with sharp, stale sweat.

I couldn't help but grin. Blood pounded in my veins. Sand fell from my hair. I might have to harm them in public. My heart raced, and I straightened my smile into a grim line. Tyler had been clear about not getting into skirmishes.

The younger man leaped at me over his companion. He held a small blade barely longer than his thumb.

I scored a slice across his knife hand, while skipping clear. I drew them away from the car and the windows of the apartment.

"Ahnjii?" Tyler had stepped out and stood on the other side of their car.

Mrs. Forster's door was cracked open.

The young man did not drop his knife. Blood poured from a carefully placed wound just behind the first knuckle of his thumb. I'd been precise. *They truly felt no pain.*

The gray bearded man scrambled up clumsily, but quickly. I had two opponents. Tyler foolishly raced around their car.

I had no time. The thralls would not react like typical opponents. They were thin, but still had bulk on their side.

I feinted toward the young man's cut with my blade. Expecting the same stroke, he jabbed, but I'd already begun to spin. I caught his knife with my heel. The force flung it to the ground, but not far enough away. I continued my arc, which offered me an opportunity for a low cut on the backside of his calf. Pain or not, a severed tendon would slow him down. He dropped to the ground, struggling to reach for his knife.

The gray-haired man nearly caught my shoulder with an overextended slice.

I had only a moment before Tyler reached us. Slapping the older man's blade with my vambrace, I opened his stance. I sliced into his fingers and drew my blade up his palm, sure to catch tendons. His knife fell, but he leaped for me. Jaw open, he appeared deranged.

I managed a quick spin, caught an elbow, and drew him into the dirt face first. However, Tyler had reached the younger man by then.

The young man stood with an impossible wobble. His knife retrieved, he cut across Tyler's chest at the right shoulder. The movement twisted the thrall, and his leg buckled again. People underestimate an opponent's pain in battle. Considering my lesser weight and stature, I counted on it.

Jumping over the bearded man's feet, I kicked the younger man into the back of the truck. Dust blossomed at his skidding feet. A breeze I hadn't felt pulled the cloud away.

"Tyler, stay back," I yelled and spun to place myself between Tyler and the thralls.

The older man growled as he rose. He'd lunge again; next time I'd aim for a slice behind the knee.

The muscles in his face relaxed.

I stepped backward, pushing Tyler toward their car.

Emotionless, old man and young turned for their truck. The remaining knife clattered from relaxed hands. The young man stumbled, but managed to lean on the vehicle and hop along the side to the passenger door. They were leaving. Why? They wouldn't have held a chance against me, but seconds before they had not appeared to care.

"Hey, stop." Tyler pushed against my back.

In any circumstance, I could dispatch these untrained attackers quickly. It didn't seem smart to harm them in public and bring out the local authorities. However, the thralls could not be beaten into submission. It would be best if they left. Tyler had no idea what we were dealing with. I put out my left arm and leaned back. Had the thralls been recalled somehow? Did this wight have a connection with them?

"Are you okay?" I asked. The cut hadn't looked deep, but I'd only caught a passing glance. I sheathed my knife as the truck doors shut.

"Who are they?" Tyler relaxed, letting me guide them back toward the car.

"I don't know who they are." Once the two thralls had moved for their vehicle to leave, they'd never even glanced at us. Spewing smoke, the truck roared into life, and I turned to shove Tyler behind their car. "We need to get out of the way." They might try to run us over with their vehicle.

Tyler's short cut stained the armpit of their shirt with blood. *Deep enough.* We'd have to get it bandaged.

The truck thudded into gear. Why had they attacked us? The wight must have tracked me and wanted to stop me from searching. Shailagh had said the wight and thralls would be connected. Emery Porter knew my name. They would have killed us if they could. I wouldn't have allowed them to harm either one of us, but they'd seemed crazed and intent on trying. Perhaps the wight recognized the futility of the attack. They'd given up too quickly.

"We can't just let them get away." Tyler moved toward their door as if to follow the truck.

We could. Mrs. Forster had mustered enough courage to show her face in the doorway. One of the downstairs neighbors peeked around a curtain. The police had likely been called. Tyler had warned about this. I had appropriate papers, but they were forged.

The truck, with mud up to the doors, dents, and scratches deep into its previously white paint, backed up slowly. They didn't appear to plan on running us over. I frowned. None of this made sense. The wight had gone through the effort to find me, that much was sure. Then it had given up.

Tyler paused at their open door. "We need to call the police."

The men's faces were devoid of the earlier rage and intensity. They appeared emotionless, like Emery Porter. If they were recalled by the wight, they might be returning to it.

As if they were heading home after work, they pulled casually onto the street, changed gears, and drove away.

Mrs. Forster yelled from her railing, "See?"

Smoke trailing thickly behind, the thralls drove off at an

unhurried speed. "Don't call the police," I said quietly to Tyler. John could be with the wight, and these two could lead us to him.

I jumped around the front of the car toward the passenger door. "We need to follow them." A cold chill ran down my spine. Maybe the wight wanted us to follow. I wished I knew.

CHAPTER 31

My heart raced as I jumped into the car. Throwing away the can hadn't gotten rid of the stench, and my tussle with the thrall had smeared me with it. Tyler hesitated at their door.

I shoved my blade into its sheath, but left it and the vambraces on my arms. "Let's go, we need to follow them."

Tyler spread out their hands as if in confusion, then winced. "Shouldn't we call the police?"

I gestured toward Mrs. Forster and the apartment building. "They've already called, I'm sure. C'mon."

Reluctantly, Tyler climbed in. The engine was still running. Tyler had leaped out to come to my rescue. Sweet, but they should know it wasn't necessary. I glanced out the back, trying to see the thralls' truck; their exhaust left a trail.

"Ahnjii," Tyler paused, putting their seatbelt on. "I was overexcited when I said we couldn't let them get away; we don't have to worry about them."

I'd have to explain about John. "Please. I'll tell you everything, just follow them. Without being seen, if possible." The thralls likely wouldn't notice anything, but if the wight was connected, it might spot us. I couldn't even be sure they were headed to the wight, but it was the best lead I had.

Tyler still hadn't moved the knob thing so we could drive. I had never wanted to learn Earth cars until now.

"We can't lose them," I said.

Tyler tapped on the steering wheel. "I don't think this is a good idea."

"It's life or death."

"Whose?"

"John's. I think. If I'm right." I closed my eyes in frustration.

My expression must have meant something. Tyler pointed toward me. "You'll explain?"

"Yes, yes." I didn't know where to start. I had promised Vivianne that I would tell no one about the Fae, her secret. This was an emergency situation.

My heart leaped as Tyler put the car into gear. As we backed toward the street, I fist-bumped Tyler's shoulder in excitement. "Thank you."

They rose in their seat, swearing.

I winced when they cried out. "Sorry." I would have to bandage that wound while we drove. "Do you have any cloth or paper? Something clean?"

We moved forward onto the road, with dirt grinding between tires and asphalt. The truck had gotten a good distance ahead of us, but the smoke would help. Tyler swore under their breath and pointed. "Napkins in the glove box."

I shook my head. I should have remembered. Half of the pile I'd put in there myself from takeout. Some Earth medicine would be preferred since they had concoctions way beyond the compress which the Queen's physicians might offer. I released my harness and the car started beeping. Tyler often wore long sleeves with a low neck; this black top fit tightly. The thrall's knife had cut the fabric but left their shirt intact.

I folded a small bundle of napkins, enough for some compression. The car continued beeping, but I ignored it and knelt to lift the edge of cloth at their chest. The shallow cut had barely opened, and most of the bleeding had stopped.

I slid the wad under Tyler's shirt despite a little squirming and loud protests. Earth humans had some interesting curses.

"Sorry. Done." I pulled my hands back, lifting them into the air.

Tyler gritted their teeth. "Buckle up." They let out a sigh. "Start talking."

I settled back into my seat and delayed by buckling my harness. I sighed and started slowly. "There are other people here on Earth, other than humans." I turned from checking on the thralls' truck to catch Tyler's reaction.

They tilted their head. "Do you mean more people like you, from your world?"

No, but I had exposed the gate back on Duruce. Perhaps someone would follow. "No, not humans. The people from your stories. Fae." I wanted to mention the Nedjir, but didn't need to.

"Fairies?" Tyler blinked. "With wings?"

"Yes. No, not the wing part, not that I know of." I could ask Vivianne. Woo hid theirs pretty well. "I don't think they call themselves fairy." I studied Tyler's blank face. "Do you believe me?"

Tyler took a breath to pause, knowing about my truthsense and phrasing their words carefully. "I'm having a hard time accepting, but I don't think you're lying."

Truth.

"Okay. There are two types, the regular Fae and a group that call themselves high Fae. The high Fae call the other group low, but the other group doesn't, so there's that."

Tyler nodded and turned to follow the truck on a left turn. We weren't moving very fast, and there was traffic. From stories I'd read, I expected chases to be much faster and less boring.

"I met a high Fae the other day and helped her with a problem." If I mentioned the wildlings, then I might have to mention Nedjir. It didn't have anything to do with the wight, thralls, or John. "She came back asking about a case I'm working on for Bill. We're sure that the client is a thrall." That's confusing. "Let me back up."

"Please." Tyler shook their head. "I've got questions piling up."

A huge car with pointy corners pulled out between us and the truck. Tyler had to slow down abruptly. I steadied myself with a hand on the dash.

"Okay, I'm a bit confused on this part myself. Wights. It seems they are very old Fae, high Fae. Some have an ability to make people obey them, thus thralls. She uses dominar as a title or an ability, not sure."

Title, Mistress.

Shh.

"A title. But it's not important. Those two that attacked us, I believe are thralls, and they might lead us to the wight, which could mean we'll find John."

"What?" Tyler swerved, tires ground into grass and we missed a mailbox before getting back onto the road.

"Yes, um, John might be a thrall." I probably could have explained it better.

Tyler gestured into the air with their right hand, winced, and audibly took in a deep breath. "Walk me through that statement."

"Remember the roots?"

Tyler nodded quickly. "Cool. Please tell me how they fit in." We came to a slow stop as the truck and the big car pulled up to a stoplight. I didn't have to wonder if the thralls saw us, as blue-gray fumes pumped out of the back between their bumper and the next car.

"The Fae use them. They call them sigils. They look like squiggly designs. On humans they can make you see or believe things. The roots I found say not to look. We found others that said follow us, or something like that. Which we did."

Tyler swore as we turned onto a four-lane highway with a median in the center. "This road, 319, goes all the way to the gulf. How far away is this wight?"

I shrugged, hands raised. "I have no idea. I'm only hoping they lead us to it."

"I was supposed to pick up Deanna's investigator at the airport." They waved in the air, dismissing the comment. "Explain why you think John is a thrall. You were on sigils."

"The investigator can Uber." Even I could do that. "We found sigils where Emery Porter disappeared weeks ago. They led into the woods. We know those were related to the wight and thralls. So having sigils, the roots, at the last place we knew John went to made me worry."

"Emery Porter?"

"Bill's client. He's a thrall."

Tyler raised their eyebrows but didn't comment on my last statement. They tossed their phone in my lap. "Text

Deanna. Tell her that I've gotten sidetracked on some Ahnjii insanity. She'll argue, but make arrangements for the investigator."

I reworded the text slightly differently, but sent the message to Deanna. "The sigils were the important part of the story," I said to Tyler.

Their lips tightened and they nodded. "I get it. The sigils where Emery Porter disappeared, did you follow them? Maybe they led to the wight?"

"Yes. No." I shook my head. "Ended at an ambush where a thrall attacked us. And snakes. Sorry. We had to kill a bunch."

"Thralls?"

"Snakes. They killed the thrall." We were a fair distance back from the truck, but the area had turned rural with few side streets. The excitement and urgency to chase the thralls had dwindled with the slow driving and long explanations. "You believe about Fae now?"

Tyler, bit at their bottom lip. "Yes."

Truth.

I would have to apologize to Vivianne later. I *had* to tell Tyler, or else none of it would make sense. We had to find the wight and she'd have to agree to that. I wanted to explain more. However, I'd risk Laura's secret if I got into the wildlings. So much had happened in the past few days.

"You can't tell anyone else about the Fae, not even Deanna."

"Why?"

"I promised." I smiled smugly. "Remember when I told you about people with horse's ears?"

Tyler frowned. "Yes."

"Those were Fae. I can see them. You can't. Sigils."

Tapping their finger in rhythm on the steering wheel,

Tyler nodded slowly. "And humans would freak out, dissect them, try to kill them all if we knew."

I grimaced, but guessed Tyler might be right. "Oh. I found an animal that no one on Earth seems to know about. I call them Woo. I left them at the apartment."

CHAPTER 32

I GRABBED the handle over the window as we veered again.

"What kind of animal?" Tyler refocused on the road quickly.

"They're adorable. Like a color changing round rabbit, with huge eyes." I couldn't help but smile. "They whistle."

"You left it in your apartment?" Tyler sighed. "What does it eat?"

"Pistachios, so far."

"Well, rabbits can be trained to use litter boxes. You'll have a mess to clean up." Tyler shook their head slowly. "How could the Fae be real? Surely in today's world we would have evidence. Other than ears, what do they look like?"

"To me? Tall ears and long fingers, otherwise mostly humanish."

"Humanoid," Tyler said, then sighed. "Okay. Fae exist. Turn into wights. Turn humans into thralls."

I'd explained it all really badly. Shailagh wouldn't be happy. I should tell her about the thralls attacking. I dug into my pants pocket. "Only old Fae turn into wights. And none of them are supposed to turn humans into thralls, anymore." I showed Tyler my earring. "That's why Shailagh is investigating them and we're trying to stop all this."

"Shailagh being high Fae." Tyler shrugged and their tone indicated a comment, rather than a question.

"Exactly. I've got to let her know what just happened. The attack and all that." I pressed the post against my neck.

"How?"

I showed Tyler the earring again. "It lets me contact her," I said with a proud smile. I'd love to hear Tyler's opinion on the compass, but that couldn't happen. "Between our minds."

"An earring?"

I nodded and placed the post back against my neck. "It's Fae magic."

"You've got a magical mental phone to the Fae?"

"You make it sound weird."

Tyler chuckled, the first mirth from them that I'd heard. "I can't make it sound normal."

"Shh." I imagined the thralls attacking us at the apartment, their truck we were chasing, and sent it to the earring at my fingertip.

Nothing happened; there was no sensation and no response, only failure. An empty hole bubbled up in my chest. Just like the compass, I didn't have any powers outside of truthsense.

"Anything?" Tyler asked. "I should call Deanna and let her know."

"No. Remember, don't tell anyone. Shh." I looked at the carvings, put the pin against my skin, and tried again. I didn't focus on the attack and just imagined the road, Tyler's car, and the truck ahead of us with the two thralls. I bundled that thought up and pushed it into the pin, imagining it reaching Shailagh and the pin in her ear. I felt the odd sensation at my neck.

Here. I sensed woods, wet musty earth, and birds singing in trees.

"Yes." I'd reached her. Shailagh was in the woods. Now what?

Another more complicated sensation flooded into me. *Following.* I could see myself holding the post to my earlobe.

"Did it work?" Tyler asked.

"Shh." Following? Yes, I was following the thralls, but that hadn't been what she'd meant. Was I holding it in the wrong place? I moved the post up to my earlobe and went through the entire process once again.

I follow. Shailagh sent. The image of me holding the post remained the same. Did she need the contact to follow us? That could get tiresome quickly.

Khimmer. I need an ear clip to hold this post against my skin.

Is that wise, Mistress?

Do it.

A trickle of Nightarmor trailed from my choker up to my ear, forming around the post at the edge of my fingertips. I pulled my hand away.

Tyler glanced over. "That's cute."

I flipped the visor down and checked the mirror. Nightarmor formed a dark clip around my lobe with silver and gold markings, eerily similar to the engraving on the pin. "She's following," I said.

Tyler checked their rear-view. "What does she drive?"

Trees. "The Fae don't like metal. They use portals in trees to move around."

"Of course." Tyler stretched out their right arm, wincing. "After we follow this through and find John, we need to have a long talk. Right now, I need to call Deanna."

"What are you going to tell her?" She hadn't believed that I fell out of a gate from another world, and she wouldn't believe in the Fae or wights. But, I'd promised not to tell anyone too. Tyler had to be convinced to follow. However, if Tyler told her and she did say anything, it would just make things worse for Vivianne or others of her kind. If anyone believed it.

Tyler sat in silence, tapping lightly on the steering wheel with one finger. "You're right. I could at least let her know that we have a lead."

"She'd want specifics." I touched the ear clip and felt the pin sticking out. I'd have to ask Shailagh about the connection when we met.

Where were we going? Surely the wight didn't have a house on the side of the highway. More likely it would be hidden in the woods. "If they pull over, you'll drop me off, and then you can call Deanna."

Tyler snorted. "I'm not dropping you off on the side of the road."

I couldn't let Tyler try to fight. They weren't trained. "You're not going to engage these thralls. They feel no pain." I motioned to their shoulder. "Less than a minute in and you're bleeding."

I had no idea what to expect from this wight. As an assassin, I'd never had partners, but Shailagh appeared better suited than anyone. Cold panic gripped my chest. I couldn't risk Tyler. The wight could have John in that case.

"And yet . . ." Tyler didn't finish their statement. They could be infuriating when they locked in on a cause.

"When we met, you were running for your life from highwaymen."

"Mobsters."

They'd had guns, which Khimmer still called Eldritch weapons. "These are worse."

"I'd finished helping those kids, and just needed to leave." Tyler pointed ahead toward the truck. "We are trying to save John."

John couldn't be saved unless I killed the wight, and Shailagh wouldn't like that. "Let me do what I'm good at."

"I'll let you and your armor lead the way."

"This wight has Fae magic. The trees will stab at things. I'll be protected."

Tyler raised their eyebrows. "That's good to know. Keep it distracted, armor and all, and I'll grab John."

They had no idea how dangerous this could be. "What if it makes you into a thrall?" I flicked the end of my braid. "I don't want to lose you."

CHAPTER 33

WE DROVE through a cluster of houses where it seemed a town might spring up before it quickly died. The air coming through the vents smelled like a swamp, but all I could see were trees, pines, according to Tyler. It had been a few hours since I'd abandoned Woo at my apartment, and Tyler chastised me for not leaving out water. The sun had reached a more comfortable angle near the horizon to my right, leaving us shaded with only a spattering of light through the forest.

The truck rode far ahead, unmistakable with its pluming exhaust. Dread had climbed up in my chest. Tyler refused to stay safe, and it was my fault for involving them. I had had no choice at the moment and couldn't decide what I would have done differently. I needed to learn driving. It didn't look that complicated.

Tyler glanced over. "Your bunny will drink out of the toilet. You said it could climb."

Woo? That was a disturbing thought. "Don't change the subject. Think what it will do to Deanna if you're hurt or killed."

"Look up Koala on your phone. Maybe you found one of those."

I tightened my jaw. Tyler was infuriating when they chose to ignore an argument. My mouth opened to continue, and I sensed Shailagh. *Near.* I could smell the wet forest around her, stagnant water that pooled around trees.

"She's close," I hissed.

Tyler leaned forward, looking at the sides of the road. "Okay. That's ominous."

I bundled the image of the truck in the distance and the highway that had narrowed to two lanes.

I caught a sense of quickly passing trees and splashing water. Shailagh was running.

"Hey," Tyler pointed one finger from their grip on the steering wheel.

The truck had turned off the road and was driving into the woods. Tension rose in my chest, and I tried to send an image of the chase but failed.

We reached a short patch of asphalt that ended in the grass. The woods beyond did not look like a road, but Tyler pulled into the brush. The scraping on the bottom startled me. "Drop me off." I could track the thralls' truck on foot.

Tyler spoke loudly over the noise. "Not happening." Vegetation folded under the front of their car and tore under us, threatening to rip off the bottom. "Prius. Not much clearance."

"Stop," I yelled.

Tyler didn't, and the brush let up as we found an open trail leading toward the sun. I squinted while Tyler dug out their sunglasses. The grass and weeds scraped against the bottom, but not as perilously as our first intrusion off the road. Exhaust or dust hung in the air far ahead of us with the glare of the sun hiding the horizon. Brush snapped at the side of the car, reminding me of Fae magic. I couldn't let Tyler risk themself.

I had to admit to enjoying the quick skirmish with the thralls, but I couldn't let Tyler continue. I winced as we drove over a small shrub in the middle of the trail and it scraped under us. On each side, the trees stood a good distance from each other, and the trail we drove cut a distinct line through them, allowing brush to hedge along the sides. Deeper in the woods appeared dark and sparsely grown.

Tyler was not easily swayed from an idea. I had a dangerous task ahead. Maybe Shailagh could persuade Tyler to stay back.

Leaves shaded the sun momentarily as the brush on my side of the car pushed into the path. I flinched at the sudden movement.

A dead limb that looked more like the stump of an arm swung from above and smashed into the windshield. The glass webbed with cracks before we scraped past. Branches clawed at my window, forcing me to lean away instinctively.

Tyler swore while they jerked the car to the left. The headlight smashed and the front corner shrieked as it tore against a tree on their side.

The bush that had smashed the windshield followed and broke the window behind mine. The animated brush hinted at Fae magic. Had the wight found us?

Full armor.

Yes, Mistress.

Amid a flourish of leaves and branches, I could make out human flesh, a man's chest. Green and brown splotches grew on pale, taut skin. The sun still shone brightly ahead of us, so my vision seemed questionable until Nightarmor flowed over as a helmet. The man attacking us appeared overly large and wore branches as camouflage.

Tyler had come to a stop, and I threw open the door, prepared to do battle. Inside the car, I was at a disadvantage. I managed a knee toward the opening before the harness pinned me in my seat.

Cut bindings.

Yes, Mistress.

Khimmer rose blades out of Nightarmor where the belt pinned me into the seat, and I yanked against the restraints. The tough fabric sliced open.

By then, the creature had reached me. Limbs and hands reached together as if bound into one creature. It stunk like the depths of a bog.

Jerked into the air, I stared down at something not quite human.

CHAPTER 34

WITH MY RIGHT HAND, I grabbed a human arm; with my left, a thick branch that grew out of flesh at the side of his ribs.

Short blade.

Yes, Mistress.

The man's face had tiny branches poking through skin in random spots. Tiny dark leaves sprouted just over the flesh, covering parts of his eyes and mouth. A beetle crawled on a section of his forehead that looked like paper-thin bark. I had possibly found the wight.

Nightarmor reformed the sheathed blade on my left vambrace. I hung in the air, with no solid footing. I released my grip of his arm, reaching for the blade. His face and neck were vulnerable.

The club that had broken the windshield, yet another appendage, slammed onto my helmet. Nightarmor cushioned the blow, but my head rocked from the impact, and I failed to pull the short knife.

The creature's grip slipped, and all I managed was a clumsy kick into his chest. It freed my left side, though branches had wound around my middle. Spinning without any control, my boots tapped the back of Tyler's car.

I had to break free. Enough pounding by that club, and I'd become dazed.

Kicking out for the car, I managed to make contact with a heel and shoved myself into the half-human creature. Using the momentum, I swung, twisting limb and flesh. The last branch snapped at my waist, and I rolled free onto the spongy floor of the forest.

Sword.

Yes, Mistress.

Through Khimmer's vision I could see the red-orange core of the man speckled with darker growths. It certainly seemed I'd found the wight, but the ears and fingers appeared human.

I stepped back as I drew my sword. Quick glances positioned the trees around me, and I crouched into a one-handed stance. Tyler moved by the car, but hadn't approached the back of the creature stomping toward me.

Its movements were cumbersome and stilted as it wielded seven upper appendages atop two mostly human legs. My first cut left the branch ending in the club dangling at its side. I could sense its rage as I darted behind a tree forcing it to follow me deeper into the woods. The next cut glanced off its thigh where bark grew as if armor. No blood followed.

The legs and torso were wrong for a human. Its hips were level with my solar plexus and its chest hung above my head. If this wasn't the wight, what was it?

The upper appendages were higher, but I had a better chance at damaging those. I feinted to force a slap from the thin branches growing out of the bottom of its rib cage. Slicing through, I leaped to the next tree as a human fist swung through empty air. The half-human shrieked, in anger I assumed, though the sound barely imitated any animal I'd ever heard.

My next step ended a few inches deeper than I expected as the ground gave way to mud. Dropping to a knee, I avoided a thick branch and took another shot at the creature's legs. The sword tip sunk into wood and bound there as the half-man bore down on me.

Khimmer withdrew the sword tip, melting and thinning the blade until it released. Still, the creature managed a blow to my shoulder that slammed me to the ground. I had nearly freed my boot.

Foregoing fists, the tree man raised a bark-covered stump of a foot. Through Khimmer's vision, warm light shone where its crotch would have been, though little seemed to remain.

I jabbed upward and found flesh and bone, driving the blade a hand's width deep.

The creature teetered, balancing on one stump. Still pinning him, I managed to draw my boot out, accompanied with a satisfying sucking sound. Blade tip still embedded, I thrust deeper, grinding against bone, and tilting toward the back. I hoped for the spine while the tree man lurched backward. I could not guess what it might take to kill the creature. Beheading? I would have to bring it lower to accomplish anything that far up the torso.

The tree man's foot stepped back. Freeing my sword, I jumped to my feet and thrust again. Aiming for the stomach, I caught it mid turn as it stumbled back to stop from falling. I pulled back with my blade scraping on ribs. In Khimmer's vision, it appeared that it bled.

I had it staggering.

Khimmer, dory.

My Nightarmor blade elongated the hilt into a staff, shaped the small tip into a sharp blade with a wide base, and the butt became a blunt point. I added my left hand, stepped forward, and thrust. The thin tip sliced through light vegetation and entered the throat. The creature's own hand pushed my weapon aside, ripping the blade through soft skin.

I jumped free, concerned for my footing, and waited in a crouch.

What seemed to be blood, through Khimmer's view, poured freely. No man would survive such a wound. I held tightly to the spear. This was no man. A freak of Fae magic. Shailagh would need to explain.

The more I'd been involved with her, the more I understood Vivianne and Laura's warnings about the high Fae. What was this thing?

The creature's knees bent, but only at a small angle, as if too stiff. I backed up another step, testing for purchase with my toes. My heart thudded in my ears, seeming to echo inside Nightarmor's helmet.

The tree man crashed to the forest floor and rolled to his side.

Tyler had just made it to the edge of the woods, easily ten steps away. Tempted to wave them back, I paused with my spear readied. A man's eyes stared out at me, dead and glazed.

Are we clear?

Yes, Mistress.

The tree man had delayed us. The thralls' truck had continued, or stopped, but they hadn't come to join the fight. I couldn't let them get away, not after witnessing what the wight could do. Deanna would not be happy if I brought John back with extra limbs.

Remove armor.

Yes, Mistress.

Nightarmor and the spear flowed back to its smaller components. A sickening putrid smell filled the cool air, worse than a bog. Lesions in the skin surrounded the protruding plants. Where the vegetation had grown out in limbs, the flesh had torn during the battle, though no blood flowed there. The forest had turned quiet around us, as if waiting.

Tyler stopped within sight of the creature. "Are you okay?"

My head pounded and my heart hadn't stopped racing. "I'm good."

They swore. "What is that?"

"When Shailagh gets here, I'm going to ask."

"So, we're safe?" Tyler peered around us.

"For the moment, we're clear."

"What now?"

Tyler would never leave John. I took a breath in and out. "We get back to your car and find the thralls' truck." *Shailagh, where are you?* I would likely need her help.

CHAPTER 35

I TOUCHED MY EAR, confirming that Khimmer had kept the clip attached and the sigil post earring safe. The stench coming from the carcass hastened my move toward Tyler. Their car waited at the trail with both doors open and a window half shattered.

The truck we'd been following was long gone, but I couldn't imagine this trail went very far.

Taking a deep breath of fresher air, I calmed my heart and rested my hand on Tyler's good shoulder. They were pale and visibly shaken.

"Let me see where Shailagh is."

Tyler pointed into the woods. "Is that what they'll do to John?"

I hoped not. "No." Grabbing my braid and flicking the end, I forced a smile.

I focused on the image of the dead creature who I would likely never forget. *Wight?* It would make everything simpler, but I still doubted that it had been that easy. I pushed through my earring toward the pin in her ear and felt the familiar pulse.

More images came of the forest; the scenery didn't look different from the last time, nor from my present surroundings. *Wait,* she sent to me.

I squinted down the trail at the low sun and the long-gone truck. Perhaps Shailagh had her nifty tracking sigils. Those had been cool.

Tyler still stared back into the woods. It made me shiver. What could turn a human into that? "Do you think they led us here — to be ambushed?"

I raised my eyebrows. The sigils we followed into the woods seemed to have that intent. Likely Emery Porter had been trapped along that path. "Maybe." I remembered the snakes; Tyler would not be able to protect himself. "Let's wait at the car."

"Are we going to follow?" Tyler glanced toward the low sun. "Or do you think it's a trap?"

"We'll wait for Shailagh."

Tyler peered at my eyes, then to the ear clip. "Oh, the magical mental thing."

I checked the woods, looking for any motion. "Yeah. Let's wait by the car."

Khimmer, keep an eye out for snakes, or anything.

Yes, Mistress.

Tyler hesitated, then frowned. "Do you think they'll come back?"

I pointed toward the car and tilted my head in that direction. "Snakes. I'd feel better if you could get inside the car if we need you to. My armor can protect me."

They peered around, then started walking. "So many questions. Always questions." Tyler gestured in frustration. "Where does the mass go?"

I followed them closely, but tried not to seem in a hurry. "What?"

"How does your armor turn from enough to cover you and make weapons to a belt and shoes?"

I shrugged. "You've asked before. I don't know."

Khimmer?

Compression, Mistress.

"Compression," I answered.

"No, no, no." Tyler sounded stressed. "Metal doesn't just do that. I mean it can, but the weight would be the same." They stopped and flipped at one of my bracelets. It jangled loosely against the others. "It would hang on your skin like a string tied to a lead ball." They turned, kicking at the leaves and needles, heading toward the car. "Okay, how do branches grow out of someone's ribs?"

"Don't know."

Tyler stopped, just a few steps away from the car. "This doesn't bother you?"

"It does." Branches growing out of people was very disturbing. The idea that John might be a thrall tortured me for what it would do to Deanna. Nightarmor had long since lost any curiosity for me. It simply was and had been since my earliest memories. The last of its kind, a relic in Duruce, bequeathed to me by its choice, ancient from a time when our planet had nearly destroyed itself in war and the gods had declared that there would be no more armies or devastating weapons. Considering the wars on Earth, and wights, a god or two would be helpful.

I motioned to my passenger seat. "Sit." Strolling around to the opposite side, I closed the driver's door. Crumpled metal dangled over the tire. Any sign of the thralls we were chasing were long gone. Except for distant birds, our surroundings were deathly silent. The air hung with heavy musk from the wet woods and an occasional taint from the putrid creature.

Tyler had accommodated me, and I took a position leaning against the back door housing the broken window. If we had visitors, I could have him close the passenger door and I would just have to make sure nothing got in. The shattered glass of the front windshield didn't have any holes. I'd rather they just drive away.

"You should close the door in case there's any . . ." I trailed off, searching the area around us.

"Snakes?" Tyler sat with their legs out. "We should be following these men, thralls, finding John."

"We'll wait for Shailagh. You should really let us handle this."

Tyler shook their head. "You're not going alone."

Mistress.

Leaves rustled behind me. I jumped up, ready to call for armor. Red hair bouncing and flowing as she ran through the woods, Shailagh had arrived.

CHAPTER 36

I RELAXED and waved at Shailagh. She barely acknowledged me, veering off course to approach the fallen body of the tree man. What would she tell me about this? Had she known it was possible all this time?

Tyler stood as I jogged to meet her at the carcass. The stench had gotten worse.

"This isn't the wight, is it?" I asked.

She took deep breaths as if winded from her run. She stood too close beside the creature. With a glance at Tyler, a smile played at the edge of her lips. "No. This was human."

"Was." I agreed with her on that account. "Did the wight do this?"

It was the only answer I could have come up with. This tree man had been here where the wight's thralls had driven into the woods. However, I was still new to Earth.

"This should not have been done." Shailagh knelt beside the carcass, far closer than I might have considering the reek. She'd been truthful, but had not fully answered my question.

"Did the wight do this?" I asked again.

She nodded, stood, and glanced at Tyler standing at the edge of the woods. Leaning in toward me, she asked, "What do they think this is?"

"We were waiting for you. This had to be Fae magic, right?"

Her eyes squinted and her face tightened into a frown. "You did not tell them who I was, did you?"

"A Fae?" I nodded and gave a quick shrug. "Tyler knows. I had to tell them. They're cool with it."

She made a quick flicking gesture and spoke in a whisper. "They can't know." Her eyes searched mine. "I forget. A witch would understand this from a young age, but you've had no one to train you. We avoid having humans learn about us; a witch, a strong enough empath, knows already. The few who have spoken of this to the outside world we fashion as unreliable. We make a mockery of them, and the other humans believe they are deranged. Do you understand?"

"Sure." It did make sense. If Deanna truly knew about Fae, wildlings, or this tree man in the woods, she'd be freaked. Tyler had barely believed me.

"These are rules, a code, that we have kept with all the peoples for a very long time." She stopped as Tyler approached.

I stepped back from Shailagh and smiled as if we weren't conspiring to hide things. Keeping secrets was difficult when you cared about the people you hid them from. My face flushed. I did not want Shailagh or her people making Tyler or Deanna out to be deranged to cover all this up.

Tyler paused, studying both of us before they gestured at the corpse. "What is it?"

After being admonished, I tried to remain silent, but

Shailagh didn't respond. What was I supposed to tell Tyler? I felt trapped between a good friend and a new friend who portrayed a sense of authority. The longer the awkwardness left us listening to distant birds and standing too close to the stench, the more I felt I had to say something.

"The Fae aren't supposed to do this. It's like a crime." I gestured up and down the tree man. His pants had split to allow the growth of bark around his legs; from this angle, the damage I'd done to his crotch wasn't visible.

Tyler's mouth opened as if to speak, but again silence hung between us.

"We should go." With almost no sound in the leaves, Shailagh turned to pass Tyler and walk toward the trail and the broken car. "What did you do to your shoulder?"

"Are Fae doing that to John?" Tyler stood their ground gesturing to the corpse, their tone rising.

Shailagh stopped and faced us, drawing a long breath. Her tone was softer than I'd heard her use before, almost compassionate. "Not likely. This process would take months and constant attention. I'm assuming. To my knowledge, it hasn't been done in centuries."

Tyler studied her. "Why would someone do this? Why would your people do this?"

She smiled and took a step toward them. "You can sense my difference?"

"Something." Tyler's tone came off sharp and quick.

"An empath, though I imagine too slight to have ever been considered a threat or worth training."

Shailagh thought Tyler an empath, a witch. I couldn't help but bounce on my heels. No wonder we got along.

Tyler stiffened. "Considered a threat by whom?"

"The Fae or the witches." She grew a sly smile. "Don't be offended. All creatures have some measure; yours is low, but not negligible. If you were born to a witch family, they would have trained you." Her glance flicked toward me. "How did you meet?"

Tyler turned to me with hesitation. I didn't want Shailagh to know of my true origins, not yet. I had questions and a sense that it would be more threatening to her than it had been to Tyler.

"In Slovenia. Tyler was rescuing kidnapped children, and I'd just been injured." I'd just fallen through the gates, and the most debilitating of my injuries came when John hit me with their van, but that part she didn't need to know.

Tyler nodded.

Shailagh shrugged. "Secrets." Again she walked toward the trail, and we both followed this time. "You were following thralls."

"We were. They continued down the road." I jogged to Tyler's side and tapped their arm, speaking low. "A witch. Tidy."

The phrase is "neat," Mistress.

"Neat," I corrected.

Tyler's dark eyes focused on the ground, and they shook their head. "We've got to find John."

I gestured to Shailagh. "We can handle it."

Tyler's jaw tightened. "I'm not leaving because of that." They motioned toward the corpse. "We need to find out what they know about John."

"Let's see if we can find them, first." Shailagh's head shifted slightly, as if she were going to look at me. "Tyler, is the vehicle drivable? Perhaps you could follow us?"

CHAPTER 37

It took us a couple minutes to tear the torn bumper from the car. Tyler and I tried, then Shailagh ripped it off with one motion. How strong was she? She had a frame only slightly thicker than Tyler's. Was this a Fae thing?

Tyler drove behind us as we walked. The stench had disappeared, but the woods still smelled wet, like a swamp.

"You fear for Tyler's safety?" Shailagh asked.

"Of course."

"Then tell them they can't come with us."

I focused on the trail ahead. The sun had dropped behind the tree canopy and only stabbed through on occasion. There was no sign of the truck. I'd already tried being firm with Tyler. Shailagh didn't know them.

"It won't stop them." I flicked the end of my braid.

"They care for this John that much?"

I chuckled. "I don't think anyone cares about him that much, except for Tyler's sister, Deanna, but that's enough for both of us."

Shailagh's expression turned grim, and she gestured ahead. It took me a couple more steps before I recognized the tail end of the thralls' truck at the right edge of the trees. I gestured for Tyler to back off.

The depths of the woods around us had turned dark. Sunlight cut lines in places, but most of the color had disappeared, leaving deep browns that blended. The sky hadn't turned gray yet, but the blue had lost some of its vibrant brightness.

I became conscious of my footsteps in the grass and padded more carefully. There were still a few birds out, cawing in the distance. The loudest sounds we made were the tires of Tyler's car grinding through sand, grass, and leaves.

Shailagh walked as quietly as I did. To my right, she separated from me so that we each walked in one of the faded ruts of the trail.

The truck had pulled nose first into the woods. No real attempt had been made to hide it.

The brush near it looked suspicious, but no half-man waited there. The trees closest to the parking spot had dead needles clustered on the ends of their branches. Even the tops of the woods looked brown.

The driver's door was open. A darker shadow took shape against the passenger window. Had they left, or did they wait for us? My heart began to race. I considered calling for armor.

Khimmer, do you see anyone?

Yes, Mistress. There is a man inside the truck. Just one.

I flicked my hand to catch Shailagh's attention. Once she turned, I raised a single finger, then pointed at the truck. She nodded in acknowledgment.

Vambrace and blade.

Yes, Mistress.

Armor poured down to cover my forearms, and I drew

the short knife quietly. I studied the silhouette in the window. It looked like the younger man leaning against the door.

Our approach would leave Shailagh the closest. I sped up, wanting to circle around the back and creep up from the driver's side. She would be in the most dangerous position. I raised a hand, hoping Tyler would halt.

As I passed the rear of the truck, I could see the man's head clearly through the back window. Indeed, he rested against the door. Did he wait for us? I had cut his leg; perhaps he'd lost too much blood to continue. Surely, they would have bound it.

Scraps of wood and rope littered the back bed of the truck. I motioned for Shailagh to wait while I crept to the open door. Needles crunched underfoot as I stepped off the trail into the edge of the forest.

The thrall appeared unconscious. Blood matted his pants where I had cut him. Who would not bind that? I had not intended for him to bleed out.

Shailagh appeared at his window, a hand positioned against him opening the door. The young man didn't move. He'd been bleeding for an hour.

I sheathed my knife and walked back around the truck. Shailagh studied me, but I waited until I was close before speaking quietly. "He's unconscious. We should focus on the older thrall; follow him." I'd dealt with Emery Porter. I didn't think that any amount of interrogation would get details out of a thrall.

Her face grim, she glared at the thrall through the window. "They are her eyes and ears," Shailagh said.

What did she intend? I tilted my head. "She?" Did Shailagh know this wight? My whisper turned into a hiss. "So you know this Fae?"

"Perhaps. It is only a guess." She gestured me back. "It does not matter. It affects nothing. We should kill the thrall."

Was she so quick because it was a human? "How about we bind its leg and leave it here?"

"Because the wight will know everything they see and hear. She will be alerted."

I could leave the man to die and better the odds to rescue John. Shailagh had obviously made her decision. I had killed guards in pursuit of my targets before, but avoided it when I could. Worse, this man had been coerced into the position.

"It won't matter then. The half-man, plant thing would have alerted the wight. They know we're coming." I peered at the young man's face. He had a light fuzz growing on his chin, barely a man. "What if I can knock him out without waking him?"

Shailagh sighed and shrugged. "Truly, I don't know. You handle it." She stepped backward and turned to head for Tyler.

I walked around to the driver's side. *Weighted gauntlet, right.*

Yes, Mistress.

As Nightarmor coated my fingers, I had to resist the pull of gravity. How *did* Khimmer make the bangles light?

Electron alignment, Mistress.

Why did I even ask? I placed a boot on the inside of the driver's doorframe and adjusted my weight so that the truck shifted slowly. Balancing on the one foot, I watched the young man as I brought my other knee up to the seat. I could smell the blood.

The front seat was one cushion for both driver and passenger, so I let it take my weight in increments. I didn't want to jar him awake with sudden movements. Struggling in this confined space was not my plan. A quick jab to the jaw and I could hopefully incapacitate him, then bind the leg and leave him here. His breathing seemed so light, I wondered if he would survive this much blood loss.

I reached my bare left hand to the steering wheel to pull myself up. With pressure, it shifted an inch in my direction before a "click" sounded.

I froze, intent on the man's face. His eyelids shifted as if he slept, but he didn't move.

The blood had fouled on the floor, a distinct smell. His arm farthest from me hung between the door and his hip. The closer hand rested on the seat.

Lifting my other leg, I placed a second knee on the cushion. I would need to be just a hair closer.

Grimacing at the noise, I slid my knee forward and lifted my right hand up by my ear.

His eyes shot open. Not groggy, but wide awake.

With a jerk, he looked right at me. The wight inside him saw me. She had been alerted.

I punched.

CHAPTER 38

IT WAS POSSIBLY MY IMAGINATION, but the woods smelled fouler. I bound the young thrall's wounds and put him in the bed of the truck. How could I leave an innocent to die?

Tyler parked behind, blocking the trail. What kind of risk did I involve them in? I couldn't see a way out of this.

Shailagh sniffed the seats and floor on the driver's side of the truck. For some reason, it made me hungry. Possibly since it had been a long while since I ate. I stood behind her quietly, and Tyler joined me. The woods turned darker every second, and no moon showed in the gray sky.

Tyler motioned toward Shailagh. "Did she lose something?"

"Our thrall's scent," Shailagh said as she leaned in, holding her hands behind her and avoiding the metal doorframe, her hair and the tops of her ears pressed against the dash. Long red curls dragged on the seat and floor.

"Are you going to do the blue light thing?"

She sounded stressed or weak. "Fachgen, yes."

Translation? I thought to Khimmer.

None, Mistress.

I crossed my arms and tapped on my armband, waiting as it grew darker. Perhaps we wouldn't need her magic. Checking the ground, I could see some disturbed needles leading into the woods. The Aegis monks had done little training on tracking, more to keep me from leaving an easy trail than to find one.

A faint blue glowed from the interior of the truck, and Shailagh backed out with a sigh. Blue footprints glowed around Tyler's and my feet and led into the woods.

"I'll lead. Ahnjii, keep your eyes out on our surroundings. Tyler, take the rear and make sure no one hears you."

Tyler was wearing their short boots and had never been particularly stealthy in them. However, if they were going with us, I needed them nearby. As Shailagh walked into the forest with her sigil in hand and blue glow lighting the ground, I spoke quietly to Tyler. "Stay close."

The sigil's light made the rest of the forest that much darker in the dwindling sun. *Khimmer, light helmet.*

Yes, Mistress.

Nightarmor flowed up, and Khimmer enhanced their sight for the night, turning everything blue-gray except for Shailagh's warm orange figure. I could make out the trees and the specks of orange for birds or small animals. Thankfully, there was no army of snakes. Why not? Surely the wight knew we were on their trail, or her trail, if Shailagh did know who the Fae was.

Birds called from the canopy above, growing quiet when we approached too close. I could see pairs and groups hidden in the trees.

The larger dull orange shapes, perhaps raccoons, rabbits, or foxes, hunkered down motionless when we got close enough for me to see them. Amid the foul-smelling woods, I did not see any larger, human-sized threats.

One small blob nestled in the branches ahead of us, likely a raccoon. I frowned. Woo must hate me for leaving them alone in the apartment. I hadn't even thought of food or water. In my defense, I had planned on being home in the evening. So far, I had done Woo no favor taking them out of their little cave.

Shailagh's gesture alerted me as we circumvented a pool of stagnant water. The blue tracks shimmered, and the thrall had obviously climbed out of the muck to the side. Lifeless puddles scattered between trees along with a familiar rise that looked like stone pushing up from the forest floor.

Assuming the wight was expecting us, she made no move to stop our progress. The eerie darkness of Earth's night had almost completely taken the woods, and only Khimmer's vision and the blue glow of Shailagh's magic kept us moving forward.

The sound of Tyler's footsteps stopped, and I swung around. They stood, immobile.

"Tyler?" I whispered.

Shailagh returned from behind me.

Tyler looked up over my head, their expression calm, almost pleased. I nudged their chest, rocking them. Their eyes remained locked.

I turned and scanned the trees. Shailagh watched us with a frown.

Moss hung from a branch, and I squinted, trying to see if some sigil hung there. Vines dangled in a snarl from the tree. Stepping back to Tyler's position, it appeared he stared at the tangle. Was there a pattern to it?

I gestured toward Shailagh and pointed at the intertwined mass. She backtracked carefully. "Liam's lips, it is a sigil." She studied it a moment before she spoke. "It will keep him locked here."

She nodded to me and started to turn Tyler away; they resisted immediately, with an urgency. I wrestled my friend's shoulder and Shailagh an arm, to get them to face away.

Remove helmet.

Nightarmor melted, and cool air brought a stronger scent of swamp. Shailagh gripped their shoulders, and I took Tyler's face in both hands and watched their frantic eyes.

"It's okay. It's me. Shh." I kept my voice low and soothing.

They blinked and relaxed tense muscles.

Our little foray into the wilds had just gotten more interesting. We could backtrack to their car, the safest option. Perhaps now they would see the danger.

"We need to get you out of the woods." I stroked the sides of their face, hoping to calm eyes that were beginning to flicker with panic.

Tyler swallowed. "What happened?"

"You looked at a sigil. It did something to your mind. A lie of sorts." I shrugged. "Fae stuff. Wight stuff."

"Like the roots."

"Exactly. Shailagh uses it as well, to hide among the humans."

She gave me a foul look.

"What do you mean?" Tyler started to turn, and I pressed their cheeks to keep them facing me. In a slightly higher tone, they asked, "What does she really look like?"

Shailagh sighed and stepped around so he wouldn't be

tempted to turn back toward the vines. The blue light glowed in her hand.

I glanced at her face, curious. "What do you see?"

"Tall, slim, beautiful. Maybe late thirties." Their voice tinged on the edge of resentment or fear. "No branches."

Shailagh's eyes widened, and her lips tightened in anger.

I chuckled. "No branches or anything like that. All of what you said. Bright red hair?"

Tyler shook their head. "Auburn at best, wavy."

I reached up and touched the tuft of fur sprouting off the top of Shailagh's ears. "Ears up to here?"

She flinched away with a scowl.

"No." Tyler said.

"Sexy long fingers?" I asked. I got a quick smile from both of them for that one.

"No." Tyler sounded more relaxed.

"Basically human, but the ears and fingers would make you wonder." I'd have to ask her about the hair; did she get to choose? Vivianne had made it sound like it happened when she was an infant.

The forest appeared more menacing. Shadowy bushes threatened to hold waiting death. Dangling moss and vines warned of traps. A lone bird cawed from behind me, and its call seemed to echo.

Tyler let out a long breath. "And your truthsense, it protects you from the sigils?"

I nodded, folding my arms across my chest. Tyler needed to be somewhere safe.

Shailagh's expression remained in a scowl. "We need to get you back to the car. There might be more, even worse sigils."

"No," Tyler answered quickly, then frowned. "Like what?"

"A command to kill everyone." Shailagh answered flatly.

I raised my eyebrows. That would be inconvenient. Tyler's eyes widened, but they shook their head obstinately.

"What do you propose?" Shailagh asked.

"I'll close my eyes. Ahnjii can lead me."

"And if something attacks, and you open your eyes at the wrong moment?" I asked. "We'd have to protect you, unless of course you start trying to kill us."

"I won't." Tyler gestured into the woods. "With my eyes closed, you'll have to protect me anyway. I'm coming. I wouldn't forgive myself if I didn't try."

I wouldn't forgive myself if Tyler died. However, I knew their determined look, and I couldn't win this argument. A chill ran up my back. "Okay."

Shailagh glared.

CHAPTER 39

I COULDN'T LOSE TYLER, even for John. We appeared to be entering a foul swamp where the wight likely holed up with her thralls.

We argued for a couple of minutes before Shailagh gave up. "It amazes me how quick humans are to throw their lives away with false bravado. Your lifespans are short enough. I guess it's because you breed like rabbits." She dismissed Tyler with a wave. "Your choice."

"You see how dangerous this is?" I asked Tyler. "We'll have to worry about protecting you."

Tyler stiffened. "I can take care of myself."

"With your eyes closed?" I snapped with a sarcastic tone.

They looked at the ground, but they weren't backing down. I'd been insulting. The last thing I wanted was for Tyler to be harmed, the second to last thing was to hurt their feelings. "I'm sorry," I apologized. "I don't know what to do."

Tyler leaned toward me. "Respect my wishes. I can handle this."

Mistress. Someone approaches.

Armor.

Nightarmor flooded over me, and I spun using Khimmer's vision. My pulse quickened.

Red motion raced toward us from the right. Shailagh turned to face the figure. It appeared the wight had decided to stop us.

Sword and spikes.

Yes, Mistress.

Trees whipped branches, but our attacker moved gracefully around them. A wildling who moved with agility had only been hinted at by my earlier encounter.

I pulled Nightarmor's sword and moved to intercept. Preferring that the fighting stay away from Tyler, I ran. The wildling scraped a paw and claws on one of the moving limbs that Shailagh activated with her Fae magic. They spun higher in the air, arcing for a landing close to her.

A second, Mistress.

I faltered mid-run, checking behind me. Like true hunters, one had distracted while the second brought up a deadly attack from behind. We'd left Tyler exposed.

My boots slipped in wet needles and leaves, causing me to lose a precious second. Heart racing, I scrambled.

Wide-eyed, Tyler had peeked over their shoulder at the wildling vaulting through the air at Shailagh. They had no hint of the approaching threat from their other side.

"Behind!" I yelled, both for Tyler and Shailagh.

Her magic had sent supple roots up to entangle the first shifter, and the wildling hit them, shredding into the vegetation with their claws.

My heart pounded hot in my chest. I managed a foothold and launched toward Tyler. Even after my warning, they hadn't taken their eyes off the wildling that threatened Shailagh. I hoped she could manage her own threat. Through the dark woods, the second shifter raced low on four feet, unfettered by any of her Fae magic.

"Tyler, to me." I had at least two steps before I reached Tyler. My throat and chest tightened.

Tyler watched Shailagh's attacker, not even registering my shift in direction. I not only had to reach them, but get around to intercept the attacker.

I could see the heat of the wilding bearing down on Tyler. Red-orange muscles glowed with shaggy hair that masked the sides of their head. A hot mouth dropped open with each stride. Had the wight turned them into thralls?

My friend finally turned from his locked gaze with Shailagh's battle. The wildling leaped before I reached Tyler.

I threw myself in the air, sword thrusting to meet the point where the soft throat would soon reach. I would not have risked such an attack if it were not to save Tyler's life. The extended arm would leave me off-balance, but what choice did I have?

Whether these were the wight's allies or thralls, these wildlings intended on harming us — killing us.

The tip of my blade tugged into fur, but the attacker had twisted, avoiding the point. I adjusted, bringing an elbow and spike into play. The full force of the wildling's jump slammed into Nightarmor.

I felt the flesh impale and tug at my elbow. Then we hit the ground together, skidding on the wet litter of the forest. My helmet slid into thick ridged roots and a trunk, pinching my neck toward my chest.

With the elbow spike caught in the wildling's side, my sword proved uselessly pinned. I tried to shift. The wilding scraped nails across Nightarmor and ground teeth against the helmet. Khimmer melted away the spike embedded in flesh and released me; I drew my sword across the wildling's stomach. They roared in anger, though their strength ebbed.

I shoved at them with my left gauntlet, but their weight was too great. Their attack futile, and their blood pouring out, they lifted up, hands upon my chest.

Tyler had been right behind me. The wilding might use its last strength to seek a softer target.

Yelling, I twisted and drove my boot into soft soil. My knee shifted into its side, and the wildling lost balance, rolling away from the tree with me. Each pauldron on my shoulders had three spikes: top, back and front. I maneuvered the short front spike on the right shoulder into the wildling's neck. They gurgled, and I knew I had pierced their throat.

Lurching my torso up, I freed myself from their claws and slashed with Nightarmor's sword. Their head tilted from their body as I jumped clear. Twitching, their flesh glowed hot red as it reverted to human form.

Shailagh's shifter still snarled behind me.

Tyler stood open-mouthed just an arm's length away from me. He could die in these woods. He had no training, no weapon.

Short blade.

Yes, Mistress.

I shoved my arm toward Tyler as the knife formed. "Take it." I risked Shailagh with precious seconds.

Tyler's eyes remained focused on the body behind me. Shailagh had pinned her wildling, but it wriggled and spun like Deanna's cats getting a bath. She had a gash on her left arm, and blood trickled down the fingers she splayed toward the ground.

"Damn me to Hades," I swore, leaving Tyler and racing

for Shailagh's trapped wildling. It tore through vines as quickly as she wove them.

Spear.

The hilt of my sword rounded to haft, blade turned to staff, and I thrust the thin tip one-handed into the wriggling mass. I caught a hind leg before nails shrieked on Nightarmor and flicked my spearhead into the ground.

A root burst through ribs and I paused. Eerily reminiscent of the tree man we'd just killed, I had to wonder whose magic was at play.

Three more roots thrust out of the body, ripping it apart. *Shailagh, then.* I pulled back my spear and glanced to Tyler. They still stood staring at the corpse I had nearly beheaded. Taking a deep breath, I walked toward them, pulse pounding in my ears.

I rested a gauntlet on Tyler's shoulder, and they flinched, trembling. "What is it?" they asked.

"A wildling, like your werewolf story, but not the same." I'd read through every book in Tyler's bookshelf and their Kindle. What I had considered their myths came uneasily close to reality.

"A shifter." Tyler spoke the words dully, as if not fully released from shock or sigil. "Fae, swamp creatures, wights." They stiffened. "John."

"We'll find him." What would I do then? Kill the wight despite Shailagh? How would that go over?

Tyler turned, glancing first at me, then at Shailagh and her dead or dying wildling. "The shifters work with the wight?"

"News to me." I shrugged. "I've just learned about all this over the past couple of days."

I'd been on Earth for over ten months. Laura and Vivianne had been an odd happenstance that opened my eyes to the Fae and Nedjir. These past few days had been too much. John's predicament forced my hand; otherwise, Tyler would be safe elsewhere.

"We should really get you back to the car." Would even there be safe?

Tyler's expression calm, they stared up into the trees.

I spun, catching sight of the vines twisted into sigils. "Merciful Rhys, again?" So much for Tyler closing their eyes.

CHAPTER 40

I TRIED to shift Tyler away from the sight, but we just struggled. "Shailagh, could you help?"

A small, orange form shifted in Khimmer's vision. It jumped to the side, and I recognized the dull orange of a snake beside the first. Releasing Tyler, I made a slow circle, scanning. "Crap."

Snakes, Mistress.

I noticed. Sword.

Slithering at us from all directions were the snakes again. This time, other creatures had joined, but they did not seem to mix well. "Snakes. We have to protect Tyler," I said to Shailagh, but her finger had already tensed, pointing to the ground.

Vines dropped to my side from the trees. Wrapping around a transfixed Tyler, they lifted their body over my head. He dangled calmly, eyes still focused on the tangled sigils.

"That works." I smiled inside my helmet. With Tyler out of the way, I only needed to protect Shailagh.

Her magic had already sprung up in the forest in front

of her. Pine branches elongated, stretching down and skewering writhing snakes. I took her back and faced away.

Shailagh offered up one of her odd curses and said, "Pine trees are the most difficult, next to palms."

It did seem they were stiffer, less agile, and therefore less deadly compared the other gray barked trees she'd used in the past. She worked with vines as much as branches. There had been mainly moss dripping from limbs when the first thrall had attacked us near the small cave.

Hopefully, Woo had learned to drink out of the toilet – if I left the lid up. I grimaced. They would be hungry. I wasn't a very good companion.

I slashed at the two snakes that reached us, dancing to keep a good view around Shailagh's ankles. A third I stepped on, slashed a fourth, and checked on Tyler. They hung limply overhead. Gratefully, they wouldn't see me hacking snakes into pieces.

The winding snakes almost appeared to avoid me, trying to get around to Shailagh. Was that from the wight, or did Nightarmor not seem appealing enough? Some did blunt their fangs on metal before I swept off their heads.

Winded from leaping and dancing from one to the next, I wished I'd brought water or food with us. Even the sour energy drink seemed like an option.

"Did you bring pistachios?" I asked over my shoulder.

Shailagh grunted with a hint of humor, but didn't respond. I had been serious. Had she gone someplace before coming out here to look for the wight? Where was home for her?

A small possum almost made it to us, and I felt bad when it died from a snake bite. The wight had called up a force that might have taken down Shailagh were she alone. Certainly, it would have dispatched any wayward human interlopers. The killing became mechanical, a gruesome process without the same excitement that the two wildlings had brought.

Had the wildlings been recalled here to protect the wight, or were they stationed in these woods as guards? What size force did the wight have? Why didn't she hold them back for one heavy assault?

As an assassin, I had always laughed when a target filled a hall with guards and I slipped in through a privy. The wight kept her forces spread out. There had been at least one waiting by Emery Porter's construction site. Two more had been sent looking for me. Still, that did not speak to the guards who waited ahead of us.

As the horde of snakes thinned out, I found myself ranging out toward them. I didn't know what type I killed, or if they were even deadly. The wight had sent them, that much I knew.

Unbidden, Khimmer adjusted Nightarmor, growing thicker on my left side. *Eldritch weapons, Mistress.* I recognized the tense tone to their thoughts.

Khimmer took guns seriously. They had warned me that Nightarmor's defense against them was limited. I found a shape heading toward us. It might have been the thrall we were tracking, considering the direction. The figure crouched as he approached, as if intending stealth.

Neither Shailagh nor Tyler could survive against gunfire, though I had a chance. She would have to deal with the last of the snakes. I broke into a run that would draw the fire away from Shailagh and bring me closer to our interloper. Nightarmor shifted at every step, subtle changes, but I could feel them.

What are you doing, Mistress? We should leave.

Tyler dangled in the air, and Shailagh's roots wouldn't stop bullets.

My helmet shifted and rang. The bullet that hit me came from farther behind our approaching thrall. The flash glowed bright in Khimmer's vision, like a lone star in Earth's black night. A dull crack of the gunshot echoed in the forest. Birds called out in annoyance.

A moment lapsed as Nightarmor shifted. The closer attacker sprayed gunfire, rattling my armor and staggering my footsteps. His gun lit like a setting sun.

The noise shattered the night, and I vaguely heard bullets thud into tree trunks around me.

Mistress?

Do your best.

I used the trees as I could, running directly toward the closer attacker but knowing where the second fired from. Each step I planned to be water or spongy soil. The terrain appeared dark in Khimmer's vision and left me guessing.

Bullets rattled my front, and the Nightarmor warmed to the point where one bullet strike on my upper arm burned skin. The small skirmish I'd had in Slovenia, protecting Tyler, Deanna, and John from two gunman, had been short lived.

If I wanted Tyler to survive these thralls, I had no choice.

Pain seared my right shoulder across the back.

Sorry, Mistress.

I felt blood on my back and Nightarmor reform. The solitary shots seemed stronger, though I didn't see the shooter nor hear their lone bullets. The thrall ahead of me was my present target. Perhaps Shailagh had moved Tyler away by now. I was close to the thrall. Holding my blade to the side and slightly behind, I planned to kill the man with one strike to the chest.

Six steps away, I veered around a tree, and the bullets staggered me into a slide. My right boot sunk, and I barely kept upright with my left hand. The noise from the weapon drowned any sounds except the rain of bullets on my helmet. If the other gunner still fired, I would never hear it.

Mistress!

I clawed up and questioned my original decision as a final flurry threatened to knock me over. Somehow, Nightarmor stopped them all. Burns prickled my front.

A dull ringing took over for the constant gunfire. As the bullets stopped, I lunged forward, dragging my boot out of the muck.

The thrall, a thin man with long draped hair, hunched over his quiet weapon, removing pieces and attempting to fix it. I gave him no time as I swung my sword in the rhythm of my steps. Twisting between rib bones, I thrust the blade deep through his heart.

I crouched as I withdrew the blade. The dying thrall laid weak hands on my left shoulder, but his body already failed him. I noted a flash ahead and swore a bullet tore into a tree behind me, but I still heard little more that ringing in my ears.

Sucking a lungful of hot air, I could smell my own burnt flesh. My thighs, arms, and chest burned with close bullets that had taxed Nightarmor's abilities. Beyond a blessed blade or a fall off a cliff, I had never thought anything could threaten me inside Nightarmor. The blood trickling down my back told a different story.

I had only one attacker left with their eldritch weapon. Gritting my jaw, I started toward the last gun flash I'd seen. I splashed as the forest floor gave into water. A bullet nearly stopped me as it slammed into my chest. They aimed for my heart. Nightarmor continued to flow with each step.

Even the boots seemed to adjust, knee high in water at points. They slid out of the muck quicker.

I could see the man wearing a tight fitted hat. Kneeling a few steps away on firmer ground, he managed another shot, always aiming for my heart. The stench of burnt skin filled my helmet. If I measured his timing correctly, he would get off another shot before I reached him.

I needed Nightarmor to be as thick as possible. Leaning close to the water, I trailed my sword in the submerged grass at my side.

A step away, the shot came through Nightarmor into my left shoulder. Deflected, it tore across skin, though I swore it missed muscle. The wound burned, and the bullet rolled hot down my back inside Nightarmor.

I slashed, catching fingers of the left hand that held the long rifle. Dull orange chunks of flesh dropped. It did not stop him. He held the weapon with what hand he had left.

I flipped my wrist as I knelt with one knee on firm ground and brought the back swing into his right wrist. Weapon and hand dropped to the ground.

CHAPTER 41

I STEPPED on the rifle as the thrall fumbled for it with a left hand that was missing too many digits. My breath came in ragged draws, and fire burned across my shoulders and dotted my front.

I had come close to dying. "Damn me to Hades, that sucked!"

Blood poured orange from his dying body, yet the thrall tried to stand. I could not save him. Tired, I impaled his heart to end his agony. Did he feel pain?

Everything okay with Nightarmor? I thought to Khimmer.

Yes, Mistress. That was not wise. We do not have the proper shielding for Eldritch weapons.

Create an opening to get rid of the bullet.

Yes, Mistress.

Shailagh and Tyler still waited where we'd been attacked by the wildlings. How many more thralls did the wight have at her command?

Water sloshing around my legs, I made for them. From

their dim shapes, it seemed that Tyler had been lowered to ground level again.

Remove helmet.

Are you certain, Mistress?

Tired and sore, I cursed. *Keep an eye out for me.*

Nightarmor flowed off my head, and I took a deep breath of the reeking bog, a slightly better smell than my own burnt flesh. The stars had come out, sparkling through the thin canopy.

"You're going to get yourself killed," chided Shailagh when I reached her and Tyler.

"She won't tell me what you did." Tyler faced the way we'd come, before arriving at the sigil that immobilized humans. "Was it your idea to hang me up in the trees?" They rubbed at areas of exposed skin reddened with lines. My makeshift bandage had soaked through with their blood.

"No," I said, "but I agreed it was for your benefit." I pointed a few feet away at the headless body of a snake. "You weren't very responsive when we had to deal with that problem. We can't keep going like this. It's too dangerous."

Hopefully Tyler could see this now. They'd been left dangling during much of the latest skirmish, but a wildling had tried to gut them.

Tyler's face hardened. "Burden or not. I'm going to help. Maybe I can free John while you keep this wight and her friends occupied."

"You might not get that far." John might not be very open to the idea, if he were a thrall. "Supposedly this wight just needs to look at you." I looked to Shailagh for support.

She shrugged. "Or you. You're assuming that truthsense will protect you. I'm not so sure. Enthralling is a form of persuasion, at a level about as equal as my empath abilities are to your truthsense, so I'm not counting on it. When we get to wherever she's holed up, I'll know when we're close. I should go in alone."

I could understand her concern, but I had to try and kill this wight to free John. Standing to the side with Tyler wouldn't accomplish that goal. Shailagh might kill John.

Khimmer, if the wight takes me, don't obey it.

Yes, Mistress.

Also, if I become enthralled, remove any armor or weapons. I couldn't risk being a danger to Shailagh or Tyler.

"So, let's get going." Tyler closed their eyes and held out a hand. "Try not to lead me into any holes."

"Tyler, you shouldn't." I'd started to waver. I couldn't send them back alone, they'd have to be escorted. Knowing Tyler, they might try and follow anyway. Back at the car might not be safe either.

They just struck a pose with their eyes closed, impish grin on their lips, and a limp hand poised before me. Shailagh chuckled as I took Tyler's hand.

Snake, Mistress.

I nearly called for my helmet, but vines whipped to my left, and the snake writhed under Shailagh's magic.

CHAPTER 42

I WALKED SLOWLY behind Shailagh as she lit up the ground and the thrall's footprints with her blue sigil light. The stagnant water stunk and had killed some of the trees, leaving only their bare carcasses. The star-filled Earth night hung above us. The onslaught of snakes had not stopped, merely thinned to occasional attacks that Shailagh took care of with her high Fae magic. I carried my sword in my right gauntlet. Tyler held my left.

Tyler stumbled more than walked, but the occasional tangle of vines that hung from limbs kept me from suggesting any change in the arrangement. We would have to deal with this the best we could.

Could Shailagh be right about the wight's ability to enthrall me? I'd sensed a true concern from her. She walked too far ahead of us for me to speak without being loud.

We passed an outcrop of rock which pushed up through a wet puddle. Brush had attached and grown up as if keeping its roots out of the water. The dark edges at the bottom reminded me of Woo.

I heard the splash behind me before Khimmer thought a warning. *Another behind, Mistress.*

I let go of Tyler's hand and sloshed through a forest floor that gave way to water at each step. The snake rippled through a low puddle, wove up the edge, and raced through wet needles. I lopped off the head with a quick slash. My dislike for the wight had increased with each creature she sent after us. She seemed to stir every animal against us, except birds, and she hadn't seemed to have an effect on Woo. Perhaps she had limits.

Shailagh waited for me to return, the blue glow lighting her feet. The heavy cloak of silence around us highlighted my noisy splashing. Did it matter? The wight knew where we were, or close enough to ambush us.

When I reached Tyler, I took their hand. "Who is this wight?" I asked Shailagh.

Her lips pursed, either from my breach of the silence, or the question. "Theovole, perhaps."

"Do you know her?"

She sighed and returned to following the blue footprints. "Of her. There was a wight in central Florida, about three hundred years back. As humans moved into the wetlands there, she disappeared. She had never been known to dabble in persuasion and certainly not as a dominar, but things change. She vanished about one hundred and fifty years ago. One of my assignments had been to locate her, one of my failures. I have never met Theovole personally."

Shailagh glanced up at a motion, and a root splashed into soggy ground with the call of her magic. Her left hand had splayed toward the ground, but she never missed a step. "There is another wight hidden in the fading swamplands on the southern tip of Florida, but that one is still there."

"You checked?"

"Of course I did, as well as north Georgia and western Alabama. They are happily enjoying their seclusion."

I ran the timeline from when Shailagh had first approached me for information about Emery Porter and wondered if she ever slept. How long had she been investigating?

"When did you know there was a wight? A dominar?"

"When Emery Porter was first spotted."

So I'd been one of her first stops. She might have visited these wights prior to even checking with me. Had she been on this case since our trip to Orlando?

"Do you sleep?" I asked.

Instead of replying, she pointed ahead. The blue footprints led into a gully where roots bundled along the edges and bottom. It descended into the darkness ahead.

Snakes ahead, Mistress.

Shailagh moved forward, where the blue glow caught the wet gleam of the sloping trench.

Helmet. I needed to see.

Yes, Mistress.

Nightarmor flowed up, and Khimmer's vision showed me the squirming mass below. "Shailagh, wait."

She stopped, and I placed Tyler's hand on her shoulder. Both of them flinched, but I stepped quickly past with my sword ready.

The gully formed by the roots dropped at a sharp slant into a pool of darkness that could be liquid. Either way, a score of snakes were writhing over each other, waiting for us. On each side of the walkway, water pooled between trees that would have filled the trench were it not for the lip. Moisture trickled along the edge of smooth roots, but Khimmer adjusted Nightarmor's boots for traction.

The pit of snakes did nothing until I was only a footstep

away, then they swarmed. Splashing sounded before they struck the hard metal of Nightarmor. I slashed into the mass of them, not neatly as before, but with wide strokes that left carnage and partial snakes still attacking.

Vines poured in from the forest, and I stopped my butchering to allow Shailagh's magic to finish the job.

I could hear Tyler hissing to her in the background as I waited.

Ahead of me the opening continued into a shaft. No puddle of water, but certainly plenty leaking in through the sides and top. Individual drops splashed onto the sickly tangle of roots. Despite the apparent height of the opening, I crouched down for a better view. The tunnel appeared to be comprised of high Fae magic, tightly woven, with twisted creations like the sigils.

I didn't turn as Shailagh and Tyler approached and the blue light showed the tracks leading down. "Do wights like to live underground?" I asked.

"Of course." She carefully removed Tyler's hand to my shoulder.

CHAPTER 43

I wondered if she would tell us to wait, but she just led on into the depths. Water dripped down on me as I followed with Tyler's hand in mine. The scent of swamp hung humid in the root-lined shaft. The height would have accommodated the tree man back near the road.

"Where are we?" asked Tyler as the floor leveled.

"A tunnel." I raised my voice slightly. "I'm assuming the wight made this, with Fae magic?"

"High Fae magic, yes. Your little friend would have no such abilities."

Did she mean Vivianne? Had I ever mentioned her? I stiffened slightly at the tone, more than the concern that Shailagh might have investigated me. She'd obviously known about my abilities before we met, so she must have done some research.

Tyler however, had not known. I swallowed and glanced back. Their eyes were still closed, and they appeared to be focused on their footing.

I'd rather we changed subjects away from Vivianne. "This kind of tunnel is common with wights?"

"It varies, depending on the environment."

I saw the motion as Khimmer alerted me. I dropped Tyler's hand to protect Shailagh from an approaching pair of snakes. The tunnel had plenty of room to pass, the glow marked the floor, and Khimmer's vision showed their forms easily. Before I could swing, roots reached out, grabbed them, and crushed the heads back into the wall.

I paused and she passed with a snort.

"I thought the wight built this?" I commented with a questioning tone.

"And?" she asked. "I can rebuild it, if necessary."

I shrugged, slightly deflated, and headed back to Tyler who stood looking around at the walls of the tunnel.

I coughed. "What are you doing?" I didn't need a berserk friend to deal with.

"Are we underground?" Tyler's face had gotten wet from the dripping. "Under water?"

From the reek, we were likely under a swamp. "Close your eyes." Could the wight just open the roots and flood us? Drowning was an immediate risk for Tyler and I assumed Shailagh, and an eventual danger for myself; Nightarmor could seal itself, but I would run out of air.

Tyler swore but complied and reached out their hand. As we progressed, Khimmer alerted me twice to snakes that followed from the opening behind. Puddles formed on the curved bottom, and slime grew on smooth roots. A droplet of water splashed on my forearm and sprayed into the air. The trickling sounded from every direction. Nightarmor provided traction for myself, but Tyler and even Shailagh slipped on occasion.

Nightarmor compressed the area of my wounds, but they stung. Blood stuck my bodysuit to skin and some of the burns had raised blisters. I would be happy to be out of here

234 / KEVIN A DAVIS

and apologizing to Woo, assuming we survived. Whatever excitement I'd embraced at skirmishing over the past few days had worn out its welcome. *I need to keep in better shape.*

Shailagh stopped us, and our silence highlighted the constant dripping. I could feel the weight of water above.

"We are close," she said. "You two should remain here. I can sense her. It is still a female wight, if not Theovole."

I couldn't leave Tyler behind, not with the occasional snake still following. They couldn't use a sword if I left them one. The decision to kill the wight, despite Shailagh's plans, had been made long ago. John had to be set free.

"We're coming with you. I'll follow behind far enough that you can try and get control of the situation, but we'll be close enough to help. Don't harm John."

"You'll stay here." Shailagh turned to stare at me.

I had seen the way her vines avoided touching Nightarmor; she couldn't bind me. "We'll follow."

Her face tightened and I swore her ears twitched at the top. "You're putting us all in danger."

You remember my instructions, Khimmer?

Yes, Mistress.

"You won't be in danger from me."

"You can't be sure." Shailagh seemed angry, I could tell.

"I am. Surely you can sense my confidence in this."

Her muscles at her jaw relaxed, but not fully. "False confidence."

"I don't believe so." If the wight took me, I'd be little more dangerous than Tyler to Shailagh.

"We have a lot riding on that belief."

"Trust me. It's going to be alright." I grinned. "We're going to have fun." I'd chosen to follow this through, for Deanna and Tyler.

Shailagh snorted. "Keep behind me."

CHAPTER 44

TYLER and I stayed far enough behind that Shailagh's form dulled in Khimmer's vision and the blue glow at her feet barely showed. The rancid water at the curved bottom of the tunnel let out a fouler miasma than before, like we splashed through the putrid remains of rotting bodies.

Shailagh slowed, but I found nothing approaching us, and no snakes slithered or splashed in the water. Sword ready, I shifted to the side to see past her.

Dim lights speckled the circular opening ahead. We appeared near the end of the tunnel. So far, the swamp had not been released on top of our heads. If Shailagh sensed the wight ahead, surely it worked both ways.

I hesitated as she did, holding back Tyler with a press of my hand.

"What is it?" Tyler asked.

"An opening. Looks like a cavern of some sort," I said.

"Under a swamp. Of course. Do you do this all the time?"

We had no wights in Duruce, so no creepy underwater dens, but we had plenty of sewers and dungeons to crawl

around in. "Not lately." Though, I had found the gate that
brought me to Earth underground, below the remains of an
old battlefield. I studied the walls of pallid woven roots. In
no other place had I ever worried that the very walls might
attack.

Shailagh descended in front of us, as if climbing down
stairs. The glowing yellowish dots gave some sense of the
space beyond. Surely a cavern from the apparent distance.

I tugged Tyler back into motion, not looking back to see
if they'd opened their eyes. In the darkness, I doubted they
could see any sigils. The way they gripped my gauntleted
fingers, they probably had the same dread tightening their
chest.

Each step widened my view into the chamber beyond,
but I could make out no other people in Khimmer's vision.
Shailagh grew dim, hidden behind soil or root.

At the first sign of danger, I planned to leave Tyler
behind and finish this wight quickly. If the wight had as
much of a reaction to metal as Shailagh did, I assumed
Nightarmor's sword would be effective. If we still had
thralls to contend with, then I would adjust, but my goal
was clearly a blade in whatever this wight considered a
body.

I reached the edge of the opening, and a gaping empti-
ness appeared beyond. Water dripped from the ceiling
stretching out in front of me to splash in pools below. It
trickled down walls in mini waterfalls. A mere dull glow
of orange, Shailagh walked far from me at the bottom.
Putrid air seeped inside Nightarmor and made me not
want to breathe. Other than the yellow glows marking
what I swore were the outer walls, nothing moved, and
Khimmer's vision picked up no signs of life beyond
Shailagh.

Where was the wight? I tested the first step, wet and slippery. "Be careful," I said to Tyler.

A club swung out from the wall of roots just inside the opening and Nightarmor thickened. The blow caught me on the right shoulder with enough force to send me flying forward, launching me into the abyss ahead. After watching Shailagh's magic, I should have been prepared.

My helmet and chest caught the edge of the stairs at least one body length below. The sides dropped off sharply from the way my body spun into a free fall off the left side.

Nightarmor drew in my blade, absorbing it into my gauntlet while the yellow dots spun past. What I splashed into on the bottom felt like a thin pool of water shielding solid rock. My head slapped inside the helmet and wrenched my neck to the left. My hip and shoulder took most of the impact, but I'd been unable to position for the landing.

Tyler. I forced myself up on one arm, reaching out with the other to brace on something, anything. The yellow dots shifted across my vision.

Climbing down the stairs, Mistress.

"Tyler, wait." My voice barely had any volume, croaking out.

A second root slammed into my back, low near my hips. It vaulted me forward, and I used the motion to crawl and scramble until my right hand felt the side of the stairs. They mounded upward, and I caught a brief glimpse of dull orange that would have been Tyler. At least they had not been hit by the club.

Wood scraped and snapped ahead of me. Shailagh's form shifted in motions that appeared a battle. I couldn't focus.

Drop, Mistress.

I had barely started crouching when the log-sized root skidded off my shoulder and slapped the stairs. The impact shifted me forward, but it could have been worse.

I needed to keep moving. Nightarmor's soles dug into the roots, not stone, below the water, and I launched myself toward Shailagh. *Sword.* I reached over my shoulder, wincing, and grabbed the hilt.

From left, Mistress.

I dodged to my right and swung, catching a piece of the club. Nightarmor released quickly, and I continued stumbling toward Shailagh.

Around her, the roots from the floor fought each other, grappling with sharp points, and I could see hot wounds in her thighs already. I had to find this wight.

Khimmer, any other signs of life?

I made it another step before they thought, *Other than Tyler, there is a mass below the center of the chamber, Mistress.*

Shailagh's magic would react to Nightarmor's presence as well as any other. Hacking at roots would obviously cut her defenses as well as the wight's attack.

Behind, Mistress.

I spun, cleanly lopping off a pale gray limb the color of death. It jabbed forward, and I sidestepped with an upswing, taking off a larger section. I'd never cut wood with Nightarmor before, though Khimmer could make the blade sharp and strong enough to cut through thin armor and bone.

The center of the cavern, where Khimmer believed something awaited submerged, lay ahead and to the left of Shailagh. I thwarted two more attacks before I arrived, my head finally feeling less dazed. I could see the dull glow and sensed life down there, perhaps more than one. The blade might not reach, but I needed to stir her into showing herself.

Under a hand's depth of water, blanched roots had swirled into a center, seeming to indicate I'd found the wight's nesting place. I'd be a sitting target for longer than seemed wise, but what choices did I have? *Come out and play, Beastie.*

Two-handed, I raised my sword high and thrust it to the hilt into the roots. I finished kneeling and panting, prepared to pull it free and strike again. I felt the sword hilt bulge and flow as more metal joined the blade. Pressing down I gave Khimmer leverage; they had to be seeking out my target.

The roots around had stiffened, while others lightly squirmed at the proximity to metal.

A club slammed into my side, and I held onto the hilt to keep from being thrown aside. A second battered my back. Nightarmor kept them from causing true harm, but the pressure felt like it might squeeze out my insides with each teeth-jarring blow.

The root around my blade cracked. Water poured down as if into a drain. A creak warned me before the floor exploded upward, sending me flying into the air with shards of snapped root and a trickle of liquid Nightarmor between my palms.

CHAPTER 45

AFTER THE FLOOR of the cavern erupted, I flew backward. Nightarmor absorbed my sword and braced my back before I splashed like a discarded fish. The roots under me groaned and scraped as they pulled back to expose the wight. I kicked with my heels trying to get some distance from the growth.

Layers of roots unfolded, exposing a rising pile of orange shapes. They formed a mass that burst up as I skidded away. The impact sucked out my breath and I drew in a deep lungful of the miasma.

Roots lashed out to hold me, stiffening in futility when they touched Nightarmor. Shailagh grunted behind me. I raised my head to study what I had brought up from the depths.

Mistress, alerted Khimmer. Nightarmor reformed on the front and where the stiff roots rested.

Two bulky thralls leaped off the dais toward me. I had no time to study my true prize, but I could make out orange shapes above. Lunging my torso upward, I snapped roots and scrambled to gain some footing.

Sword.

I felt the weapon growing on my back. The closest thrall slammed into me before I'd risen to no more than a crouch. The man could almost pass for a wildling he had so much hair on his face and bared chest. Entangled, we skidded through the shallow water.

I spun from under him by digging a heel in the roots and kneeing his stomach with the other leg. *Two guards, and one might be John.* I could not guarantee that I would spare the slob grappling with me. What would I do with John? How could I get past him to the wight?

I slammed my right vambrace under his beard, hoping to get enough force to knock the man out. I just pinned him back.

He pounded on my left arm, with no effect. The jolting was annoying at most. His weight could have easily gained control of the two of us, but he had no skill.

I smacked my helmet into his forehead. It would not likely incapacitate, but it might stun.

A second body landed on both of us.

John? I thought to Khimmer.

With the wight, Mistress.

So, John had not attacked me. Pinned under two hefty strangers, I swore the roots below tried to recede but were too brittle. I wasn't getting buried into the floor.

They had too much combined weight. I had armor, but less strength than one of them, much less two. Agility and training counted for less when your opponents felt no pain and had you pinned. Regrettably, they would have to die. I couldn't let them stop me.

I imagined their positions against Nightarmor. It would be a quick death for each of them. Each thrall and snake I killed tallied against the wight. My teeth ground at the score.

I thought to Khimmer, *Spikes.*

Two thin spikes protruded from Nightarmor. Khimmer could see the placement in my mind: one from the right side of my chest into the bearded thrall's heart; the second from my left bicep into the chest of the attacker on top of me.

The bearded man cried out in a plaintive howl that tugged at my emotions. I could not waver. John, Tyler, and Deanna were counting on me.

With my heart pounding in rage at what the wight had forced me to do, I rolled the thrall off of me. John would survive. I would make sure.

Tyler?

On the stairs, Mistress.

Shailagh's battle had not gotten any better. Writhing roots fought in a tangle that defied determining whose magic controlled what. They formed a loose cage around her. She had scores of cuts, and blood ran hot from her arms and chest. I hoped she would understand that the wight must die.

Left, Mistress.

I dodged over the fallen thralls, reaching over my shoulder for my sword. The club clipped my chest. I staggered and grasped the hilt. My slash caught the root as it returned. I hacked off an end and bound for the dais in the center of the cavern.

I would have to keep moving since the wight had endless roots at her disposal. From a steep sided platform, a large orange glow started at my height and rose as large as the tree man I'd killed. I would need to scale the side quickly before roots could knock me off.

A second form huddled in her arms, like a suckling

babe. John? I would need to be closer to see any characteristics.

I caught the movement of a swinging root from above before Khimmer alerted me. I managed two hacks, dancing so that each step brought me closer to the foul high Fae rather than away.

Still a score of steps distant, I sensed the wight like a light shining on my soul, calling my emotions to her. *Wet and slimy lies.* Like a song, her magic hit me in waves. Even though I knew the truth, a part of me wanted to believe the slick vows. They promised comfort and relief, love and belonging.

My footsteps faltered as my own fears were stirred. Returning home to my life as the Queen's first assassin. Training with the Aegis monks and killing the country's enemies. Worse, never finding my way back to the gate or home and not fulfilling my contract with Nyx's blessed blade and leaving the King Dior of Tahnet alive. I had a duty to perform for country and Queen. A promise to satisfy for my goddess, Nyx. It was a friendless life I'd never known as empty until I met Tyler and the others.

For a moment, the wight's peace seemed reasonable. No more duty or fears. *Lies.* My heart pounded, and my ears rung with the rushing of blood and the pounding this creature had given me.

No.

Mistress?

Hearing Khimmer realigned me even more. Anger flashed in my blood, and my chest tightened. The wight, Theovole, had tried and failed to enthrall me. Disgust over her tasted more rancid than the malodor that I breathed.

Are you okay, Mistress?

I locked my focus on the malevolence standing upon the dais. *I am now, Khimmer.*

Theovole recoiled in surprise. She sensed my hatred. Her emotions closed off in a heartbeat, and the room burst into a flurry of roots.

CHAPTER 46

Two ROOTS HIT ME, despite Khimmer's warning. The thud of wood on armor rang through my teeth. I caught a glimpse of the wight and John as I launched off the ground.

A third root tried to smack me in midair. I caught the tip of my sword into it with a clumsy swing, and the impact flipped me into a spin. The cavern echoed with scraping wood, yellow dots flashed around me, and my stomach tightened from disorientation.

When we hit, Nightarmor absorbed what shock it could, and I rolled in a random direction knowing Theovole had not given up.

Wood splashed into water, spraying up dark droplets. I scrambled to keep in motion. Khimmer's warnings kept me from being pinned, but even the skimming hits were taking their toll. Each turn brought me closer to the dais, but often I managed little more than avoiding the whipping roots.

The floor had turned from a flush, orderly pool to a tangled mess; many roots lay scattered where they'd been used and discarded after the wight's attention. Passing or jumping over these raised my pulse with concern that they'd reactivate, and some did. Theovole appeared to be leaving more of these closer to the dais. Unintentionally, I'd worked around to the opposite side of the cavern from Shailagh.

Jump, Mistress.

Instinctively, I obeyed. The floor and the surrounding water sucked into a gaping hole below me as the roots pulled back. My earlier concern of being trapped underneath crossed my mind.

As I stumbled into a run on the other side of the new pit, I imagined that this tactic could be very effective against Nightarmor and myself. I needed to end this. The difficulty rose in avoiding the swinging clubs and making it onto the platform.

Mistress, Tyler is moving toward the wight.

My hesitation cost me a blow from a club I'd been avoiding. Skidding backward, I lost some ground toward the dais. I'd been rounding toward the stairs and back to Shailagh, perhaps hoping for help. I could make out Tyler's orange shape. They were so close to the dais they were nearly out of my direct line of sight. They moved swiftly toward the wight.

Enthralled.

I fear that is the situation, Mistress. Left.

I dropped and rolled, imagining the floor opening below to a watery grave. By the time I'd sprung up and raced toward them, Tyler had climbed stairs to the platform.

My closest friend had been taken by the wight. John mattered nothing, compared to this, but I'd known there was a risk. I dodged into a run with a hollow in my chest that hurt worse than any bruise, burn, or wound in my flesh. Getting on that dais was the only way to stop the wight.

The Aegis monks had a trial path that these swinging

roots reminded me of. In an underground chasm two stories tall, I had regularly jumped the gaps between posts jutting from the top on each side. Spring and human-powered paddles had spun at various angles along my path, which I had to time perfectly or risk the fall. Khimmer had not been allowed to engage Nightarmor on the exercise. I had developed some unusual methods.

I changed my motions from a straight run leaping over inactive club-like roots to springing between them. It left me in the air more, but with less control for evasive shifts.

Mistress, this course might be unwise.

I hoped the opposite. The activity might appear foolish, leaving me vulnerable mid-jump. The wight must have sensed this and brought an idle root up to bat at me in midair.

Mistress.

Fortunately, the angle proved correct at the first attempt. I spun in the air, raised my knees up, and aimed the soles of Nightarmor's boots toward the root to take the initial impact.

I caught the swinging club with both feet and pushed off, launching myself toward the wight. The combined momentum of the root and my own legs sent me soaring toward the dais in a slow somersault.

John sat in what might be construed as the wight's arm and suckled on the ruins of her chest. Parts of Theovole looked like rotting wood, other areas fresh bark. I could make out no skin. Her large eyes seemed like the only part of her that had not turned to vegetation. Branches with leaves had replaced her hair, and numerous worn limbs comprised her arms. Stems at the end worked like fingers splaying out in thin mimicry of knuckled digits.

Her cheeks were so pitted with rot that I could not be

sure if she had a mouth or if it was an illusion created by one of the holes. The closest resemblance to her Fae ancestry rested in her face and moss-covered wooden ears, which branched up to join her leafy hair. Beyond the absence in her eyes, I could sense her hatred, tinged only now with fear.

I would just make the edge of the platform. Theovole's surprise caused her to pause, her moving limbs coming to a stop. John, dressed in his dirty blue work shirt and jeans, lifted his head to glare.

Tyler reached out and took the branches Theovole had offered as a hand.

I hit the edge of the dais hip first, and rolled quickly to a crouch. The cavern groaned in movement as roots scraped from every direction. Theovole's presence radiated across the platform, and her hatred of humans seared into me like Earth's noonday sun. This close I could do nothing but sense her emotions. Among the abhorrence of my kind was weariness. Our intrusion had taxed her energy.

"Destroyers!" A haunting screech emanated from what I had supposed her mouth. It might have been Earth English, or I sensed her well enough that the meaning came through. In my mind's eye I saw the big yellow bulldozers and falling trees. She had only been trying to protect her domain.

While Tyler and John were at risk, her plight and concerns didn't matter to me. The thralls that had died were no proper payment for her distress. Construction workers like John and Emery had threatened her habitat. Tyler would not pay for that offense.

I slashed the branch that clasped Tyler's hand and body-slammed my friend off the dais. Dazed, they barely reacted, and I could only hope they did not break bones on the fall. Enthralling might take time or contact. I knew nothing of this, but to save John, the wight had to die anyway.

In the two moments I'd taken to protect Tyler, Theovole awoke from her surprise and reacted. Her branchlike limbs flailed against Nightarmor and kept me from striking into her body while roots rose around the dais. John leaped off his perch and lunged for me.

Clubs slammed into the back of Nightarmor and cracked into the platform at each side before John reached me. His usual clean-shaven face had grown an unpleasant stubble that mixed with smears of dirt. Golden-orange hair that he usually kept coiffed in the air like a horse's mane had plastered to his skull from the dripping water of the cave.

His grappling would have threatened to knock me down, were it not for the barrage of wildly slapping roots pounding my back and sides. Theovole reminded me of an excited octopus from one of Tyler's books.

I could not stab John and then save him. He wouldn't react from the pain, so a wound serious enough to disable him might kill him in the end.

Theovole had effectively pinned me two steps away from her, and eventually the beating I was enduring on my back would bludgeon me senseless. I swallowed back the concern that I might not survive even one step closer. My stomach churned, either from the stench of her, the swamp leaking in, or the rising sense of futility.

I sensed pain, and surprisingly fear, from Shailagh through our connecting pins. She'd been stabbed, but not killed. Did Theovole have compassion for her own kind, no matter how far removed? *Kill her*, Shailagh sent.

At least I wouldn't have to face Shailagh's ire, if I could figure out a way to reach Theovole. I sensed the wight's pleasure and satisfaction that Shailagh and I had been stopped. Even her rotting wooden face seemed to smirk.

One of the clubs skimmed John, shifting his weight off me. I needed him hurt badly enough that he couldn't impede me, but able to move afterward.

I released my grip on my sword's hilt, and Nightarmor absorbed the trail of liquid metal it formed. Taking advantage of John's imbalance, I shoved a knee under his to drop him and maneuvered him into a head lock.

The two dizzying slams from roots nearly loosened my grip and would have broken John's neck, had I not been in the way.

Arm shield. I imagined the placement and configuration for Khimmer.

Yes, Mistress.

A tall black shield grew from my right vambrace, detailed with the signature gold and silver filigree. I had never used the protection; it seemed useless considering Nightarmor's inherent defense. The Aegis monks had required at least perfunctory knowledge in its formation. In this case, it protected John from head to groin. He struggled against the grip around his throat, hampered by the black wall of the shield.

As he straightened, trying to throw me off, I dangled, swinging my airborne legs to the side, and twisted his body. A club slammed onto the shield, where my back would have been. The impact caused John to grunt, and he would likely be bruised.

The next slapping root connected with one of his legs. I heard the bone crack and felt it through my grip.

John screamed. Evidently, unlike the other thralls, he could still feel pain. Perhaps it took more time at Theovole's breast. I couldn't imagine mentioning any of this to Deanna, if I could avoid it.

We both dropped, and I stopped us with ready feet. Releasing my choke hold, I threw my right arm and shield wide. I shoved him off the dais with my left.

Remove shield.

I spun, finally facing Theovole alone. She shrieked and three roots rained down on me. I could sense her power waning. The barrage dropped me to one knee, but I stood, gaining another step closer to her.

Don't kill, Shailagh sent to me. She had changed her mind. I could sense her, bloody and staggering but free, as Theovole focused on me.

The wight sent more roots, but they came with less frenzy and power. I knew nothing about how Fae magic worked, but there seemed to be limits. We had worn Theovole nearly to submission, and she appeared to shrink back from me. I sensed her panic and the urgent calls she sent out for protection. There were more thralls, or snakes. Were they close? If I acquiesced to Shailagh's desire, John might never be free. Worn myself, I felt bruised from every pounding of her clubs.

Theovole's body, no more than a gnarled trunk for legs and roots for feet, had a torso of sorts. Did that mean a heart still beat there? I could clear her branch-arms and hope for a swift kill. My own pulse raced, and I gasped rancid hot air from inside Nightarmor.

Shailagh sent a desperate image of a metal cage around Theovole, trapping her and dulling her powers. She wanted me to save the wight and possibly lose Tyler.

My high Fae friend would have to be disappointed in me.

Spikes. Like a pork pine pig. I envisioned the image for Khimmer.

Porcupine, Mistress?

Yes.

Thin spikes, as long as my arms, sprouted from the chest plate of Nightarmor. Theovole's limbs slapped at them. Fixed in front of me, I could do little but stave off the flurry with gauntleted fingers spread wide. My salty lips bled from the pounding. A needle tip snapped off, turned into liquid metal, and poured into a lower spike.

From behind, thick but weak roots slapped at my sides, some catching spikes and breaking them. Nightarmor liquefied each and retrieved them. I imagined the metal would damage the magic and the Fae body. If not, I'd call for a sword and begin hacking.

I stepped forward and Theovole shrieked. Her lies poured into my thoughts in a last attempt.

Shailagh screamed at me through our connection, a dull recrimination.

I stepped forward with force, and some spikes snapped while others drove into the wood or rotting pulp. Theovole's tortured howls brought me to suddenly feel cruel and question my actions. Tyler and John joined her cries below. Their screams bolstered my resolve and set my teeth on edge. Water rained down on me, splashing off the leaves that made the wight's hair.

A final shove drove most of the needles deep, and Theovole's shrieks turned silent in the chamber while they tore at my mind. Every horrible memory I had rose to the surface. The last envisioned me kneeling beside my mother's head, severed by my own hand and sword. That pain nearly broke me. My legs felt weak as I strained, embedded into the dying wight. Any blisters from earlier had become chafed holes in my flesh. With my helmet tilted back from Theovole's chest, I could only see the orange-hued wood in Khimmer's vision, rotting in most places.

Mistress?

Theovole died in quiet silence. I leaned against the trunk of the corpse, panting.

Mistress, we need to leave.

We were safe. How badly had I hurt Tyler? Had John been freed? Water poured across my vision. Nightarmor's spikes receded into the chest plate.

Mistress, the water.

Like the bottom side of a sieve, the roots forming the top of the cavern had loosened, and the swamp was pouring in around me.

CHAPTER 47

I STAGGERED BACK, searching for Tyler to my right. They were struggling frantically to help John, who appeared unconscious. Water splashed into the bottom of the cavern all around me in a cacophony that defied any sound except the pounding of my heart. Shailagh stood farther back. I could sense her rage and pain.

"Tyler?" I stumbled to the edge.

Water swirled around Tyler up to their hips. John rested in their arms, water up to his chest. Torrents poured from above through random holes and splashed down the stairs. Had the wight's last defense been to drown me? It seemed the entire forest drained to this pit. The yellow lights had faded, dying with the wight.

I vaulted beside Tyler in a splash. "The tunnel?" I grabbed under John's arm. "Hades, he's heavy."

Tyler was crying as they held John, and the look in their eyes stopped my heart. "What happened?" They shook their head and shifted John higher.

I sensed the panic from Tyler. We needed to survive, then I could worry how much damage the wight had done to my friends. The tunnel I'd hoped to escape through spewed water like a sewer pipe. Shailagh glared, unmoving, as water churned up to her hips.

I leaned to John's ear, yelling above the rushing deluge, "John!" He would still have a broken leg, thanks to me. "Wake up."

I motioned with my head to the dais. Tyler nodded and we dragged John's body toward the stairs. In another minute the rushing water would cover our heads. Surely the flood would ease soon. How much water had the forest or swamp above held?

"You go first," I said to Tyler. Water trickled in through the vents at my chin. Nightarmor would seal if threatened with submersion.

Water dampened my clothes inside Nightarmor. Shailagh remained, standing chest high in water. I didn't want to lose her either. I held John with one hand and beckoned to her with the other. She glared, but didn't move. I'd really pissed her off.

Tyler slipped off the stairs, going under and coming up sputtering. John's chin rested on the water. What smelled like a sewer splashed up on the stubble of his cheeks.

Khimmer, tether John at the shoulders.

Yes, Mistress.

Nightarmor poured a line around John's chest and shoulders that remained loosely connected to me. I gestured for Tyler to go up the stairs. "Get up to the top. I've got an idea."

"Okay." Tyler's eyes flicked about frantically, the rest of his face slack. "We've got nowhere to go from there."

Tyler climbed with hands and feet. The root stairs were barely the width of their shoulders and slippery.

"Drowning isn't a good option." I could only hope that

the platform was high enough and the water would subside. I could pray it wasn't a lake or river above us. The water smelled stagnant at best. "We need to get John out of this."

Extend the tether up to Tyler.

Yes, Mistress.

A loop of Nightarmor rope grew between myself and the tether around John's shoulders. Tyler grasped it hesitantly. "Got it."

"Pull," I said. More water seeped inside Nightarmor, and my clothes were soaked. "I'll shove him up to you."

Pushing John on his back up the stairs, I felt Khimmer close Nightarmor's vents at my neck. The water would be over my head soon. I smelled like sweat, blood, and worse.

"He's too heavy." Tyler slipped as they yanked and dropped off the platform, and John slid down the stairs and underwater.

Crap. I had not gone through all this to have everyone drown. If anyone, Tyler had to survive.

I managed a boot on a higher stair, shoved John to the surface, pinned his chin against my shoulder, and found Tyler's arm as he grabbed onto the stairs. I pulled Tyler higher. "Get up there. Be careful."

Through the connection of the pin, I sent Shailagh an image of our predicament. *Help.* She could use her Fae magic to get us onto the platform.

Anger seeped back from her, and a torrent of water opened onto us from directly above. Was she the one trying to kill us? The waterfall knocked Tyler back into my helmet, and I went under with John.

I pushed Tyler up with one hand on their back. They seemed to grasp something, then surprisingly continued to shift on their own, rising into the air above the water. Tyler's legs scrambled against a stair, then relaxed.

Then John jerked off my shoulder and started to follow. Somehow, they were both being lifted out of the water.

Release tether.

Yes, Mistress.

Vines curled around my gauntlet, then stiffened.

Hold on, Shailagh sent an image of me grasping the bundle of greenery. I obliged, and vines yanked me above the surface of the water.

Tyler and John dangled above me, drifting toward the hole she'd opened. Free of the water, I spun, and my arm ached, but I held on. Shailagh followed, and together we rose above the cursed cavern.

Nightarmor vented in fresh air, though it smelled no sweeter. The water above had turned to drips and flows of mud or slime from the edges of the hole that Shailagh had made. Beyond that, I made out stars, one of the more endearing features of Earth's sunless nights; I loved stars, more so at the moment.

Tyler and John were wound tight with the vines. Nightarmor prevented such a blessing. By the time I reached the edge, the joints in my hand ached, and my shoulder would have wrenched from its socket were it not for Nightarmor. As we neared the opening, Earth's moon hung large and white behind gray clouds that left only the top curve visible, but still it lit the treetops as if a lamp hung there. I had not gotten used to seeing a planet so close in the sky.

The skirmish with the wight had proved that I was out of shape. The sparring with Aegis monks had been a daily routine for me, and I'd needed it. On Earth, I'd grown soft with little to challenge me physically, and that had been a mistake. Earth was far more dangerous than Duruce. *Wildlings and wights*. I'd nearly lost Tyler. Where would we have been without friends like Shailagh? "Thank you," I called down to her.

She spoke, hard and sharp, with three syllables. I didn't understand her response. *Translation Khimmer?*

None, Mistress.

I reached the edge as Tyler pulled up a still unconscious John. Scrambling, I released the vines and we eased John up, dragging him a good distance from the hole. It was a relatively easy task through the mud of a drained swamp. John's left leg wobbled loosely, and I guessed the break had been low under his knee.

"We can't drag him all the way back," I said.

Tyler barely huffed a reply. "Agreed."

Shailagh climbed out behind us and stormed toward me in a pace that made my chest heavy. I'd broken her trust, and I still didn't know if it had saved John or not. *I had to try.* Tyler and I reached a lip of somewhat dry grass, and she stomped the last steps while we dragged John onto it. I guessed we were still above the cavern, but the ground felt firm.

Shailagh slammed two palms into my chest. "I told you not to kill her."

I didn't like her being mad with me, but I couldn't have left John a thrall. "I'm sorry."

Her ears twitched and her lips thinned. "Remove your armor. Tell it to go away."

Tell it? Had she gleamed Khimmer's presence in my mind from the contact pin?

Remove armor.

Are you sure, Mistress? She seems to mean you harm.

If Shailagh needed to punch me to get this out of her system, then so be it. I couldn't fault her for being mad. Theovole had been one of her people. Her clothes were pierced with holes, though the dark stains around them didn't seem to be from fresh blood. Could she heal that quickly? I owed her my life and Tyler's. And John's.

Remove armor. If you see a tree about to skewer me, you can bring it back. The few trees around us looked brown and sickly.

I need to leave the pauldrons on, to staunch the blood. You will need your wounds to be taken care of, Mistress.

Very well.

Nightarmor melted off, leaving me with thin, unadorned pauldrons clamped tightly over the two wounds on my shoulders. The fresh air smelled like a swamp, a far more pleasant odor than the cavern below or even my own body.

"I'm sorry," I repeated. Reaching up under my ear, I thought to Khimmer, *Remove ear clip.* The post dropped into my hand, and I offered it to Shailagh.

She didn't take it. Her fingers flashed in an angry, unfamiliar gesture. "I should have given you to the Council, let them use you, derive the secrets of your armor."

Had she considered this? When? Every time I'd gone through the portal, I'd trusted where she was taking me. Perhaps too trusting. I blinked and, after all that I'd been through, wanted to sit beside John. I swallowed. "I'm glad you didn't."

"I treated you better than a human should be treated. Even after you ruined any chance I had to get out of this duty in the next decade. Don't kill a wildling; you kill it. What did I expect this time?"

Technically, the rogue had been more of a mutual mistake. I didn't get the sense she wanted a response from me. I was sorry if I'd messed up her job.

"What were all the bugs on the walls?" Tyler asked.

He had been able to see the yellow dots I'd seen through Khimmer's vision.

"What?" Shailagh turned to them, then glanced at John at the ground. "Those were the wight's eyes."

"Creepy," Tyler said. They were distracting Shailagh.

Shailagh sighed. "How do you plan to get him back? I'm nearly drained."

A flicker of hope lit inside my chest. Tyler had gotten her off her rant, and she didn't seem about to abandon us. We'd saved Tyler and John, so far, and I didn't want to lose her as a friend.

Tyler smiled, glancing at me. "We can make a litter. I made it as far as Webelos." They waved off the comment. "Too long of an explanation. Some poles for each side, then tie some vines between and strap John to it. Between the two of us we should be able to drag him back to the car.

Shailagh grunted. "Smart." Splaying her hands toward the earth, she winced at the motion, but vines rustled behind her. Closed, pink wounds dotted her arms and the exposed portions of her chest. She gave me one last glare and turned to face the construction.

I dropped beside John, and Tyler joined me, reaching for my hand. They trembled.

"I don't remember anything after stepping on the stairs. I guess the wight got me?"

"Yes. Scared me there for a minute."

"I felt so lost. Standing there with John and the ceiling caving in, raining down on us. I couldn't remember anything for a minute, then the glowing bugs on the wall." Tyler swore. "How did you . . . ?"

"Kill the wight? Metal."

Wood snapped loudly as Shailagh finalized a stretcher of vines tied between two branches. She brought it to us, motioning Tyler out of the way. "Lift his side to you." Vines knotted and twisted; the construction appeared both pliable and sturdy.

I grabbed John's shoulder and hip, leaned against his weight, and managed to tilt him. Shailagh shoved the litter underneath, tucked the top and bottom under John, and jerked her head for me to let him back down. While she and Tyler pulled, I helped push the body onto the knotted vines. Leaves rustled under his weight. John would be a heavy load. I hoped Tyler could handle their side.

I started for the front, but Shailagh waved me off.

"Wait one moment." She laid her hands on his leg, dark in the starlight, and I could sense her magic working.

Was she healing him? The older Virgins of Gerais could bring forth the god's healing blessing. She was. This I could sense. Shailagh had convinced me of my empath ability, and somehow that had helped it grow, or at least my recognition of it. Her soaked, red hair plastered over her strained features. Without her, I would have lost Tyler. I'd betrayed her trust and planned to the whole trip. That didn't make me a very good person.

Shailagh sighed and spoke quietly enough that only I could hear. "You did what you had to for your friends. I understand." She glanced at me with a weary expression.

Had she forgiven me? I started to smile.

Shailagh frowned "That doesn't mean I forgive you. The Council will be livid, and I'll take all the blame. They don't expect anything but violence and death from a human." She stood, shaking her fingers out as if they ached. She flicked her left hand at John and walked away. "Let's get moving."

Violence and death from a human, what about the wight? I smiled. At least she wasn't really mad at me.

Tyler managed to carry their side, and we dragged John slowly behind Shailagh. The night darkened as we reached healthier trees, and each footstep seemed treacherous. We would need to get John medical help, and Tyler could use a real bandage. My own wounds might need a stitch. I hoped that Deanna's questions could wait; she'd be excited to get her boyfriend back, but what kind of condition would he be in, mentally?

None of us talked. My arms wanted to break at the joints, and Tyler had us stop twice to rest. I needed to get back to Woo and apologize.

Despite the nightmare with water, I was thirsty. How much farther? *Khimmer?*

Thirty minutes at least, Mistress, at your present rate.

John started awake with a cough, and Tyler lost their grip on the litter. I dropped before we toppled. John swore when he smacked to the ground. "What's going on?" His voice sounded raspy and dry. "Where am I?"

"It's okay." Tyler knelt.

"Tyler?" John glanced at me. "Ahnjii?"

Tyler nodded. "You're okay."

John tried to sit up, groaned, and swore. "What happened?"

If he didn't remember the wight, which seemed likely after Tyler's experience, then it would be better if we came up with an alternate explanation. How did I explain why were in the middle of the woods? How had he gotten a broken leg? I'm glad he wouldn't remember fighting me.

Shailagh stepped up beside me. "You fell into a sinkhole, and we've managed to get you out."

"Who are you?" John asked while his eyes furrowed.

"I, unfortunately, am an investigator."

CHAPTER 48

I DIDN'T KNOW how much farther I could carry John. Each step through the leaves rustled, and any twigs snapped quickly under our combined weight. It had to be longer than thirty minutes by now.

The reflection off a window ahead flickered twice before I recognized it. The thralls' truck faced into the woods, and the windshield caught the starlight above. The sight made me doubt I could take another step and encouraged me at the same time.

Shailagh paused as if listening. Did she expect trouble?

I stumbled noisily. "What?" I whispered. My arms shook, and Tyler sagged beside me shifting some of John's weight.

She raised a hand, but I could feel John shift. "What's wrong?" he asked. The pain in his leg had kept him quiet during most of our hike, after his initial outburst.

I hoped we didn't have more snakes to deal with. So far, John knew nothing of Shailagh's magic, nor the wights. I intended to keep it that way. He knew of Nightarmor from when we'd met months ago, and that was enough.

Khimmer?

I detect the man you left in the truck, Mistress. Birds and very few animals, but none of them appear hostile.

Impatiently I sighed, started moving forward, and spoke. "We're clear." I needed to get us to healers. Shailagh had her own healing abilities, though her skin still showed the wight's attacks. I doubted my wounds had stopped bleeding. If Shailagh had been inclined to heal me, she would have offered.

What could we do for the man in the truck? If he were like John and Tyler, he'd have no memory of the wight's control. We had to call someone out to help him. However, his cut had come from me and been witnessed by Mrs. Forster. I'd have to deal with her, and possibly the authorities, when I got home to Woo.

John started swearing and rolling in the litter. I almost called Khimmer to make gauntlets just so I wouldn't lose my grip. "Where are we? My leg is killing me."

Tyler's car reminded me of Thina's waterfall at the end of the Aegis monk's ledge trial. Shining in the starlight, it looked spectacular. "Almost to Tyler's car. Hang on."

Shailagh walked beside me. "I need to take care of some things." She nodded to her left.

I was too tired to guess. "What?" She wouldn't ride anyway. I had assumed she'd leave us here at the car.

Her face tightened. "I need to get rid of something."

Six more steps and we'd be at the car. I had no energy or time for games. "Okay. Thank you for helping . . . for finding John."

Her expression turned uncomfortable, then dark. "Put him down and come talk with me."

Four more steps, and I'd be happy to let go.

"What's going on? Did Deanna hire you?" John asked.

He needed to stop moving. "You're not with the police in that getup."

Her green skirt torn and stiff from being wet, Shailagh stepped aside as we trekked the final steps to the side of the car. "I'm just helping Ahnjii."

My knees complained as we let down the litter. I trembled as I forced myself to straighten. Shailagh watched me with a frown and flicked her fingers for me to approach. As soon as I took a step, she led me away. I wanted to sit, not walk.

Tyler worked with John, helping him climb into the back seat. John, thinner than I'd ever seen him, complained about the broken glass.

Shailagh turned so she could watch them and me. "Make sure Tyler keeps quiet about this. There may be consequences from the Council, so if I show up with another high Fae, be respectful and honest. Except, don't mention your armor."

Her previous comments about the council and her thoughts of betraying me stiffened my posture, despite the aches. "They don't know? What would they do if they did?"

"Whatever technology the humans develop always interests them. We have remained hidden among you for a long time, but the risks grow higher. If there is a war, we need to be informed."

I had always thought of Khimmer as a gift from one of the gods, like a blessed blade from Nyx. *Khimmer, are you technology?*

Technically, yes, Mistress. Constructed intelligence.

Nightarmor?

Picotechnology with chain framework, Mistress.

I don't understand.

Most humans wouldn't, Mistress. Does this bother you?

Nah. I shrugged, catching a probing look from Shailagh. Since my earliest memories, Khimmer had always just been in my mind. Khimmer choosing me and providing me with Nightarmor had pointed me toward being an assassin. The Aegis monks had made that clear. I knew now that they'd stolen me from my parents for my truthsense, not rescued an orphan as I'd believed most of my life.

Shailagh discretely motioned behind her. "I'll get rid of the wight's reconstructed thrall. Once it decomposes, there should be nothing to alert humans."

That had been what she tried to tell me earlier. I needed some sleep, but water first. Maybe some stitches.

"Okay. I'll see if I can call for some help for the thrall in the pickup. Get some healers out here."

Shailagh smiled. "Where's your phone?"

I reached into my back pocket. It stuck against the wet jeans, but I pried it out. It didn't turn on.

She laughed. "Water and human technology, they don't mix. Look in the truck. I saw a phone wedged in the seat. Wait until you're about to leave, dial 911, and leave it with him. The police will take a while to track it. You should be gone by then. Avoid leaving fingerprints."

We seemed to be on friendly terms again. However, I'd trusted the Aegis monks for most of my life. "So, you won't give me up to your council?" I asked.

Shailagh's face darkened. "Not if I can help it." She turned and walked down the trail.

I watched her for a moment before I recognized John's swearing and went to help Tyler. We would have to come up with a story about how we found John, who Shailagh was, and why we went out without calling Deanna or the police.

CHAPTER 49

WHEN WE HAD John resting across the back seat, I motioned to Tyler to follow me to the truck. The night air seemed fragrant from all we'd been through.

"We can't tell John anything," I said.

Thin gloves, I thought to Khimmer. They formed agile metallic gloves over my fingers.

Tyler snorted and their voice pitched sharply. "No one would believe it." They gestured to my hands and glanced over at the once-thrall unconscious in the back of the truck. "What are you doing?"

Tyler's reactions to me had changed. Since I'd arrived on Earth, they'd taken a protective position warning me of any pitfalls that could occur if any authorities found out about Nightarmor or my abilities. During this trek to find John, they'd ranged into nervousness around me, though at the moment they seemed just as weary as I was. They did not grow up around the constant physical violence that the Aegis monks had imposed.

I didn't answer his question as I opened the passenger door. "Are you okay, with me?"

Tyler rocked their head from side to side. "I know you killed people in your previous life. I can't say during that first attack there was a person anymore, with branches like arms, but I could see a person inside there."

Killing the tree man had bothered Tyler, but it would have harmed him. "I didn't have much of a choice." I found the phone and tried to open it, but a keypad asked for a code. Turning the face toward Tyler, I said, "I want to dial 911 with his phone, so they find him before he dies."

Tyler paused. "The gloves are so you don't leave finger-prints. Smart." The surprise in the last comment stung a little. I wouldn't have thought of it if Shailagh hadn't reminded me, though I had read some crime dramas of Tyler's. "Swipe up from that corner, emergency call."

I wasn't as smart as Shailagh or Tyler. When a woman answered, I lowered my voice and said, "Help." Careful not to hang up, I placed the phone in the back with the young man.

Silently, we walked back to Tyler's car. They would remember how easily I'd killed the tree man, little else except perhaps the wildling that nearly tore them apart. I hoped Tyler would still be a friend. I'd been proud to be one of the Queen's assassins in Duruce. The gods prohibited war, but assassins had been the ones to make sure it didn't happen and bring down their wrath. The Aegis monks had trained me that providing the function released the pressures between kingdoms and kept the farmers' children from heading off to the horror we thought of as war. On Earth, they seemed to accept this mass killing; some glorified it. That seemed more terrifying than the scores of people I'd killed.

John swore in the back seat. Tyler stopped me at the bumper of their car. "We're okay, me and you. This is a lot for me to absorb." They pulled the side of my head to theirs and leaned against me. "Thank you. Let me spin the tale for John, Deanna, and the police. You're a lousy liar."

John cursed us when we climbed in. "I need to get to a hospital. I've got a broken leg."

As the car started and scraped across brush in a turn, the odor of the swamp filled the air and soaked into our clothes.

"It's an hour to Tallahassee, but I'd rather get you to a real hospital. You look like crap," Tyler said.

John grumbled. "Call Deanna."

"Lost my phone digging you out of a sinkhole." Tyler sped faster down the trail than on the way in, ignoring the noise of weeds against the bottom of their car. Loose metal rattled at the front. "How'd you get down there?"

I kept a straight face, peering out the passenger window.

John sputtered. "You tell me. How'd you find me?"

Tyler drew in a breath. "Well. Deanna had a bunch of investigators out looking, and when Ahnjii's friend offered to help, I did some analysis on where they and the police hadn't been looking. Sort of a technical process of elimination, but she found the trail. What were you doing this far south? Everyone else was looking on the north side."

"I don't remember a damn thing." John grunted with a barely audible groan. "You got anything to drink?"

I glanced at Tyler hopefully. We were near the end of the trail; I could make out power lines along the road.

"We'll stop and grab something along with some gas." Tyler patted their pants. "Ahnjii's buying."

The dangling metal from the front of Tyler's car tore off as we drove through the higher brush near the road.

"She's buying with the credit card you gave her." John had always been annoyed with the help Deanna and Tyler offered me. He'd been part of the reason I'd moved into my own apartment.

I wouldn't be alone now, if Woo didn't hate me and want to run back to their cave for leaving them alone. I would ask Tyler to get me back there once we got the healers to look at our wounds. I needed pistachios.

John swore. "How'd the window get busted?"

"A branch," I said.

CHAPTER 50

Tyler convinced a skeptical attendant to use her phone to call Deanna. I managed to find pistachios and added a bag to a pile of snacks and drinks on the counter. Bottles of tea and water and cans of energy drinks clanked as I shoved them forward.

"We'll meet you at the emergency entrance," Tyler said. They rolled their eyes, and I could hear a hysterical Deanna even through cupped fingers.

The young woman on the other side of the counter glanced up at us between scanning every item. I offered my best smile, but smelled like a marsh, had started to bruise, and had two reduced pauldrons clamped to bare shoulders. People on Earth didn't wear armor.

Tyler handed the phone back. "Thank you. Rough night." As we headed back to John in the car with two bags, Tyler shook their head and said to me, "I don't think we should have you go into the hospital." They tapped one of their shoulders. "If they recognize GSW, they'll have the police all over that. We're already going to have trouble explaining everything as it is. How bad?"

GSW? I thought to Khimmer.

Gun Shot Wounds, Mistress. According to a television show you watched.

I smiled. "I need stitches and a compress, or medicine." If I'd been on better terms with Shailagh, I would have asked for some healing. My left shoulder hurt the worst.

Tyler nodded apologetically. "I have an idea, but I'll need Deanna's phone."

When we opened the car doors, John groaned from where he lay in the backseat. He drank readily once I passed him a cold water. We'd bought him cheese crackers, and those kept him quiet. I gobbled down salty chips. None of us spoke much, so I dozed off at one point during the drive back, waking when we stopped at a red light near the airport.

"Where is this hospital?" I asked while opening a barely cool tea.

"Northeast from our house." Tyler looked ragged and pale. I still didn't know how much the wight had affected them. They drove us through the city to a massive complex of concrete buildings that stacked against each other. A sweeping ramp led us into a lit garage.

Deanna had tied her hair into a ponytail that swayed and slapped as she paced outside a bright entrance. She dressed as if heading out for dinner, but her eyes were red, and her face flushed when she ran up to the car with heels clattering on the drive. She barely gave Tyler time to come to a stop. "John, John." Tears had stained her cheeks, even knowing we were bringing John back. In a voice she rarely used, she screamed at an attendant as two automatic doors slid open. "Get a wheelchair!"

John rumbled curses under his breath, but shifted in the backseat and flicked crumbs off his ruined shirt. I couldn't even smell us anymore. Getting a healer sounded less important than sleeping. Feeding Woo topped the list.

Deanna opened the door at John's feet, then clattered around to the other side where she could gently touch his matted hair. "Are you okay? What happened?"

When I reached for my handle, Tyler motioned for me to stay.

"Leg hurts like all hell," John grumbled. He avoided the explanation as much as Tyler and I did.

Deanna waited, then her hands pulled back and she stiffened. Tyler had started to get out. She shot me a quick look and noted the armor on my shoulders. It wasn't the first time she'd seen it, but it had been a few months.

"What happened?" she repeated. Her tone had cooled, and her syllables were crisp.

"We found John in a sinkhole." Tyler rested their hand on her shoulder, and she flinched, turning to appraise them. "It was a bitch to climb down and get him. He's been unconscious for a while. We got some fluids and food in him." One of the attendants from the massive building, the hospital, approached. Tyler motioned to the far door where John's feet were. "He's got a broken leg; we'll need a wheelchair."

Deanna gave us three probing glances, one to each of us. "He's back. That's what matters." Her face tightened as if she were running through all our interactions throughout the day. "When you canceled, you could have told me."

Tyler hugged her. "I couldn't get your hopes up on a whim."

She wrinkled her nose, but took the hug. "Thank you. God, thank you."

"Lost my phone down there. I need yours for a minute while I drive Ahnjii home."

Her expression turned suspicious again, but she gave them her phone. "You'll be back?"

Tyler snorted. "Yep." They still had a cut on their chest to be looked at. Tyler never mentioned Shailagh. I sat uselessly in the front seat while Tyler helped the attendant slide John out.

I sat watching John being wheeled through the sliding doors with Deanna while Tyler typed on the phone. Driving off slowly, Tyler kept checking Deanna's phone. We had made it as far as College Town when they grunted while checking at a stoplight.

"Can you make it 'til morning?"

Deanna had packed what she called a medicine cabinet with supplies; Khimmer would remember what each was for. "Sure." I'd wash up and get some sleep.

We were driving down the street to my apartment when Tyler asked, "What did Shailagh mean about an empath?"

I shrugged and winced. "I don't get it myself. She thinks I'm an Earth witch, so I guess they're common. From her description I'd guess that witches are empaths, but she expects them to know all about Fae . . ." I stopped myself, almost discussing Nedjir. Tyler knew about wildlings, but I didn't remember mentioning anything else. I thought of Darren McGyver, who might actually tell me about witches. "I'll ask around and see what I can find out."

"Other Fae?" Tyler asked. "Do you know others?"

I hadn't intended to breech Vivianne's trust and would want to talk with her. "Yes, but she asked me to keep it a secret."

Tyler nodded and appeared to accept that.

We pulled up in the dark outside my apartment, and I checked the cars. It seemed days ago we'd been ambushed here. Mrs. Forster had her lights on. "I've got to race Mrs. Forster," I said, and jumped out of the car. "Tomorrow."

"Tomorrow," Tyler replied.

Pistachios in hand, I raced up the stairs, boots clacking noisily, and had my keys out when I reached my door. Chains rattled quickly on her side as I flipped the lock and turned the knob. As my door closed and I locked it, I could hear her talking. She rambled just outside. Mrs. Forster might call the police, but I didn't have the energy to deal with her.

I flicked on the light and searched for Woo. My heart skipped when I didn't see them. We'd left cups on the counter. "Woo?" I whispered.

I looked at the cabinets carefully, in case they were camouflaged. I flung open doors, but they weren't inside any either. A hollow dread opened in my chest. What if they found a way out and left me? It had been horrible to bring them from their cave, no matter how dank, and lock them up in my apartment. The kitchen window was intact and closed.

"Woo?" I headed for the bathroom.

They whistled a low wavering note before I reached the door. Camouflaged, they hung from the pole that held my shower curtain. Their liquid black eyes studied me and betrayed their hiding spot. The fat fluffy tail spiraled down the black rod.

"I'm so sorry." I reached up with a twinge to my shoulder.

Woo let loose a series of whistles that I was sure chastised my negligent behavior. Their fur blushed pink and they leapt for my chest with a forgiving tone. I caught them with a smile, and they shoved their forehead under my chin, trilling in low notes.

"I didn't mean to leave you for so long." I paused. Someone had left potato chips in the bathroom sink. There were no potato chips in the apartment, just ramen noodles. I reached out to grab them and Woo let out a low apologetic whistle.

Perhaps a tissue would be in order, Mistress; those might be excrement.

I halted, glancing into Woo's liquid eyes. "Woo poo?"

It would seem only fair. I had left them alone. Should I get a litter box? I doubted I'd be walking Woo on a leash like Earth people did with their dogs. Holding them against my chest, I pulled some toilet paper, cleaned up the chips, and tossed them into the toilet. Woo whistled a low plaintive note before I flushed. I would have to get a proper bowl for them to drink out of.

"Pistachios?" I asked.

Woo seemed to know exactly what I offered. I left them feeding on the counter while I stripped off my clothes, tempted to throw them outside.

I had showered and cleaned out my wounds, but my left shoulder was still bleeding when the police knocked on my door. Woo hid on top of the cabinets in camouflage. To hide the bandages, I grabbed a T-shirt Tyler had given me.

Two heavy officers waited outside my door, seeming annoyed at having to knock so many times. Mrs. Forster was talking off to the side in a non-stop stream, as usual. Perhaps they were irritated by her more than me.

"Ms. Fate. Are you alone?" The man had a handsome cut to his chin.

I leaned against the door as if my shoulder didn't hurt. "Of course, is everything alright?"

"We were called out for an altercation, with knives, earlier this evening."

"Some beggars were here, looking for gas money. We just drove off." I laughed. "They didn't pull any knives. They might have been homeless, or on medicine."

The colloquial term is drugs, Mistress.

"Drugs," I corrected.

Mrs. Forster turned rabid outside of my vision and the second officer had to move off to deal with her. I grimaced and shifted as if to see her as she babbled in an increasingly higher pitch.

"So, no weapons?" His jaw tightened, but the frown he gave was toward Mrs. Forster.

"That would be scary," I said. "I don't think that happens in this part of the city, in broad daylight."

He sighed, took out a card, and said, "Call us if you have any trouble." From his look at my neighbor, I almost felt sorry for Mrs. Forster.

I leaned against the door when I closed it. I needed some sleep. It had been a very, very long day.

CHAPTER 51

I WOKE in a haze to crisp knocks on the front door. Cinnamon-scented Woo, sharing my pillow with their forehead tucked under my chin, let out an inquisitive whistle. The sun had risen. My shoulders stung. Had I been asleep more than an hour? It didn't feel like it.

Tyler had said someone would be here this morning. What time was it? I'd gotten used to my phone to tell me the hour.

As I slid my feet off the sheet and disrupted Woo further, my visitor knocked again.

Boots, I thought to Khimmer.

I staggered as Nightarmor formed under my soles and stumbled noisily. "Wait a minute." I whispered. The blue T-shirt had bunched up around my underwear and I tugged at it before reaching the door.

Laura waited outside holding two cups of tea and a bag that smelled like pastry. Her ears twitched and lowered as she saw me, and her smile disappeared. "Are you okay?"

Mrs. Forster's door opened.

I stepped back and nodded Laura in. A vague memory of her wanting to visit lingered at the edge of my mind. "C'mon."

She skipped in and headed straight for the counter, but her neck twisted trying to find Woo. "You're bleeding."

I glanced at my left shoulder and could make out the dark blotches on the T-shirt. "Hades." Mrs. Forster had just started to say something when I closed the door and locked it.

Laura put down our breakfast, smiled as Woo crawled out of the bedroom, and gestured to my shoulder. "What happened?"

"We found John. Have you ever heard of a wight?" I blinked, unsure whether I had planned on telling the story to Laura. Not that it mattered, since Shailagh was likely still angry at me.

Laura's tiny mouth formed a circle and her round red eyes widened. She stepped on a dropped pistachio shell with a crunch as she approached. She didn't answer my question. "Let me see. I might be able to help."

I pulled off the shirt, wincing, and she helped. Blood had soaked through the left bandage.

She peeled it off carefully and frowned in a Nedjir kind of way. "This is bad. How did it happen? Better yet, what caused it?"

"A bullet."

"Then it could have been worse. Do you mind if I try and heal it?"

I needed some tea; my mind hadn't woken up yet. "Heal? What gods do you call?" Earth humans had plenty of gods, but none seemed to actually exist. Perhaps the Nedjir had different deities to call upon.

She laughed. "No gods. Everything is connected. The

Fae call it universal threads. We Nedjir have a name for it, but nothing translates." Woo shuffled past her legs, distracting her. "They are *so* pink."

Woo whistled at the compliment, climbing the corner of the counter.

"Yes," I said. The virgins of Gerais had worked on me plenty of times when their powers were needed above the Queen's mundane herbalists and healer. "I would appreciate it if you can heal these."

Laura looked confused for a moment and then placed furry fingers at each side of the wound, pressing them closed. We stood the same height, but I lowered, wanting to shirk away at the pain. "No muscle is torn. That's good, or it would take longer."

I focused on Woo and gritted my teeth. The stinging ebbed stronger. I focused on remaining relaxed. They offered a numbing tea at the temple of Gerais which the Aegis monks had not allowed me to sample. I would have been happy to try it now.

Laura took long enough that Woo had thoroughly sniffed around our breakfast and moved to the kitchen window to peer outside. Their fur camouflaged with a slow ripple before their face neared the glass.

"There." Laura nodded toward an ugly pink scar where I'd been bleeding earlier. "Let's see about the other shoulder. So, can you tell me what happened? That high Fae was involved, wasn't she?"

Telling her about the wight took my mind off the pain, though I didn't mention that Shailagh had thought Tyler might be an empath. When she finished, we continued talking over breakfast. Woo showed no interest in pastry. I'd need to find out what they liked to eat.

"Are there a lot of witches?" I asked.

Laura gave me an odd look, reminding me of Shailagh's disbelief when I was ignorant of Earth's witches. They both expected me to know. Tyler was a human who didn't have any clue of witches or empaths, nor any Nedjir and Fae. Why would they expect me to know?

Her face tight, Laura nodded slowly. "Yes, there are large families and clans of witches. They hide themselves like we do, and protect their own like we do. There's even a group of witches called the Knights that work against anyone exposing us, but their methods are questionable and their intent, suspect. They track anything considered paranormal to humans. There are always non-witch humans searching out rumors of us for governments. A couple thousand years ago, organizations were still hunting Nedjir, Upre, and Fae." She looked over at Woo. "Witch families search out young, empath children if they are strong, like you. They train them in the ways of the world, so that they do not expose themselves."

A chill ran over my neck. I tilted the empty cup of tea to hide my expression. Any human growing up on Earth with a power as strong as mine would have been noticed, contacted, and taught. Shailagh and Laura both knew that. My ignorance said I wasn't from here. Instead, the monks had noticed and stolen me from my parents, orphaning me.

We changed subjects and focused on Woo. Laura agreed that I needed to get something to provide water and a litter box. She warned about experimenting with food too much.

I still hadn't put on a fresh shirt when someone else knocked at the door. Earth humans had more concerns with clothing than my people living in the warmer climates of Duruce. At the farthest habitable edge of the sun side, few wore clothing at all. Woo camouflaged, and I dashed into my bedroom for a bodysuit. I could handle the straps on my shoulders now.

A very handsome man, a couple years older than me, waited outside with a duffel bag. He had a fashionably trimmed beard along the jaw and the strange blue eyes that some Earth humans had. "Ahnjii Fate?" he asked. His eyes flicked inside at Laura. Mrs. Forster swept in front of her door.

"Yes."

He frowned as he studied my shoulders. "Tyler asked me to come by."

I motioned him inside. Mrs. Forster didn't say anything. As I closed the door behind him, I said, "You're the healer."

"EMT." He had a fit form, like a palace guard or workman.

Khimmer?

A healer, Mistress.

"I'm good now." I pulled down each strap.

He flushed and focused on Laura. I looked back to check on Woo, clinging on cabinets. How did he not see those big liquid eyes? He coughed and motioned for me to return my clothing. "I see that. Tyler had made the wounds out to be more serious."

I should have just sent him off to start with. "Tyler worries about me." If Laura weren't here, and if the healing hadn't tired me, I would have attempted to distract him with sex. After everything over the past couple of days, I could use a little distraction myself. "I'm sorry to waste your time."

I stepped to the door and opened it for him, keeping hidden from Mrs. Forster. "Tell Tyler I'm okay?" Would my phone work again?

The handsome healer frowned, but nodded. As he climbed down the steps, Mrs. Forster clicked her tongue and brushed more leaves onto my mat. She started saying something, but I'd frozen.

Leaning on what I'd come to consider Shailagh's tree was Darren McGyver.

CHAPTER 52

I PAUSED a little too long at the sight of Darren McGyver adjusting his straw fedora and smiling up at me.

Laura must have noticed; she rested a hand on my shoulder. "What is it?" she asked.

"Darren McGyver. A novelist. A witch according to Shailagh." I spoke in a quiet whisper.

Mrs. Forster was saying something to me, but the noise of her voice dulled into the background of birds, cars, and the murmur of the city. Should I ask him about witches? It would only highlight to another person that I might not be from Earth.

"What does he want with you?" Laura asked.

Tyler's healer navigated through Mrs. Forster's pink birds to his car. Darren made a gesture for me to come down. Shailagh had warned me about him.

I took in a deep breath. "I'm going to find out."

Laura followed me, closing the door behind us. I wasn't sure what to be concerned about; Shailagh hadn't given me any specifics. Working with the high Fae had raised some disturbing considerations here on Earth that I hadn't dealt with on Duruce. I recognized how little I knew.

Darren watched us descend, his smile never diminishing. When we reached the bottom step, he tipped his hat at Mrs. Forster and stepped to the side of the tree. The breeze flicked brown leaves down the street and brought a light scent of exhaust.

"What do you want?" I asked.

As if it had been waiting in his hand, he handed me a gold card. I recognized a sigil bordered within the logo and the wording was simply Darren McGyver, Knight of the Ascendant Concors.

"Who are the Knights of . . ." I wasn't great with pronouncing some English words.

He snorted. "A true Verity. I wasn't alive during the last one."

My face heated. He'd tricked me much as Shailagh had when we first met, but she'd been sexy when she did it. Darren just angered me. The sigil on the card probably hid the writing and I'd just blurted it out.

"Be careful," Laura said from behind me. She had heard me say Knight, and she'd just mentioned them.

Mistress? Khimmer thought. They would want Nightarmor protecting me.

Wait. "What do you want?" I repeated, keeping the card.

He tipped his hat to Laura. "This does not involve the fallen gods, Mrs. Laura Nelson. Go back to your studio."

Laura took in a sharp breath. "I'll see you later," she said to me in a whisper.

"Yes," I said, but didn't turn to watch her walk through the leaves. This man disturbed me, not just because of Laura and Shailagh's warnings.

He waited calmly, though his eyes did flick between Mrs. Forster and Laura. "We don't know you, Ahnjii Fate. You've just appeared along with a mess in Orlando where you left one of the forsaken wildlings dead. Something happened last night. We haven't put the pieces together, but we need to know if there is anything we will need to clean up. Is there?"

"What do you have to do with anything?" I hated not knowing so much about Earth, but I would not be asking Darren McGyver for a lesson about witches.

He scoffed. "The Knights maintain the veil, as you know. Everything the witches and non-humans do can leave a trace, and we need to make sure that the mundane humans do not rise to a panic." Darren stiffened, snapping to peer around the tree.

Glowering, Shailagh stalked toward us down the street. Her steps crisp and long, she wore fresh clothing, and I couldn't see a mark on her for all the stabbing the wight had inflicted on her. She might still be a threat considering her mysterious council, but I trusted her more than Darren.

"Look who found me," I said in a fake, cheerful voice, as if we were all good friends. Before she got too close, I held up his card. "Turns out, he's a Knight."

My comment stopped Shailagh in her tracks. Her fingers stiffened and I half expected her to skewer him.

He turned back to me as if she hadn't reacted. "So, our services will not be needed?"

I shook my head, pursing my lips. "Nope."

Darren lifted his hat to me. "Very well. We'll see. Make sure your friends Tyler and Deanna Ramnath are under control. Hopefully, they don't know anything. We'll be watching."

His lack of knowing that John was involved gave me

some hope, or perhaps he chose not to mention it. Darren's attitude and Shailagh's comments about keeping things hidden left me with a better understanding of how Tyler had never suspected anything of people like Vivianne and Laura.

Darren took casual strides away. Shailagh and I both watched him cross the street to a beat-up blue car.

"You'll have to be careful with the Knights now." Shailagh spoke quietly and acted as though I should know about them.

I needed to find a friendly witch to give me some tips. My list had grown long enough for today. Woo needed food options, a water bowl, and something to leave his chips in. John would likely be back from the hospital, and I should check in with Tyler. They'd been hurt, though not seriously, and I did want to make sure they were okay. Maybe they could help with getting a new phone or getting my old one to work. I wouldn't get to Vivianne today.

With long fingers, Shailagh brushed my shoulder, sparking a response. "Did your Nedjir friend heal you?"

I wanted to ask her why she didn't tell me Laura could heal, but that would emphasize my ignorance of Earth.

"Did you come by to check on me?" I asked. That would be nice.

"Partially, but also to deliver a warning. I've given the council my report, leaving out mention of your particulars." She gestured to my collar and armbands. "I told them you used knives and are very adept."

I smiled. I was good with blades.

"However, they may still send another investigator to verify my report. This remains to be seen." Shailagh's grim face told me I didn't want this to happen.

"Okay, I'll be careful."

"Good. I don't want to be stuck in this job for another century." Shailagh watched as Darren drove away.

I would have rather hoped she'd be concerned that the council didn't try to harm me, but I'd take her lying for me as some measure of friendship. "What are you up to?" Maybe we could have tea.

Shailagh sighed. "Some trouble in a rural town east of here. Yourself?"

"Some shopping for Woo, then check in on Tyler and John."

CHAPTER 53

By the time Deanna brought out some iced tea, I had stripped off my clothes to skinny dip in their pool. Tyler sat shirtless in the lounge chair with a bandage on their shoulder.

Deanna tsked as I grabbed a glass. "What is it with the skinny dipping?" she asked. "I bought you two suits."

"Which I wore to the ocean when we visited, just like you asked." I'd checked, and no one wore bathing suits in a shower or a tub. How was the pool any different? On Duruce we didn't wear clothing into the baths.

"Whatever. Tyler, are you making lunch?" Deanna asked.

Tyler held up their book. "End of the chapter. Promise. Will Grumpy be eating?"

Deanna's face tightened. "He's in pain. I ordered soup for him."

"He's going to love that." Tyler laughed and grabbed a tea.

I slid into the water, sucking in a breath. The temperature was cooler than in the summer. I hated the smell, but wanted to work out some sore muscles from last night's skirmish.

Deanna headed back in with quick steps. She'd been hovering around John while he was awake, and most of the time when he slept. Tyler and I had skated for a bit this morning, which prompted me to want to cool off in the pool.

I rested in front of Tyler with my elbows on the concrete. "I had a weird visitor today. A human, a witch."

Tyler peered over their book. "Okay." They hadn't mentioned their own abilities, what Shailagh had said about them, or even anything about last night.

"This guy warned me not to let anyone find out about what happened. I don't know if he knew you were there, but he warned me not to let you say anything."

"Like some sort of witch mafia?" Tyler smiled. "Don't worry. I haven't done any weird internet searches."

They were blowing off any concern, but Tyler tended to mull things before breaking out in a long theory about the topics.

I blew out a breath. "Just wanted to warn you."

"Because you love me?"

"Yes, of course." We stayed off the awkward discussion of physical relations. During my first month on Earth, the attraction had been obvious. The first week. By then, we'd become friends and I had to face my issues between friendship and sex. I'd almost told them about my mission back home and the blessed blade that I'd hidden at the skating rink. I'd carried it here from Slovenia, but Tyler thought it was part of my Nightarmor. When they suggested I hide it, they assumed it would turn into bangles or bracelets. It wouldn't disappear until I'd used it on the victim Nyx had consecrated it for, King Dior of Tahnet. I would have to be on Duruce to do that.

Tyler put down their book, climbed out of the chair, and sat down on the pool's edge beside me, their face grim. "I worry about you, too." They rubbed the pink scars on my shoulder. "How do I get you to stay safe?"

Pulling my braid over my opposite shoulder, I flicked the end, spraying water against my cheek. "You've managed so far." Without their guidance, I might have ended up in a government lab. Now, we both had bigger worries.

"Just be careful."

Tyler looked so serious, I splashed water on their chest. They sucked in a breath and started to return the favor, cupping their hand in water.

Before I dove under, I laughed and lied, "I'm always careful."

ALSO BY KEVIN A DAVIS

Please head to my website and join my mailing list if you'd like to be kept up to date on this series or my other books.

Khimmer Chronicles

Wight's Wrath - Book One

Death's Contract - Book Two

Fate's Betrayal - Book Three

High Fae's Quest - Book Four

Friday's Fifth - Book Five

If you haven't read the Origin story of the **AngelSong** series, *Shattered Blood*, then download a free ebook or purchase the paperback or audible on Amazon.

AngelSong Series

Penumbra - Book One

Red Tempest - Book Two

Coerced - Book Three

Demons' Lair - Book Four

Infrared - Book Five. (End of the AngelSong Series)

Website KevinArthurDavis.com

Facebook @KevinArthurDavis

KevinADavis on Instagram

KevinADavisUF on Twitter

ACKNOWLEDGMENTS

I'm still trying to impress my wife after two decades of marriage. April appears to like Ahnjii.

Robyn Huss, my editor, takes my roughest drafts and works magic. There should be a new character in RPG; the Editor. No matter how badly you rolled your spell, she'll fix it. Robyn would be the default image on the card. She's fabulous.

October K Santerelli was a reassuring influence by performing a detailed sensitivity read. Check out his novels and I highly recommend his services.

I blame being encouraged to bring these characters to life on Dianne and Brett from Apex, Arrash and Michele from Jody Lynn Nye's DragonCon workshop, and Katharine, Mark, Rosemary, Tim, and Vail from our JordanCon writing group (the infamous Fireside Group).

I still miss David Farland's tireless mentorship. Please pick up one of his books and enjoy the magic he endowed upon the world. Writers, study his lessons at Apex Writers.

Jody Lynn Nye's workshop will always be my go to

suggestion for an in-person critique for any aspiring writers. Her insight is invaluable.

The wonderful cover art is by Rebekah at VividCovers! Consider her for your next design.

Thank you.